SOME BEASTS NO MORE

When an attractive, red-haired young lady who has been questioned and excused in one murder case, moves to another town and takes a different name and is involved, even slightly, in another murder, it is inevitable that Scotland Yard should become interested in her. There was also, Superintendent Hawker pointed out, the curious coincidence of five unconvicted murderers having recently died themselves in highly suspicious circumstances. So young Detective-Sergeant James is sent down to Bradshaw to discover what is happening.

In the pleasant country town he finds a group of leisured, well-bred people with some curious relationships among them; the lovely Rhonda Gentry, and her peculiar relationship with a distinguished ex-commando; a landlady, who was once a music-hall star who tells a great deal but by no means all she knows; an old murder, and a new one. Harry James becomes more involved in the problems than he should be, until it comes down to a desperate search with time running out very rapidly.

Lively, diverting, and satisfying, SOME BEASTS NO MORE introduces Superintendent Hawker and Detective-Sergeant Harry James for the pleasure of readers who prefer the straight, slightly eccentric detective novel.

SOME BEASTS NO MORE

by

KENNETH GILES

WALKER AND COMPANY
New York

First published in the United States of America
in 1968 by Walker and Company, a division of
the Walker Publishing Company, Inc.

Library of Congress Catalog Card Number:
68-27389

Printed in the United States of America from
type set in Great Britain.

CHAPTER ONE

EVERYBODY HAD BEEN *terribly* nice to Harry James. He had received a personal recommendation from the Chief Commissioner, some words of praise from the judge and a signed certificate from the Home Office which mentioned 'beyond the call of duty'. And the judge had given five years apiece to the three men who had worked on Harry with boots and an iron bar in the derelict old warehouse which crouched among the new buildings on the south bank.

But somebody else had got the job he had been sweating after. He stood waiting for a break in the traffic which had assumed the tropical dawdle, bumper to bumper, which the hot sun and creeping humidity suggested. His face was still brown from the four weeks he had spent in the south of France, spending some of the accumulated pay of a five months' stay in hospital; a slight man even in these days when the police seemed smaller than they did.

He stared at the taxis, at the old crates which had survived hire purchase and patching, the neat little jobs driven by 'our representatives' and the occasional amphibean lengths of the fishbowls. Then he saw the Lagonda and grinned appreciatively at the old warrior of distinction with its hand-made headlights, wire wheels and a gentle plop plop of smoke from its twin exhausts. He registered that the driver was elderly, with a flat cloth cap, a hooked, blackened pipe and a purple mark blotching his left cheek. The traffic jammed and he dodged through it, between the Lagonda and a van proclaiming in gilt letters 'Mars Picture Corp'. A cut-out on the roof outlined a busty woman holding a machine gun. 'The Sea Gunners' shouted the caption, 'Wonderful moments...' (The Standard). Harry remembered that the critic had written something like 'wonderful moments of insensate drivel and triteness'. Bogus prospectuses should have been Harry's job, and he smiled to think of what the Fraud Squad might think of film ads. He gained the Whitehall side and glanced back. His eye checked at the Lagonda. It stood there, chromium reflecting painful flashes of light, gently vibrating. The driver's seat was empty. As he gazed a bowler-hatted head

5

appeared above the back seat, followed by an expanse of blue, sweaty-looking blue serge. The man slid over the division, legs squirming under the wheel. A whistle blew and the traffic restarted with a fume-reeking jolt, flowing smoothly, as at the release of a dam, in the direction of the Embankment. His mind was automatically checking. The old man in the cap could have got out. Nobody, thought Harry, paid any attention to other drivers as human beings. They could be nude, baboon-faced monsters, but as long as the machines made the prescribed hundred feet dashes nobody would care or notice. He thought the new driver had come from the back seat, foreshortened to the eye and over-shadowed by the untidy heap of the rolled hood.

He shrugged and turned towards the Embankment, again intent on the little blister of doubt that had prevailed for the last two months, ever since he had heard definitely that the last place in the new Squad had been filled, the place he had finagled and ingratiated nights for.

The bloody thing was that he had been ideally fitted for the job. Three years of training in a first-class auditors and not one of your catchpenny little companies with dirty teapots on the filing cabinets, but a mahogany tabled, graceful Queen Anne facaded place in Fenchurch Street where the senior partner was a peer and the chaste wooden files read like a roll call of the old city firms.

Then it had been—he grinned—the call of adventure, the sickening of calling back figures for days on end. What had her name been? All he could remember was a voluptuous expanse of thigh and stomach in a red dress and the fashionably gruff voice. 'So you're one of those funny little men who slide about big offices as if they didn't quaite belong there.' Hell, yes, she'd said *quaite*, the bitch. But she had been a catalyst for that mood. Something had reached a head inside him in the dimly lit studio where the party had been held, compounded of three years in a city suit, the cyprus sherry, and, yes he supposed, this statuesque bitch. At least he'd taken her home.

Then the years of being re-educated and the bright boy had become a detective sergeant assigned to investigative duties where his accountancy knowledge hadn't proved really adequate to get much in the way of clues from nasty little fences who didn't keep books anyway but showed a surprising intuition about what you could or could not get nicked for.

But the new Squad, that had been something, with a couple of hints and the Super in charge asking about one's qualification coming down in the lift one night, as if he didn't know. Harry considered he had a subtle mind and the new business was right up his alley. The new financial jungles, the world of take-over and prospectuses which weren't prospectuses because they referred to options to buy instead of cash on the barrel for shares, had opened new and devious channels for the rogue. That was what the new Squad was for, and during the vital months when the men had been chosen he had been on his back in hospital.

He overshot his turn-off, nearly bumping into the back of old Squires, whose life mainly consisted of tracking down smut, with immense cogitation as to what smut was. 'Used to be easy in the old days,' Squires said when he lectured on the subject. 'All turned on the D. H. Lawrence case. No body hair and it was clean; body hair and the magistrate convicted. Nowadays it's not so simple.' Yes, there was Squires walking towards West End and Praed Street, into the world where sunlight didn't filter, and the makeshift dark rooms and subterranean store-rooms must be as hot as hell this weather, sure as it was now well past ten, when Squires emerged each day on the dot.

Harry turned and as he did so drew himself up to avoid bumping into somebody. It was the old man in the cloth cap, his briar still fuming away so that the grey smoke, dribbling into the humid air, hung against the red mark on his cheek. He was bow-legged and, Harry grinned, wore plus fours with check stockings below, and a rather baggy pullover which looked expensive.

There weren't many people about, and for some reason which he didn't analyse Harry slightly lengthened his stride so that he walked half a dozen yards behind, the old man covering ground with deceptive speed, powerful thighs pushing against the grotesque-looking knickers.

The girl was standing against the railing of Parliament. She was tall, perhaps a couple of inches taller than Harry in her high heeled shoes. She had copper hair which had been styled into one of those cuts which Harry dimly realised had probably been expensively contrived to look careless. Her face was a trifle broad, but he was caught by its serenity. It made her look cool and extremely competent, and, in a street of pretty faces, beautiful. (Somewhere in Harry's mind, was recorded 5ft. 6in. 8½ stones, full figure, white blouse, grey pleated skirt.) But he got the impression that her legs were long with just a faint hint of muscle in the calves and if he had written that in a report he'd have been told to cool himself off with a long walk.

He saw her stare at him, and he gained the impression of a surprising switch of expression, as if the whole surface of her face shifted and moved. Then she had turned, and her strides were long and Harry imagined the play of thigh against the skirt, as she strode, almost running, towards the west gate.

Out of the corner of his eye he had sensed that the old man had half turned and swung his shoulder up, as if obeying some impulse to avoid being seen, the gesture of a man who is surprised by a street photographer. Then he, too, strode on, whipping the pipe from his mouth as he did so.

Harry accelerated his pace so that he came level, feeling the pull of muscle in his left leg, now a trifle shorter than the other. Not caring about the old man, he broke into a kind of trot and was a few feet behind the girl as she turned into the west gate.

Parliament was sitting and the uniformed policeman moved over. 'Not this way, Miss.'

It was as though Harry had crossed another dimension. He felt himself reach the girl's side and nod to the policeman, 'It's all right, Bert. She's with me.'

He had known Bert from his Bow Street days. The constable looked doubtful for a second, then smiled and turned away to the gate.

Harry felt his hand touch her elbow. It felt cool. 'Just walk with me.'

He turned. The old man, pipe in his mouth again, was talking to the gate guard.

The sun cross-lighted the scene, making odd plastic shadows, but in the second he glanced back Harry had the disconcerting impression that the old man was looking at him from the corner of his eyes. And in spite of the cap and ridiculous attire Harry received an impression of youthful power and vigour. He decided it was a trick of the light plus his nerves, still jangling from the drugs his system had absorbed.

He heard his feet clatter on the concrete. The woman walked by his side, perhaps four inches of clearance between their shoulders, her shadow dancing across his. He cleared his throat but could think of nothing to say. He raised his hat and walked back the way he had come. There was no sign of the old man.

Presently he found himself in his old room, a long one with a dozen or so desks. There were three people there to slap his back,

8

retail the latest misfortune of an unlucky and lecherous sergeant, and inform him that the boss would like to see him.

His former section, broadly dealing with receivers and receivers of materials and clothing in particular (although for some reason furs 'came under' another department) was controlled hierarchily among others, by a man whom one remembered as combining a horse face, very pale blue eyes and yellow buck teeth.

He was a man of considerable academic attainments and an uneasy air. He was supposed to be very good indeed in the realms of administration.

On the occasions Harry saw him, perhaps once in three months, he generally talked of wine, Harry's father having been a book-keeper for a superior wine merchant of the kind who never displayed stock. Harry's pocket did not run to wine, but somehow he had absorbed a vast mass of technical data. He preferred beer.

The boss offered coffee and a superior cigarette and much talk of France and lamentations for a highly superior parcel of a 1956 burgundy, laid down in the cellar at Highgate, and inconsequentially 'going off'.

'Such a beautiful flinty soil, too,' he lamented. 'You could taste its character in the wine.'

He gave his disconcerting smile. 'Sometimes I think that there are sturdy French knappers, shaving bits of flint into wine bottles, for wine snobs like me. Anyway I'll send you some.' He waved one long hand, 'I'll have to get rid of it within three months or pour it away. Anyway, the iron will probably build you up, and it's getting so that you can almost hear the bits jangling in it.'

Here it comes, Harry decided, the oblique reference to health.

'You must go slow at first,' the boss said, in his serious voice. 'That was a nasty time you spent in that warehouse.'

Harry sweated. He didn't like to think of it, had resolutely put it into some mental cupboard and locked the door. In spite of the patent little box which was supposed to purify the air, the office seemed stuffy and for one moment he felt a kind of upsurge and dizziness as though he was going to faint.

The voice was going on, and the eyes peering at him sharply. 'You haven't quite found your niche here James. Sometimes I've thought you were about to, but ...' He let his voice trail off and continued to stare for a fraction of a second in silence.

Harry mumbled that he was sorry.

'Oh no, we haven't any complaints.' The teeth showed wider in a grin. 'Your record is enviable. But of course it's like everywhere else. A sense of purpose is needed. Like old Squires and his postcards.'

It was over, realised Harry. The oblique lead-in, the hint of something or other that he'd have to work out (striding up and down on his second-hand Axminster with a quart of beer half finished on the mantelpiece and the stillness of the night outside the open windows).

'But, immediately,' said the boss, shuffling some papers, 'I wonder if you'd be good enough to report to Superintendent Hawker.' He saw Harry's face and hurried to say, 'Lord knows, we're not putting you on to what my old housekeeper calls stastistics. No it's not that. Hawker's got a feeling that all is not well, and he knows not what. He asked me for a bright, intelligent young detective, and I thought you might use the occasion for "running-in".'

Harry proceeded to the door.

'Oh, James?'

'Sir?'

'I've known occasions on which Superintendent Hawker was very, very and quite damnably right.'

Hawker had long spatulate fingers, a greyish skin and an annoyingly racy habit of speech. He presided over batteries of punched cards in grey Government-issue filing cabinets with disconcertingly sharp edges.

Providing lists of bald-headed, squinting burglars with a fondness for marmalade was, of course, routine to records, but it was Hawker's passion and genius delicately to calculate theories from this mess of figures, as when his statement of increased shop window breaking in Huddersfield had been carefully correlated to altered bus timetables from outside certain pubs.

'Have a look at this list, laddie.' He pushed forward a laminated buff folder with quarto pages neatly bound in rings.

Harry flipped it through, almost unconsciously making a quantitative survey.

'About two hundred and sixty names,' he said, 'about three hundred people all annotated with your cabalistic signs in red ink.'

Hawker nodded approvingly. 'They're all murderers,' he said. 'Or to my estimate 95.8 of 'em.'

Harry James sighed and prepared to listen whilst Hawker let his fingers caress the hard surface of the laminated desk.

'These people,' he said didactically, 'have never been charged. There are two fifty of 'em, collectively responsible for two sixty seven deaths. There are twelve doubles, and one man with four—all of them cheap tarts found dead around Paddington.'

'Never been charged?'

'You're giving me an excuse to order more tea. You know as well as I do that most homicides result in a trial. Of the rest, we're sure of who has done it in more than ninety per cent of the cases, and pretty sure in the remaining ten. But there's nothing for the Public Prosecutor to wrap his little brief up in. There are the closed files, the ones that the Superintendents are sure of. My opinion is that you could allow something over four per cent for errors accounted for by sheer coincidence or the Super on the case having a bee in his bonnet. You remember....'

Harry remembered the Super who had retired a year ago, a man notorious, in cases defying solution, for developing unreasonable suspicions against someone in the case.

'So,' Harry said, 'you've got two hundred and sixty homicidal ratepayers who are going about their daily jobs, singing in the choir, weighing butter and selling eggs, not liking to drink in company. I know one of them.... That fellow in Bath, I saw his name there.'

He watched old Hawker carefully, saw the tongue flick at the thin upper lip. Hawker smiled triumphantly. 'Someone's knocking 'em off!'

'Listen to this carefully, laddie. This list was unknown to you, or should be. Inspectors or their superiors know about it and can consult it if they've got good reason. But it's completely classified, as the Yanks taught us to say. It couldn't be produced in court: we'd hide behind the Home Secretary and everybody could go to hell. But the Home Secretary, worthy man, knows that it's among the documents he doesn't ask to see. In the past six years only old man Hawker, yourself and fourteen senior officers have had occasion to see it.'

'How many of these men have been ... eliminated?'

Hawker ignored him. 'Each year the local station is asked if Mr. Smith the honest green-grocer is still in business. Perhaps the locals know that it was Mr. Smith who beat in Aunt Aggie's brains ten years ago, perhaps they don't. About forty of these birds are always inside for other offences, and the returns are automatically posted. Then old Hawker gets out his quill pen and annotates. Each year seven of them die and a number, which in these days of hire purchase and bank references amounts to an average of slightly more than two, succeed in disappearing ... a phoney passport, maybe, and life anew in the great open spaces. But last year,' said Hawker, 'thirteen of them died.'

He nodded. 'An actuary's nightmare. The permissible deaths,' Hawker smirked like a guardian angel, 'is an average of seven, rising to nine, and dropping to five. Based on age, occupation and occult formulas you wot not. I tell you, my hair stood on end. I could see compulsory retirement looming. It's a terrible thing when a man sees his beautiful irrefragible,' Hawker rolled the word, 'little figures standing up and going into a polka. But I clung on and checked. One senility, two cancer, etcetera, quite normal, but five indubitable pieces of funny business.'

Harry sat back patiently to listen. It was part of Yard lore that whilst Hawker endlessly discursed, he made up for the loss of time by never going home.

'Usually the only murderers who get murdered themselves are the gangsters. Now for one, Charles Edwin Smith, forty-seven, described as a ship's painter but actually a bookmaker's minder, was beaten to death in an alley in Southwark. He lived by the cosh and died by it. No particular suspects and he was drunk when he got it. Enemies?' Hawker snorted. 'He had sixty-four known enemies in that district, none of whom we could place at the scene. But he had enemies in Walworth, enemies in Islington, and even as far away as Birmingham. Charles Edwin had committed two beatings which ended in death.' He drew pictures with his hands. 'Round the dirty little streets, knock, knock, "where were you when Charlie Smith got it, chum?" No result.'

'I was on that for a time on relief,' said James. 'A vicious bashing, didn't care whether they killed him or not. Charlie was past it, living on his rep. The younger men had kicked him off most of the streets he used to work. I thought they saw him drunk and the drink made Charlie truculent. So they took him behind an advertising hoarding for someone's trousers and smashed him up.'

His voice trailed off, remembering a rather nice faded wife and the four kids, all with snivelling colds, the night he'd knocked at the paintless door set flush on the street.

'Yes,' said old Hawker. 'Charlie's could be just a statistic, but the others ain't. Listen!'

'Mr. Guy Tavisham, sixty-eight. Might have been Sir Guy with any luck before it happened, "it" being an eight year old girl who

Guy undoubtedly and very brutally killed in 1950. As a youngster he was very promising in the Indian Civil Service, performed some obscure but worthy civilian job in Portugal during the war, receiving two minor decorations, inherited a great big house with enough to keep it up, net personality £142,000, and as mad as a hare, only hares aren't vicious, at least I think not,' he added with mock dubiousness.

'No doubt?'

'Tomlinson had the case just before he retired. He's been dead two years, but I'd rate him among the four best I've ever seen here.' His fingers sketched again, and James dimly remembered a thin little man, eyebrows still sandy below sparse grey hair, a rat-trap mouth and faded light blue eyes. A copper of the old school, prodigiously hardworking, patient and tenacious.

'No doubt,' said Hawker, 'you'll remember similar cases, been a lot of them. Girl was the daughter of an employee at a brush factory Tavisham partly owned. Indication was that the late Tavisham had known the parents and the girl over a few years. Girl meets somebody going home from school, disappears, turns up in a culvert. It's all very horridly familiar, except for the fact that Guy Tavisham was a gentleman. Imposing personality, general feeling that he had been unfortunate not to have made more of his talents, seems to have been a genuine scholar,' Hawker's Scottish burr lowered in pitch. 'Now the girl was a painfully shy little thing—it's certain that she knew the person who lured her into a car. Tavisham was thirty miles away, no alibi. Story was that he had been driving aimlessly from nine in the morning until about seven in the evening, took some sandwiches with him.'

He gestured. 'That wasn't uncommon. Tavisham was of solitary disposition and increasingly so, as you'll see in a minute. Tomlinson's squad interviewed two thousand people, a procedural classic of its kind. He was certain Tavisham was the man. There was a kind of disused cottage on the property and they got a search warrant, very tricky business as the Tavisham family was an old country one. There was some evidence of the murder, it might have taken place there, but Tavisham's car was as clean as a whistle when Tomlinson got round to sneaking a check on it.'

He gestured. 'No evidence to clinch a case. One of the forensic men went up there, took a few looks at Tavisham. He said the man could, repeat could be suffering from a kind of mania which would progressively worsen—the desire to be alone could be a symptom. Could! Could! Could!'

Hawker snorted disgustedly with a policeman's disgust at scientists who persist in seeing all shades of grey.

He looked at the younger man. 'Tavisham had a remarkable library of criminology and morbid psychology.' His mouth twisted. 'Everything published on Leopold and Loeb, the murder for thrills boys, among 'em. After the killing we were in a spot, because if the trick cyclist was right, Tavisham would get queerer and queerer and other little girls would turn up in culverts.'

He sighed. 'All very nicely done! A couple of oldish sergeants sworn to secrecy and told to keep a benevolent eye on Mr. Tavisham, spending their Sunday afternoons lying in the clover with binoculars, all very civilised.'

'Was Tomlinson as certain as that?'

'Listen to what the old dog wrote. "The enquiry, although inconclusive, evidentially leaves no doubt to my mind of the guilt of Mr. Tavisham." Evidentially! You'll find when you read the file that Tavisham, although any reasonable man would have known that he was in the position of chief suspect, showed no sign of being aware of it. Insouciant, was old Tomlinson's Sunday school word for it. You know that sign. When they're not indignant, don't even come trying to discuss it.'

Harry knew it. The worst sign. The sign that made a policeman sigh inwardly and say in his heart 'I'll have you, you cold-blooded bastard'.

'After the case,' said the old Superintendent, 'Tavisham started to look his age. He kept the house on but seemed to hate living in it. Only one thing. One of the local sergeants who kept an eye on Tavisham heard something second-hand that indicated he might have been blackmailed. Oh, yes,' he caught Harry's words and took them away from him, 'we did ask his solicitors after he died. No dice. Wouldn't play at all.

'Tavisham took a spare-time cottage near Guildford. Used to drive down and do for himself, eating out of cans. Sometimes he used to stay there for a couple of weeks. When he was in residence, a woman used to come in every three days and clean up. She found him dead one morning, flat on the floor of the bedroom. Botulism.

'Very little risk of that these days sonny, but it does happen.'

'Tins?'

'The devil about botulinic acid is that it kills suddenly, but the

14

experts quarrel a bit about how long it can lie low in the stomach without striking. When it does, it can kill you before you can reach the door. No, he'd had an evening meal, tinned sardines on toast, and perfectly good. But he'd had a piece of veal and ham pie somewhere that day and his stomach was full of the acid. That was what puzzled the doctors. They couldn't conceive how all that quantity could have been ingested with approximately four ounces, one decent slice of veal and ham pie. Again, there wasn't any veal and ham pie in the cottage. The whole county and those next to it—remembering his drifting habits—was combed until every grocer cursed us to high heaven. Nobody sold him veal and ham pie, that choice viand, and the health boys found no source of contaminated v. and h. The analyst thought the pie, might again, have been home made.'

Hawker glanced at his notes, 'Here's the next.'

'Mr. Freddy Farqueson had a wealthy aunt whose unpaid messenger boy he had been. The aunt was fifty-eight, a healthy woman of peculiar disposition who was addicted to the bottle. Addicted, and if you want to know, Tio Pepe and ginger ale, God help us all, was her tipple. She could afford it. The husband, a man named Smythe, won seven thousand pounds in the pools in 1937. Alas for the moralists, the money doubled and redoubled for him, most of which he put in his wife's name. He had a chronic heart condition and died in 1948. Auntie Smythe cut up for £78,000 when she was found with her skull stove in at the bottom of her stairs. She'd hit the newel post.

'Now Auntie wasn't a hospital case by a long sight, could have lived for years, but she'd started to hate Freddy. In fact she's told her friends that it was only fair for her to leave the dough to her husband's relations, whom she'd never met. We knew she had engaged a private detective to trace them. Smythe had been a secretive bird, and all she knew was that he had a brother somewhere.

'Meantime, Master Fred, in business with Auntie's financial backing gets himself into the sort of hole where it's money or a couple of years inside. The maid is out for the evening, the Aunt invites Freddy round to go over her private accounts. Fred is sitting there with the accounts, whilst Auntie guzzles her sherry. According to his story Auntie makes a ladylike trip upstairs and presently he hears the crash and there lies poor Auntie.

'Two flaws. One is that the maid didn't go so early as she usually did. She heard a telephone ring and Auntie told her that Master Freddy had rung her asking if he could come round for the evening. Second, witnesses saw Master Freddy emerging from a public telephone box at about that time. Thirdly, the Home Office bloke thought that somebody might, repeat might, have picked up Auntie by the hair and dashed her brains out against the post. After pushing her down the stairs, of course.

'Freddy was as bold as brass.... Lennon went up from here to take the case.' His voice had hardened and the young man grinned inwardly, for the Lennon rumour had it that luck rather than ability, and a remarkable talent for public relations, had gained his reputation.

'Master Freddy was very engaging: the phone call was to a blonde, one of many. The young man had the wit to call upon a good solicitor at exactly the right time ... not early enough for counsel to hint that he went running to a lawyer ... and there's no case, although the insurance company who had to cough up another £10,000 went blue in the gills.

'Now you take Freddy. The welfare state leave him £35,000 after cutting the estate up. He pays his debts, and has thirty thousand left. His wife divorces him, like a sensible woman, and Fred prospers in real estate. Speciality is buying new blocks of flats and selling them off as "own your own home" jobs. Two months ago, ten months after Tavisham died, Master Fred is found with his skull smashed in at the bottom of a half completed lift well in a block of flats being built in Reading. He went up by the stairs—the door wasn't on and for some reason the aperture hadn't been boarded up. He must have gone up on a pitch black night, and no torch was ever found.'

'Suicide?'

The old man grunted. 'Examination showed that Freddy's fat little hands had scrabbled desperately at the top of the well and there was a bruise that could, repeat could, have meant that somebody stamped on them. Open verdict.

'The third man was a Mr. Ron Case. Four years ago Case, a man of no visible means of support, was associated with one Joe Seddon, who had a long record as a doper of greyhounds, an agent for a marijuana ring and a landlord of brothels.

'Both Case and Seddon are listed as homosexuals.' Hawker wrinkled his lips.

'One Thursday night we find both Case and Seddon living in a rooming house, one of those shady places a couple of degrees higher than a doss-house—dark stairs, smell of frying fat, a

16

couple of dozen doors off landings with greasy gas stoves on 'em. They shared a room. Now mark this. Both of them had been dead broke, but the dead man, Seddon, had made a killing at the dog track a few days before. He had been flashing a great roll of notes around. And he'd quarrelled with Case: no doubt of it, Case was dead scared of something.

'Earlier on this evening people had heard them at it hammer and tongs. Now to the time element, at ten minutes to ten Seddon knocked at the door of another room occupied by an old man who was glad to run errands. "Nip across and buy us half a bottle of Scotch". The old man goes across to an off licence and straight back to the Seddon-Case room. He finds Seddon dead with a clasp knife in the back of his neck. The guv'nor of the place comes up and looks at his watch—exactly four minutes to ten. The local police checked the watch afterwards—only a few seconds slow by Greenwich.

'Open and shut, particularly as Ron Case never showed up! He's picked up in London next day, with a new suit on and a few quid in his pocket. There was no money found in the room, but Case had plenty of time to stash it away.

'He wouldn't make a statement, but sat there trembling. But then something transpires. At exactly ten o'clock he had walked into the Red Rose, a pub in the centre of town. Teevee was on and ten o'clock was given out just as Case, who the landlord and the barmen both knew, walked in.

'Now no one could have run from the lodging house to the Red Rose in under ten minutes. It would take, say, twenty minutes at a brisk walk.

'Oh, yes, the local police—it didn't come to us—searched for stolen bicycles with no success. Case finally got round to say that he'd walked out in a huff at 9.30, dropped in at the Red Rose for a brandy and caught the 10.25 train to London.

'He did it, of course. The knife was his—he looked guilty as hell when they picked him up. There have been many cases where the time factor doesn't jell. They hanged a man during the war who confessed to murdering a woman. Yet two truthful witnesses said they saw him two miles away near the time it occurred. There could be fifty explanations. But they couldn't find any one that would stand up in court. The Director of Public Prosecutions took exactly seven hours to send the papers back. No prosecution.

'Master Ron prospered in his nasty way—sold teevee at one

time, ran a small book, lived in a nasty little flat in Hammersmith, kept his nose cleanish. One day he doesn't come home and his little flatmate eventually gets round to telling the coppers—after he's pawned everything moveable.

'Six months ago a couple of farm labourers find him dead in a ditch down in Wiltshire. Shot through the head, with a gun in his hand.

'You know how hard it is to fake a suicide. The farm labourers had moved him, and he'd been dead four days, but the Medical Officer had a very strong suspicion he'd been shot through the head, nicely arranged in the ditch with the gun in his hand.

'No leads at all, except someone remembered him getting off a train at Swindon. He'd got fifteen hundred in the bank, by the way. The Coroner brought in an open verdict. Someone could be as clever as hell. I'll give you the first case by default, but Tavisham, Master Freddy and Mr. Ron Case have a certain familiar ring about them.'

Hawker took a final gusty mouthful of cold tea. 'Now to the catalyst, laddie!' He leered over the desk.

'Miss Rhonda Gentry would now be twenty-seven years of age. When she was twenty she lived in a country town in Sussex and was engaged to a young solicitor. He broke the engagement. It was all very civilised. But a month or two later the solicitor was returning home from the tennis club, where he'd been with his new girl friend, and collapsed a mile from home and died a few hours later. Enough hyoscine in him to kill a camel.

'Oh, yes, Miss Rhonda Gentry had been there, with forty or so other young people. It was a very warm afternoon. You know the thing. "Can I fetch you another lemonade?"' Hawker looked coy.

'The solicitor complained of feeling unwell, a touch of sun, so he made his excuses and left early, leaving Miss Rhonda to mixed doubles.

'They never found the container. Sergeant White went down, and it transpires that Miss Rhonda had the reputation of being extremely bad tempered and malicious to those she thought injured her. And her profession was a dispenser at the local hospital.'

'What about the records?'

'Three weeks earlier there had been an explosion in the dispensary—a heater blew up during the night. Cupboards blown in, bottles smashed all over the place. The hospital authorities

18

couldn't be quite sure whether or not hyoscine had gone. They thought it hadn't, but when White persisted they admitted that the required quantity of the drug could possibly, perhaps, maybe have disappeared in the shambles.

'Oh yes, everybody was certain it was Miss Rhonda, including White. She was a very collected little girl in the box: result, an open verdict. Miss Rhonda was an orphan, living with an aunt and uncle. After the case, she went quietly away, in fact to a town named Bradshaw, in Lancashire. She gets a job in the laboratory of a small chemical works, buys a cottage, and lives there in an odour of sanctity.'

'How was she killed?'

Hawker chuckled. 'She's not,' he said.

Harry refused to rise to the bait, and helped himself to a cigarette from the open packet on the desk.

'She's alive,' said Hawker after a few seconds. 'I'm stuck here,' he grumbled, 'among diligent clerks, with not even an errand boy who I can trust to do more than fetch another box of cards from the store. No, laddie, she's alive and flourishing. But, on reading through seven square acres of reports, one thing struck me: none of these people apparently had ever met each other or had any contact at all with anybody else on the list, except Miss Rhonda Gentry.'

He tapped his long fingers on the desk. 'One, Charles Edwin Smith. No contacts at all. Two, Mr. Guy Tavisham. He knew Miss Rhonda Gentry because he was one of three trustees appointed to administer her father's estate. He was a solicitor and left about twelve hundred pounds. The girl was around eleven when her father died, so there is no particular reason why he should even have met her.

'Three, Mr. Freddy Farqueson, the plump little gentleman. Gentry took her training in London and lodged in a flat in South Kensington. The next-door neighbour at that time was a Mr. Freddy Farqueson. Two little addresses in the reports.

'Four. Mr. Ron Case. I told you he cashed in a bit on the teevee boom.' Hawker registered disgust. 'The early days when there was a bit of witchcraft about the thing. Ron went to Bradshaw and opened one of his little shops—Townend Teevee—installing antennae and doing repairs. He sold out after a year.'

Harry stubbed the cigarette in the Bass ashtray. 'doesn't sound much,' he said.

'Work out the odds,' said Hawker, shuffling in his chair. 'Four of 'em could have known Gentry. Suppose you had struck one of those phoney balance sheets your old firm audited. . . .'

'Look,' said Harry, aroused, 'we did million quid public companies.'

Hawker cackled offensively. 'Should have stuck to that, my boy, you have the beautifully innocent mind. But if you had been looking for some falsification, and four out of five cheques had been paid in through a certain branch of a particular bank, you'd conclude that it might be a lead, an indication, a smell of a trail, whatever you want.'

He snapped erect and slapped his hand on the file. 'For a starter I want you to see this Gentry. Use your charms, you're a fine bronzed youth if she likes them undersized, a year or so older than she for maturity, and you know as well as I do that small men have a certain reputation.'

Harry laughed. He liked Hawker. 'Look,' he said, 'what's the cover story or do I offer her sex books on the instalment plan?'

'There's a ready-made one. I asked the Bradshaw people if they knew any connection between Mr. Ron Case and the Gentry. They didn't, although she installed a teevee the time he was starting up there—she must be doing well. But the Super mentioned casually that something peculiar found its way into the records. There was a Saturday this year when she was waiting, with about five hundred other people, for the fast train to Euston. It coincided with Bradshaw United's first and only appearance in the fourth round of the F.A. Cup. As the train comes in Miss Gentry staggers and falls. But the authorities in their wisdom had decreed that a large case of prime Irish salmon, destined for Manchester, still reposed after several days of ripening on the very edge of the platform. It ended with Miss Gentry sprawling on top of the case and just missing being hit by the train. The mob hauled her up, and into the train she went without complaint. But behind her had been standing a woman who knows her, to wit the sister of her charwoman. She was "fair flabber-ghasted", but as she said she had her ticket to think of. But on return in the evening, filled with stout and mortified by the three nil defeat of her team, she spared the time to come into the police station and meander about the dreadful thing. She had seen a plump man deliberately shove Miss Gentry as the train was coming in. She stuck to it even next morning when she was sober, and in fact had told the people in her compartment, two of whom she insisted in bringing to the station.'

It was Hawker at his worst, Harry reflected.

'Of course, somebody went round. But Miss Gentry was evasive. First thing, she had stumbled over the prime salmon, but the man stuck to it and eventually got some sort of admission that she did feel some urging pressure on her backbone. His report said "she was cool and evasive and seemed anxious to forestall any investigation." '

Hawker lit his cigarette from the stub of the old. 'Bloody things—won't live to get me pension. O' course, if you were the Gentry you'd have had a bellyful of policemen. But this puts you in, brother. I've fixed it so that you're attached to the Bradshaw Constabulary for all reasonable purposes except stipend, and your rank is so humble that your presence will presumably go unnoticed. Go and see her. Hint that there might be a Teddy gang going around barging into women on stations ... mention Mr. Case in some way. But don't mention hyoscine or her real name for God's sake. The Watch Committee is eighty per cent Labour and the M.P. loves publicity. No bashing, arm twisting, suborning or any typical tricks of the brutal constabulary. The lists of love now ... well,' Hawker leered.

The old Superintendent jerked a thumb to a stack of files. 'It's all there. Spend a couple of days reading it up and seeing anybody that might occur to you. Then, up you go to Bradshaw.'

Harry paused by the door. 'Gentry's her real name. What's she going under?'

Hawker butted his cigarette. 'Oh, didn't I tell you? Holland. Elizabeth Holland, her middle names.'

'What's the matter?' He came round the desk very fast and Harry found an arm round his shoulder as the room seemed to close in and the floor become nearer. 'It's the heat,' said Hawker.

Harry shrugged the arm off. 'I'm all right.' The room began to clear as he went through the door.

The files were depressingly dull, in regulation language, but he stuck to his note-making in spite of a headache.

Mr. Freddy Farqueson had been divorced by his wife in 1953, eight months after his aunt's death. Harry telephoned the solicitors who had handled probate. A rather bored law clerk said their deceased client had made a financial settlement with the wife and they had no record of her subsequently. Fortunately she had married again, her present name being Bayliss, and Somerset House's record gave a Finchley address for the groom.

The house possessed a telephone and a voice at the other end said that the Bayliss' had left a few years ago to live in Wimbledon.

Harry took a train out there after he had finished the day's work.

The former Mrs. Farqueson was a rather faded little woman in her late forties. Her husband was a quiet, stolid-looking man who, Harry considered, must have been a considerable relief after the roving Freddy. Two children sat in the corner of the room doing homework and Mr. Bayliss was watching the televison, so he talked to the woman in her bright little kitchen.

'No,' she said, 'I don't mind talking about Freddy. Naturally his death gave me a shock, but no particular grief. I'd stopped grieving for Freddy many years before that.'

She had a quick, open smile that was attractive.

'Before his aunt's death, Mrs. Bayliss, I understand your former husband was in financial difficulties.'

'Yes, the police made quite a point of that at the time. Mind you, his aunt was a rather terrible woman, reeling drunk half the time, and there was no reason I could see why she shouldn't have pitched head-first down the stairs.'

'How bad was his situation?'

'If you'd ever met him, sergeant, you'd know that Freddy was such a consummate liar that you could never establish anything. In 1950 he did have some kind of windfall, that's definite. Then, being Freddy, he started to go down hill again and we were flat broke. I imagine it was true, as the police said, that he had been forging his aunt's name in the months before she died.'

'You'll forgive me for saying that he was a man who would make enemies.'

'There's nothing to forgive. Freddy was a liar, a man who couldn't keep his hands off women and a cruel treacherous person in every way.' She glanced away from him.

'You didn't see him after your divorce?'

'No, I never did. I would have gone out of my way not to.'

'He seems to have prospered in business after his aunt's death.'

'Oh, don't misunderstand me. He was a smart business man, but he had no patience, with the result that he was always chronically under-capitalised. The money that came his way in 1950 should have been put into his existing business, but instead he used most of it to open another shop and was back where he started.'

'I don't think I have a note of his line of business?'

'Electrical goods at that time.'

He thanked her and started the wearisome journey back. In the train he looked at the notes. Electrical goods might mean some connection with Ron Case, the same line of country, but it would need a whole squad to cover that angle. Fat chance.

Next morning he arrived early with an overnight bag stuffed with the minimum of clothing, not for the first time thanking the Lord for drip dry, and finished the last file.

He could see no near-at-hand lead on the man Case, who had spent his last years out of London. He telephoned Hawker and said he'd take a train around two.

Charles Edwin Smith, six feet of muscle running to fat and grog blossoms grouped unpleasantly on a lardy face, might be another matter. Whoever had done Charles Edwin over had made a good job of it, he thought, looking at the harshly lighted close-ups. There was ruthless intent there, not just a usual bashing. If the police had failed to find the murderer it wasn't for the lack of asking questions or parsimony in man-hours. For a moment, Harry felt a slight tingle in his mind as though a door had briefly opened.

He parcelled up the files for return to Hawker, got his bag and went by tube to see Old Lobby, who came very high, at a fiver a time. By profession Lobby was a publican, in a very small house not far from the Oval. The long lane consisted of very blackened three-storey houses set flush on the street, with a pub of varying size every two hundred yards. Lobby's single bar, about twenty feet by twelve feet, had two battered tables and a piano which had a greenish tinge and was never opened. Lobby had been licensed to sell beer and wine for thirty years: three congealed wine bottles above the racks of bottled ale bore testimony to the vinous connexion with England's oldest ally. At one corner of the bar a door opened into a precipitous, rickety staircase, culminating in two rooms of filthy horror, in one of which Lobby slept on a rubber mattress covered with the greasy remains of three stolen car rugs. The blinds were never drawn.

Lobby was a fence. In the little room with the old gas stove which opened out behind the bar, where presumably old Lobby cooked what meals he took, quite a lot of illegal business was transacted. For himself, Lobby was well on the side of caution and dealt only with unidentifiable objects: blankets, certain types of clothing, and radio parts were the main portion of his trade. For the rest he acted as an agent. A young thief with half a dozen stolen car radios would be put in touch with the right source by Lobby who got his commission. It was years now since the police had searched the premises. A dozen blankets which Lobby would swear to as wedding presents, or half a dozen valves 'bought cheap in the Lane to try and get me little ol' wireless goin'', were poor rewards, but as an informer Lobby ranked very high in police estimation.

There was only one customer in the bar, as Harry pushed open the swing door a minute after opening time, a skinny old woman drinking stout. Harry glanced at the door behind the bar, and Lobby lifted the counter flap and beckoned. He was a dirty, small man with watery grey eyes and a few grey hairs obscenely plastered to his skull with dabs of yellow grease.

Harry ordered the ritual warm pale ale 'for the good of the house' and Lobby took a small glass of shandy.

'Know anything about that fellow Smith who got done over nine months ago, Lobby?'

The old man shrugged. ''Ad an inspector 'ere at the time. I said I couldn't 'elp.'

'No information since?'

Lobby sucked his teeth for a minute. 'Orl right, I'll tell you. There's bin a lot of talk, a lot of talk around, and nobody knows nothin' about Charles Edwin. Billy Edwards wanted to know because it's 'is territory.'

Edwards was the current 'head' of the district in which Smith was murdered.

'That's strange,' Harry commented. 'Perhaps it was a North London lot.'

'I tell yer, Billy was fair 'opping mad. He went over the river and asked what abaht it. Nobody knew a bleedin' thing. Some of the Birmingham lot who 'ad it in for Charles Edwin were down 'ere about a dog and Billy 'ad a word with 'em. They swore their gospel bleedin' oath that it weren't a Birmingham job.'

'Any ideas of your own, Lobby?'

For once the bleary eyes met his. 'I'll tell yer. I reckon Charles Edwin was in drink, and, Christ, you know what a terror 'e were after fifteen pints and a drop of Scotch. Suppose 'e met a strong ornery lad goin' 'ome from work, or maybe a couple of 'em, and started suthing. They 'ave to defend themself and Charles Edwin was a demon when 'e saw red. At the end they've got a corpus on their 'ands, so they drag 'im behind the 'oarding and just scarper 'ome, not sayin' nuthin'.'

Harry thanked him, took a sticky palm in his, and placed a fiver on the table. He used his handkerchief in the bus to scrub his hand.

The sergeant who had handled the Gentry case was now a D.D.I. in a high class suburban area in south-west London. Harry caught him as he was going off for lunch and suggested a pint.

'Rhonda Gentry, huh,' the D.D.I. said with some distaste. 'There I was sweating for the step-up and I got this turkey.' He had a beefy red face which he buried in his tankard.

'The run down was this. Deceased was a solicitor named Goldsmith who was in his uncle's office in London. Uncle had a very thriving practice and young Goldsmith could look forward in time to a partnership with his two cousins. He had a widowed mother who lived in the former gate-keeper's cottage of an estate that the uncle had bought and was hanging on to for future development.'

'Young Goldsmith was a handsome, popular youth, not too stable so I judged, who had got himself engaged to Miss Gentry when she was nineteen and he was twenty-six. After six months it was all off. Some fifteen months later Goldsmith gets himself engaged to another girl, a cowlike and statuesque young English rose. I'd have preferred Rhonda myself, but for temper.'

'That bit about her bad nature was in the summary,' said Harry.

'Well,' said the D.D.I. 'Wrexbury is one of those sleepy little towns brimful of gossip. Gentry's parents got killed when she was eleven in a car crash and she was brought up by an uncle and aunt. They treated her like a daughter.

'The uncle was in a fair line of business, just comfortable, not wealthy. Rhonda never really settled in—fiery nature which suited her hair and a lot of slow-blooded rustics who gossiped. They didn't like her, the tradespeople and such, and she didn't like them.'

Harry accepted a second pint.

'Then,' said the D.D.I., 'they had this Sunday session at the local tennis club. Deceased's there with his new fiancée. During the afternoon he is seen talking pretty seriously to Gentry. He leaves early, his fiancée's parents being present to take her home.

'Eventually he's found dead with hyoscine in him near some bushes half a mile from his home.'

'Yeah,' said Harry. 'I read the file. On paper the case looked weak, and I couldn't fathom why you were sure.'

The D.D.I. sighed. 'Wasn't too much—bad-tempered girl jilted, hospital dispenser, and the only person at the tennis club we could trace having any contact with a drug such as hyoscine—a relatively painless way to die, I'm told. The dispensary had been wrecked when the gas heater exploded and you couldn't tell with any certainty how the records stood.'

'Any suspicion she organised the explosion?'

The D.D.I. grinned mournfully. 'If she had, maybe it would have been the clincher, but she was on holiday and the gas plumbing was a scandal, right back to Flo. Nightingale and beyond.'

He doodled in a beer stain on the bar. 'You should have seen her, lovely bit of goods, long legs, well stacked up there, and a good face if she hadn't looked as though she hadn't slept for six months. You know, a nervous twitch in the forehead, eyes like a pair of oysters looking out of a tin can. Jumpy.'

The D.D.I. sighed. 'God knows I've never seen anything like it, picture of guilt. And the attitude! Just "Yes, sergeant" or "no sergeant".

'The aunt told me that the girl had been poorly for a month or so, not eating, not sleeping, something on her mind—lost about half a stone by the time I saw her.

'So after two days I asked her to come to see me at the Station, very formal. I had the idea she'd break.

'At twelve o'clock she came in, very composed except for her twitch, and I turn on the usual caution, heavy as I could, and told her that maybe she should have a solicitor present.

'She gave me a nod and said she had arranged for that, but he couldn't be present until one and please could I wait. So I let her sit there and made a pretence of working hard. Sure enough, at one there's a tap on the door and I look up, expecting one of the local solicitors who's torn himself away from conveyancing.

'I nearly keeled out of my chair when old Specs walked in.'

Harry frowned. Old Specs was the smartest criminal solicitor in London and some people said that the adjective referred to him and not his practice.

'How the hell did a twenty-one year old girl know about Specs?'

'To do her justice, her ex-boy-friend was a solicitor and Specs is a legend in the profession. I guessed he must have told her about him.'

'And ... ?' Harry's pint tasted flat and nauseous.

'Oh, Specs steam-rollered right over me. You know his fatherly act! He had his hand round her shoulders and in the neighbourhood of those luscious tits in about forty seconds.'

The Inspector wiped froth off his mouth with a handkerchief.

'She went out free as a bird with Old Specs opening the door for her. Of course there was the inquest. We'd hoped to get something there about the poison, but the Coroner saw Specs at the table and toned it right down. Open Verdict.'

'No chance of suicide?'

'He couldn't have got the hyoscine, unless maybe Rhonda got it for him—no possible contact. Nice boy, happily engaged to a girl whose family had influence, good job with prospects. We saw the uncle, trap-faced old bird like God's wrath, and he said young Goldsmith was coming along nicely in the office. No, old boy, it was her or nobody.'

CHAPTER TWO

WICKSTRAW, THE BRADSHAW Super, was a southerner who had transferred a few years before. Harry's first impression was unfavourable when he saw a fussy, stout man with spectacles halfway down his nose.

'H'm,' said Wickstraw, shuffling papers around. 'Mr. Hawker phoned me. We're short-handed and having to move men about, so you won't be noticed. I've notified the Inspector.'

'Thank you, sir.'

The Superintendent hunched himself over the table. 'This woman, Holland, I can't fault her. M' wife's on a committee with her. Tea and sherry occasionally at my place. Charming, but reserved, is Miss Gentry.'

Harry let a look of admiration cross his face.

Wickstraw smiled and Harry noticed that the small black eyes were cold and shrewd. 'I got my transfer from that area and saw her once in the Coroner's court. You don't forget her in a hurry. Now, once a year, I write one line to Hawker, "Nothing known".'

Harry decided to venture a little further. 'Is that all you wrote to him?' He emphasised the past tense.

A guarded look made Wickstraw's eyelids drop a little. 'Oh, Tavisham,' he said. 'By the time I got here the old gentleman, he wasn't that old actually, around fifty-seven, was in his shell and not coming out. There were two sergeants, one dead now, who looked after him. But you'd have seen the reports. They went each month to Hawker.'

Harry shrugged non-committally, while his opinion of Wickstraw shifted. 'I'll report to the Inspector, sir.'

'Have some tea before you go.' The Super pressed a bell.

When the thick canteen char came in its thick china, he watched the pursy old fellow shovel three teaspoonsful of sugar in.

'Elizabeth Holland,' gurgled Wickstraw, dunking a marie biscuit, 'has got a charming cottage—my wife's adjective—at the Strand, lot of greenery around, lot of retired people, solicitors, County Court judges, people out of the colonial service. Odd place for a spinster of twenty-seven.'

'Good place to go to ground, maybe,' Harry volunteered.

'Ah,' said Wickstraw, 'she fits in. A lady. The Strand has always been a desirable district. Ever heard of a man named Marcus?'

'Not particularly,' said Harry, surveying a few men of that name.

'Before your time. He was an accountant who got to be a young M.P., in his thirties, in 1937. He disappeared in 1939.'

'Disappeared?' Harry was jolted in spite of himself.

'Odd business. Before I came here, o' course.' Wickstraw emphasised the words while his bland black eyes smiled over the teacup. 'I must say I do enjoy a cupper around this hour. Yes, Marcus, patriotic bloke from all accounts, an orphan and un-married. One day he walked out of his house at the Green and never came back.'

'I don't remember....'

'No fuss, unusual circumstances, Marcus had applied for the Chiltern Hundreds a week before he disappeared, so technically he wasn't an M.P. any more. He'd had a three thousand majority and his successor was on a piece of cake. It was July, just before war came and the file went to the Yard and that was that.'

Harry had been staring abstractedly at a fly exploring his saucer, and wondering about Wickstraw.

'Well, Sergeant, I know all about the Strand. And I hope you'll co-operate as is usual.'

Harry felt his eyebrows raise.

'Frankly you're young. No local police wants to be made a goat.'

'I'll co-operate, sir, usual channels and all that.'

'Fine,' said Wickstraw. 'It's just that we've got a touchy Watch Committee—ratepayers' money etcetera.' He scrabbled in a drawer. 'If you want a lodging there's the address of a Mrs. Fanny Walsh. The Strand is outside the factory area and Mrs. Walsh has got a big old house half a mile the wrong side of the railroad tracks. Quite suitable. I'll ring her up.'

Harry got up and moved towards the door.

'Miss Holland's a member of the local tennis club. We might be able to wangle you into that,' was Wickstraw's final remark.

He reported to the Inspector, a laconic man with a broken nose. 'The Super gave me instructions, and I told Harris, the Sergeant, as little as possible. You're on plain clothes work in connection with housebreaking. That means you'll have to spend a few hours per day doing just that.'

Harris was fiftyish, moist of eye and at first glance uninquisitive. He invited Harry, his eyes bland, to a glass of beer that evening. 'No need to come on duty until tomorrow,' he confided, 'but maybe there's a few things about this manor I can put you right about.'

Bradshaw had been a largish sized Victorian town, Harry's swotting had established, because it was sited on large deposits of inferior clay eminently suitable to the mass production of very cheap crocks. 'It's Bradshaw' had been a minor colloquialism applied to something which might shatter at any moment. Later, its near neighbour, Bentleigh, given over to railway works, an ordnance factory and boiler works had first dwarfed it and then overflowed it so that now Bradshaw was an appendage of the equally depressed Bentleigh. He had not been quite expecting the faded but unmistakable wounds of gouged quarries beyond the blackened row houses, the limping pubs, the better-class houses of 1910 vintage with area steps now unwhitened, the whole broken by oases of brightly painted shopping centres. He decided that a taxi wouldn't be passed on expenses, and rejected the impulse to treat himself. The bus conductor put him off at the middle of a long, slightly crescent-shaped street of old houses.

He rapped at the door, which swung back from his hand leaving a smear of the purple paint on his knuckles. While he was wondering whether to ruin a handkerchief the door swung completely back and a woman's deep contralto, port wine in its undertones, said, 'I never know how to judge the thinners, you know.'

He blinked into the blackness of the hall.

'At any rate you've used too much this time. I'm looking . . .'

'I know, Mr. James, and I'm Fanny Walsh. Come on in. Leave your case and come into the kitchen.'

He dropped it beside an umbrella stand leaning at forty degrees outwards, surmounted by a span of antlers, and followed the shape thirty feet down the corridor and then into the surprising brightness of the kitchen.

Harry guessed that in the times when a merchant class had built the crescent, the kitchen had been of paramount importance to stomachs fed on seemingly boundless empire markets. There were various doors around, one open and leading into an old-fashioned scullery. His eyes gradually became accustomed to the garish colours, reds clashing with purple, and a frog-like green dresser rubbing shoulders with a howling-yellow meatsafe. The only thing, Harry realised, that wasn't coloured was the refrigerator, still virgin white. He was conscious that his hostess, paint tin in one hand, brush in the other, gently dripping grey plastic paint on the rose-coloured synthetic tiles, was wistfully looking in the same direction.

'I think a bit of colour livens you up,' said Fanny Walsh.

She was a big woman, a bit over six feet he reckoned, with close cropped grey curls, and a grey organdie frock which came well below her knees. She was very erect, like an African woman, and he judged sixtyish and pretty big. Her large grey eyes were impassive as they blinked at him short-sightedly.

Miss Tweddle was rather square with the impression of muscle rather than fat. Her hair, pepper and salt, was scraped into a bun, but it was her face that fixed Harry's gaze. The texture was the mottled suet of the alcoholic, the expanse of skin seeming far too small for the features, fastened like seashells daubed on wet concrete.

'Your room's number 2 on the second floor, Mr. James, and Miss Tweddle's taken your case up.'

Harry mumbled because, mounted on a raspberry painted stretch of peg board above on the door, he had just glimpsed fullplate photographs of women taken as nudes. Further he was conscious of a remarkably savoury smell, meaty in base, which pervaded the room, and was conscious that he felt hungry.

'And you'll please take a homely bite with us, dear, I always think that's the best way to get to know the landlady.' A large, paint-smeared hand gestured towards the table laid for three.

He didn't protest as he was pushed into a wicker dining chair. There was a weakness in his legs, a clamminess around his hands and the healed fracture in his left leg seemed to ache.

'You've been ill, love?'

He said he had.

'Ah, you'll have to take it easy. It's long hours in the force.'

He soon found that the stew was excellent, with curiously seasoned little dumplings lurking in it. He ate more heartily than for months past and congratulated his hostess.

'Ah, you learn cooking in the lodgings—on gas-ring things. A trick cyclist, very clever, from Austria taught me that one.' His tired brain puzzled the connexion between lodgings and psychiatry and stew and his face must have showed perplexity, for Miss Walsh vigorously swallowed and said:

'Theatrical lodgings, love. Didn't you know? That's me.' She pointed a fork towards the pegboard.

Harry squinted and saw that the naked ladies were in reality the same lady in different poses, statuesque, bosom thrust upwards by powerful pectoral muscles, strong, arched thighs, sometimes standing arms akimbo, sometimes coyly holding a fan against her stomach. The face was bold and smiling under the piled up hair which in one photograph had been hand-coloured canary yellow. There was no doubt about it, it was the Miss Walsh of some years ago.

'Ah, yes,' his landlady said. 'I got me chance during the war. I had a little put by and put it as a deposit on a lease of a provincial house when everybody else was panicking. Four shows each weekday we did, for three years. The boys had nothing better to do than to come to see me.' She gave her gusty belly laugh. 'We kept prices down, you know, but it was very good money while it lasted.'

Harry relaxed and finished his stew before tackling a large helping of crisply encrusted apple pie.

'The Super said you were on special duty when he phoned,' said Miss Walsh as she poured out thick black coffee.

'Lots of burglaries these days,' said Harry. 'We think it's a gang. Places like the Strand are a favourite mark for cat burglars.'

'I hope they don't disappear.' Miss Tweddle's voice was plummy and a trifle slurred.

Harry glanced sharply at Miss Tweddle. Somehow he had received the impression that she never talked.

Miss Tweddle gave a short laugh like a hiccup.

'They say that people disappear at nights at the Strand.' Her fat little mouth closed firmly.

'That's a local joke,' said Fanny Walsh, a trifle too quickly. 'A man, a politician or something, is said to have disappeared.'

Harry went to keep his appointment with the Sergeant who, at close quarters, emitted a rather goaty smell. Harry thought he could spot the type, originally uniformed and bicycled in a village of insanitary row houses, astute enough to wind up as a day desk sergeant, pension ahead and maybe a pothouse or some reasonable job as a superior watchman.

They had a game of darts and the Sergeant won on merit.

'The Inspector said "no names, no pack drill",' he said as he lipped a third of his winner's pint.

'Good idea,' said Harry.

'And there's the Super,' said the Sergeant as though the idea had suddenly struck him. 'The Deputy Chief of the County goes on superannuation next March and if all's well old Super will get a leg-up. He wouldn't want 'owt to interfere with that.'

'I wouldn't know about that.'

'So you're lodging at Fanny Walsh's,' mused the Sergeant, un-snubbed. 'They say she was a lively bit of homework a quarter of a century ago.'

'She certainly displayed what she had according to her photos,' agreed Harry.

'And a nice old house that I wouldn't mind myself. Nice and handy to the Strand.'

'I've not seen that area yet.'

'It's the nicest spot around, pity it's always had a queer reputation.' The Sergeant drained his pint and Harry called for another.

'Queer?'

'It started on account of a murder, way back in the '80s. The usual thing they were always having then, fellow poisoned his wife and sister-in-law for the insurance, only the doctor was flyer than most and spotted the antimony. Nothing to it, but it gave the place a bad name and values fell.'

'Somebody told me that there was a disappearance there a few years back.'

'Ah, that was a fellow named Marcus. The M.P. in those days.' The Sergeant laughed without humour. 'They had a P.C. stationed at the Strand in those days and it happened it were me first posting. One day the old housekeeper comes knocking at the door and says the master ain't been home for four days and all sorts of people have been ringing up asking where he is.'

'And he never did turn up?'

'Not hide nor hair of him. Must have gone off with some bint, you know the thing.'

'Ah, yes,' said Harry and excused himself.

He put on a clean noncommittal suit and walked round to Rose Cottage at eight-thirty. The Strand had originally been well-planned. The side posts which originally supported the barred gates to private roads still remained, as did the gate-keepers' cottages. In one of these, latterly enlarged, lived Miss Elizabeth Holland. The original high wall had been enlarged to enclose a garden and the entrance was flanked by an elaborately clipped hedge.

Closing the gate he walked towards the mellowed ground-level house. Three bedrooms, one single, he guessed, veiled by rose bushes and shrubs. It looked carelessly planned, purposely perhaps, but neat in execution. A place that one might like to live in if one could. On the right a larger house, three storeys high, looked clumsy by comparison.

A woman with a thick mane of copper coloured hair was squatting, straddled-kneed, against a flower bed working a garden syringe. The skin of her neck was tanned until the loose fitting linen jacket fell back to reveal thick creamy skin. As she heard his footfalls she turned round, resting one gloved hand on the ground.

He stood there hat in hand as she got to her feet with the ease of an athlete. Practice kept his face impassive as he met the tawny green-flecked eyes of the woman he had seen outside the Houses of Parliament.

It seemed a long second in which he could not tell whether she recalled him or not. He had the impression of a regular, oval face, with rather high cheek bones.

'I'm Constable James,' he said, 'stationed locally, perhaps I could talk to you.'

She put down the syringe. 'Oh, please come in, Constable.' Her voice was a soft contralto.

He followed her through a wide hall into a living-room, rather sparsely furnished, but, he registered professionally, expensive for what there was.

She motioned him to a chair. 'It's about a fall you had on the railway station,' he said with his best smile.

She raised one eyebrow. 'That? I had another policeman round here at the time.'

'The fact is,' said Harry, 'that we're troubled by a 'teen-age gang. They invent all kinds of new devilment and the latest seems to be creating a problem at the railway station, stealing packages and fixtures, that kind of thing. But there's a game they play occasionally which consists of barging into passengers when a train comes in. I'm collating the complaints.'

She gave him a quick warm smile. 'I'm afraid I've always been sorrier for 'teen-age gangs than cross with them.'

'Socially perhaps you're right, but it's the police who have to sweep up the mess and sometimes it's a messy mess, if you take the point.'

'Yes, I see. But when I collapsed on to that smelly fish box I'm sure there were no juvenile delinquents around. You'll have had the facts I suppose. I had an urgent reason to get to London and the first train was the one hundreds of football fans were scrambling on to. As the train came in they all surged forward—quite frightening. I suppose some zealous supporter tried to climb through me.'

He snapped his notebook closed.

'Ah, well, that's life on the force. Hundreds of useless questions per week.'

'I'm sorry I can't help you,' the gentle voice said.

Harry thought she meant it.

'Oh, we'll stop them,' he said. 'It'll mean a couple of fellows permanently there for a couple of weeks, but the Boss wants a complete report.'

'Don't you find the job boring?'   1476738

'You need a certain sense of dedication. You don't—or at least I don't—get much kick out of arresting people, but you do get satisfaction in preventing crime, seeing the rate drop.'

He noticed that a faint shadow had fallen over her face.

'I've been admiring your tee-vee set.' He walked over and examined it.

'It's getting long in the tooth as these things go,' she said. 'I was rather talked into it at the time, I'm afraid, but it's given good service.'

'May I ask where you got it? I'm dallying with the idea of getting one.'

'Townend Teevee. It's somewhere in the Old Town, but it'll be in the book.'

Harry walked back to retrieve his notebook. 'Yes,' he said, 'you get irregular shifts in my work and sometimes the teevee offers the only type of relaxation. Only thing is, I'm worried about the service and upkeep.'

'I haven't had much trouble. A few weeks after I got it something went wrong and the poor little man who sold it to me came out and fixed it. Then a shop started not far away, so now I call them if anything happens.'

'Townend Teevee. I might give them a look in. I hope they're not too high pressure.'

She chuckled. 'For a policeman you seem easy to sell. I've never been to the shop. An odd little man called in his van.' She searched a moment for the right phrase. 'He was one of the beaten, hang-dog little men, so anxious to please. I couldn't afford that set, but I found myself buying it.'

'I'll look him up,' said Harry easily. 'What's his name?'

'Just a minute.' He watched her lithe swinging carriage as she delved into a drawer. 'Let's see, should be among the t's. Here it is, a Mr. R. Case, Townend Teevee, 13 Barrett Lane, Old Town.'

'Thanks, I might get round to him. Well, Miss Holland, thanks very much and goodbye.'

'Oh, no, I was glad to clear it up.'

She preceded him into the hall. Just inside the door was a small table with half a dozen photographs on it, a pair of old wedding groups, and four portraits. One of them was Guy Tavisham, no mistaking the high, balding forehead and heavy eyes set rather close together over a fleshy nose. He hesitated a trifle too long, for the girl turned and their eyes met.

The heavy eyebrows lifted in interrogation.

'I've seen him before some place,' said Harry easily, 'but I can't remember where.'

She rested one hand against the newel post. 'His name was Guy Tavisham, he died a year ago.'

'I'm sorry,' he said. 'I must be mistaken.'

'You might have seen his photograph in the press when it happened. He died terribly and alone of food poisoning.'

He followed her to the front door. 'Poor Guy,' she said, 'he was my trustee, and I only knew him when I came here. So kind. . . .'

He spent an hour strolling around the Strand, which bore evidence of having been a small village before the tide of industry had rolled to its border. Harry wondered how it had escaped submersion, but doubtless the impetus of Bradshaw's Victorian boom had weakened before it could wash over the Georgian houses and cottages which radiated from the tiny green. He looked at a small ruined church, obviously unused, standing rather incongruously among a cluster of fairly modern houses. At its side a stone wall surrounded a mellowed, rambling old house set in about two acres of beautifully kept garden. Harry stood admiring the roses, in which the owner seemed to specialise. 'Cost a packet to keep that up nowadays,' he mused.

As he stood there the front door of the house opened and an elderly man came through, flanked by a large boxer. The man wore a neatish blue suit and soft hat. As he watched him Harry found the walk, purposeful and thrusting, familiar. It was the old man he had seen behind the wheel of the Lagonda car. The cap and the plus fours were missing, and he wasn't sure until he could see the purple mark spread over the left cheek and the fleshy, predatory line of the nose. As he watched, the man fumbled in his pocket and jammed a pipe between his teeth.

Harry moved back from the gate and stopped to adjust his shoe lace. He heard the creak of the gate and cautiously watched the blue clad legs proceed in the opposite direction. Harry straightened and at that moment the old man suddenly swung round and snapped his fingers at the boxer, lagging behind. Their eyes met for an instant and Harry was certain that the old man gave a slight start before turning and walking away.

'Curious,' he thought as he walked back the way he had come. To perfect the illusion of an out-of-the-way village was the pub, smallish, with a public bar and a tiny snuggery.

The woodwork gleamed from years of loving·polishing and the air was redolent of turpentine and brasso. He admired the row of pewter tankards and called for a pint and a couple of sandwiches from one of the two old ladies behind the bar.

There were about a dozen people in the place. He chose a wooden bench to sit beside a youngish man wearing working clothes. A gardener, Harry thought. He watched the darts players and slowly ate his beef sandwiches.

'Nice little place, the Strand,' he said idly to his neighbour. 'I wouldn't have believed it could be so near the town.'

'Fine place,' the man said. 'Quiet like.'

'Don't seem to be any houses to sell or let.'

'No,' said the man, 'they don't come up much unless anybody dies.'

'The big house, now,' said Harry, 'there's a lovely display of roses.'

His neighbour looked pleased. 'Ah, I do that garden. Me and a boy, not that boys are any good these days. No interest in the roses really. That was the old Squire Monck's house a hundred years ago. You see that old church?'

'The one that's falling down?'

'That's right, fair dangerous I reckon, but it's nobody's business. The old squire quarrelled with the church like, so the old fellow built his own with a tame parson who did what he was told. Then the old man died and the estate was split up, but nobody wanted the church.'

'Who's got the big house now?'

'Ah, that's Mr. George Stryver and a good chap he is.'

'I think I saw him coming out with a boxer dog. Shortish with a curly old pipe in his mouth.'

'That'd be Mr. George, never without a pipe.'

Harry finished his pint and walked slowly through the dusk to Miss Walsh's.

There were sounds of voices in the kitchen, so he looked through the open door. Miss Walsh presided at the top of the large table on which reposed a row of stout bottles, while Miss Tweddle had a corner seat at which she sat with a remarkably large and shapeless piece of knitting on her lap and her glass on the floor.

Round the table sat half a dozen men whom Fanny Walsh introduced as fellow lodgers. He took a chair between an elderly bank clerk and a short man in the plumbing fixture business.

'We sometimes club in for a drink,' boomed Miss Walsh, 'five bob per head.' Harry put his share into the old teapot in the middle of the table.

'What about a song, Fanny?' said somebody, and the landlady's fruity voice, which nevertheless had a considerable talent for pitch, launched into one of the bawdier Edwardian music hall songs.

Two hours later when everybody was slightly hoarse, except Miss Tweddle who refilled her glass in silence, and the company had shrunk by three men who had to get to bed early, Harry took advantage of the lull.

'Well, Miss Tweddle,' he called, 'nobody spirited me away when I went around the Strand.'

A trace of malevolence crossed her face.

Her immediate neighbour, the bank clerk, belched slightly and said, "Poppycock story, that is. Just local yokels' gossip.' He gave a glassy grin of satisfaction at having negotiated the consonants successfully.

'I dunno,' said a younger man opposite. 'You mention the Strand in any pub and people look uncomfortable.'

'Phooey,' said the bank clerk. 'There was a murder there in the last century and then an M.P. named Marcus left home suddenly and didn't come back.'

'Let's have one last chorus for the road. Fill your glasses,' interrupted Fanny Walsh.

Later, upstairs in his room, Harry found he had left his lighter in the kitchen. He walked down the dimly lighted stairs and into the kitchen in pyjamas and dressing gown. The glasses and bottles had been cleared away, and only Fanny Walsh remained wiping dishes and sipping a glass of gin.

He retrieved his lighter. 'You're lucky to have this nice old house, Miss Walsh.'

'Well, love, it was left me by a gentleman in his will a year ago. I never expected it. I made a lot of money during the war, but, well, easy come, easy go. So what I had was just enough to buy a little pub in Essex with Miss Tweddle to help.'

'Thanks, I will.' Harry accepted the glass of gin and took a chair.

'But now I do nicely.'

'Miss Tweddle a relative?'

'Oh, no, dear, she was with me in the chorus years ago.'

She watched his face amusedly. 'Yes, time do change don't they? Not but that Tweddle didn't let herself go.'

'Well,' he said, 'this house was a decent sort of a windfall.'

'As I said before, it was unexpected, but when you work it out Guy had no family and the poor dear got very funny towards the end, not liking to meet people, you know.'

A tingle ran along his spine. 'I never knew Guy Tavisham,' he said, 'though I've heard of him.'

She accepted the name casually. 'I knew him when we were both young. He set me up in a flat, that was when he was in London. He was quite different then, you know, liked his bit of fun.' She gave her rich laugh. 'Dear Guy! I remember him saying I was the vulgarist woman on earth.'

'So he remembered you, evidently.'

'Oh,' she said, 'it only lasted a year, then he got sent to India. I never saw him again until after the war. I was up in London for the day trying to get the brewers to have the public bar done up—a wreck it was—and I walked slap into him. He recognised me. We were both in a hurry, but I mentioned my pub and told him to drop in some time, not that I dreamed he ever would.'

She filled up her glass and sat down heavily on a kitchen chair.

'But he did?' asked Harry.

'Many times, usually of a Sunday around noon. After we shut he'd have dinner with Miss Tweddle and me, then afterwards he'd sit talking to me about old times until it was time to open up again. Then he'd say goodbye and I wouldn't see him perhaps for four weeks: a lonely chap.'

'Must have had something preying on his mind?'

She looked at him sharply. Her face was flushed, but her speech was still completely steady.

'Dunno why I'm telling you all this, but I've always had a weakness for policemen.'

'Oh, I like listening.'

She hesitated. 'You see, Guy came of a very old family and he was the last of them. He should have married, silly old sausage. His great grandfather was a Cabinet Minister and his grandfather a famous surgeon. There'd been judges and bishops and all sorts of great folk in his family. He was very proud of it.'

They sat in silence until Harry thought the conversation had dried completely.

'Have another?' she said, refilling his glass and her own.

'Ah, yes,' she said, 'when he died I was perplexed. I thought that above all Guy hated scandal, so I shut up.' She drew her generous lips tightly together.

'I understand he died of food poisoning.'

'Maybe. Lots of muck they sell in the shops today, and dear Guy never cared what he ate. Old books now, he'd be like a child over some greasy old thing he'd bought, but you could slave over a meal and he'd never even notice it.'

'Some people are like that.'

'Well, time for beddy byes.' She started to get up rather carefully, then sank back.

'That man, Marcus, that disappeared,' she said. 'He did vanish, didn't he?'

'We don't know where he went to,' said Harry, 'but a lot of people disappear just because they want to.'

'Because they want to.' Miss Walsh was at last showing the effect of her drinks. 'That's funny. He was a friend of Guy and it worried him when he went off. Guy told me so. I remember him saying, "Why should he want to?"' She gave a gusty, ginny sigh. 'And now young fellow remember to turn the light off.' Upheaving herself she walked a little unsteadily through the door.

At nine the next morning, his stomach queasy and a slight pain in the middle of his forehead, Harry stood outside the red painted façade of Townend Radio. He had declined Fanny Walsh's offer to provide breakfast—she emphasised eggs and bacon—and taken toast and coffee at a workmens' café in the dingy streets of Old Town. It was where the original Bradshaw development had started and it seemed impossible that a hundred years alone could have provided so much grime on the dismal warehouses and narrow office blocks.

The shop door stood open and he asked for the proprietor, with difficulty assuring the two assistants that he had no complaint of any sort. The boss was a burly man wearing an aura of harassment about him.

'I'm Mr. Harris,' he grunted.

'I'm a police officer, Mr. Harris. I just want any information you have about a Mr. Ron Case.'

'Him! I bought the shop off him six years ago and I reckon I paid every penny it was worth. I met him twice with my accountant. Slimey little man. I paid over the money and that was that.'

'Do you know where he lived in Bradshaw?'

Harris gave the heavy sigh of the man whom the world imposes on. 'I'll look it up.'

Harry looked at the stock for a few minutes until Harris came back with a slip of paper. 'That's the address he gave me.' Grudgingly, he added, 'You take a bus. It's about twenty minutes.'

Case had shown some discrimination in his lodging, a detached house in a rather pleasant, newish suburban street. He must have been doing all right, Harry thought.

The landlady was a shrewdish middle-aged woman who explained to Harry that she did let a couple of rooms to approved gentlemen.

'Mr. Case,' Harry showed her a photograph. Ah, yes, she remembered Mr. Case.

'How long did he live here?'

'Six months.' There was something in her manner which prompted him to ask whether he had been a satisfactory guest in her home.

The landlady was pleased at the way he had phrased it and said in her affected voice, 'We can't be too choosey, these days, you know, but I didn't like Mr. Case. For one thing he was always asking questions about people. Keep yourself to yourself is my motto.'

'What people?'

'Oh, well, there was Mr. Tavisham, the late Mr. Guy Tavisham, a real gentleman, for one. He was in the Diplomatic and his family had been here for generations. I happened to mention that my grandpa had been, well, I suppose you'd call it Steward to Sir Guy's father and that I'd often stayed at The Hall as a little girl. After that he was always asking questions. It got on my nerves.'

Harry thought snobbishly, 'I'll bet you're the butler's grand-daughter.' Aloud he said, 'What sort of questions?'

He realised his mistake halfway through the sentence as he saw the thin lips purse forbiddingly.

'So you see Mr. James, I really can't help you further. The maid will show you out.'

In the street, Harry consulted his map of the district. Tavisham Hall was five miles out on this side of the town. At this rate he reckoned he'd need a bicycle by the time he'd finished. With difficulty he found the appropriate bus stop and lounged around for half an hour until it arrived.

He felt very depressed, and cursed Hawker. Wryly he supposed that it was rather too late to make another change of career. A fool's errand, ruddy old Hawker's senile mistake and something which could only detract from whatever reputation he, Harry, possessed.

At the other end of the journey he trudged up a side road, his stomach and head feeling rather worse, until he reached the lodge gates.

There was a For Sale notice which alluded to a fine residence and ninety acres of land. Tavisham Hall stood on a hillside, facing away from the grimy silhouette of Bradshaw and out towards the green farmlands. As he walked up the driveway, now spotted with grass and weeds, there was the faint hum of insects and the smell of clover upon the air.

Outside the portico a man was working with a motor mower, the sun beating on his tanned arms and face. He was a big, heavy man of perhaps seventy and he seemed grateful to park the machine and walk over to Harry.

'Police, are you?' he said when Harry produced his warrant card. 'I suppose you haven't found who sold that poisoned food to Mister Guy? Well, what is it?'

'Let's see, you're ... ?'

'My name's Tallent and I was with the Tavishams for fifty-odd years, that's who I am.'

It was no good trying to soft soap this one, decided Harry. Abruptly he took out Case's photograph from his wallet. 'Ever see this man?'

The surly blue eyes squinted.

' 'E got anything to do with Mr. Guy's death?'

'Could have.' Harry shrugged.

'Now wait a minute, I'm sorry I was short, but we were all fond of the Master. He never had a cross word for anybody, though he was queer in some ways. But, damn me, a man's got a right to do what he wants to do, 'asn't he?'

'People liked Mr. Tavisham, Mr. Tallent, I know that.'

'Well then,' said Tallent, stooping to give a vicious wrench to a dandelion. 'Well then. We all thought there was some funny business about the way he died and there's surely enough policemen around to find out.'

'About the photo, now.'

'Well, as I collect it it were two, three months before Master died. This fellow starts hanging about the Old Bull, it's the house where the butler and me would take our pint of an evening. 'E gets to know us, very free with his money. But after a bit he starts asking questions. Who the master knows, who he visits, stuff like that. One day I says to Mr. Barry, the butler—'e's living in Southend now—"Johnny," I says, "this fellow must be one of them burglars asking all these questions".'

'So the next time we see this fellow, Jackson he called himself, we tax 'im. I says, "Well, Mr. Jackson for all the questions you're asking you might be planning to burgle the 'All".'

'What did he say?'

'Oh, 'e had a skin like a rhinoceros. Just gave 'is greasy laugh and ordered pints all round. But,' Tallent lowered his voice, 'we never see 'im again after that. Not once.'

'Pity you didn't inform the police.'

'What?' said Tallent, hackles up again, 'tell that stupid Fred Howard, 'im without a brain under 'is 'elmet. And tell 'im what? That we'd 'ad some drinks with a nosey parker?'

'Ah, yes, I see,' placated Harry. 'There's one other thing, Mr. Tallent. Do you remember Mr. Marcus?'

'Oh, yes, I do. Here every Sunday evening for around two years until 'e goes off mysterious like. And I don't think the police ever found '*im*.'

'I suppose he came for dinner?'

'No, the master never gave much in the way of dinners, not like years ago when every night not less than twenty sat down to table. No, an omelette and a bit of cold salmon or a cold bird, that's all master used to serve, with a good glass or two of wine. Then they used to sit in his study until all hours.'

'Did you like Mr. Marcus?'

'Not my place to like or dislike,' Tallent said in a surly voice. ''Sides I never saw much of 'im being around the grounds. Mr. Barry used to say he made him nervous, a fidgetty little man, always adjusting things on the table.'

'Was Mr. Tavisham staying at the Hall when Marcus went away?'

'No, he weren't. I remember it well because a policeman called round and Master was in Paris at the time.'

'I suppose Mr. Guy was away a lot?'

'And why shouldn't he be?'

Harry again became conscious of his headache. He jerked his finger at the house. 'Mind if I take a walk around?'

'Please yourself. It's empty.'

The compass needle in Harry's mind now fluctuated slightly towards Hawker's vague suspicions. Tallent had seemed sure of his identification. Blackmail, maybe, that would be up Case's alley right enough. He walked round to the back of the house, peering through the windows at the high-ceilinged deserted rooms. About forty rooms, he guessed. Tavisham had closed most of the house and had lived in one wing. Difficult to sell, he thought, unless to some institution.

The old stabling was at the back, part of it converted into garage space. The door of one box was ajar, emitting a faint horsey odour. He peered into the dim interior. There was a ladder in the corner propped against the entrance to the hayloft. Suddenly his eye was caught by a pair of blue coloured slacks hung neatly over a piece of wire in the corner. He felt himself frown as he glanced around. They were women's slacks.

He heard a movement and looking up saw a pair of long creamy legs come over the edge of the loft and grope for the rung of the ladder. Above were a pair of rather brief briefs.

It was a lovely body, thought Harry, standing unable to move: belly muscles firm and rather heavy, firm breasts cupped in a bra, the head appeared, auburn haired. It was Miss Rhonda Gentry. He made an effort to remember she called herself Elizabeth Holland.

Her head turned and she saw him. For a second he thought she was falling and he ran forward to catch her, rather eagerly anticipating doing it. But the smooth muscles in her arms tightened and she clung to the ladder.

'Miss Livingstone, I presume,' stammered Harry and walked out of the stable as quickly as he could.

He wiped the sweat off his forehead. An assignation? With whom? A piece of very discreet lurking was indicated, he supposed.

As he started to move away, a voice called. 'I want to see you when I've finished dressing, P.C. James.'

Convicted men had told Harry that the judge's sentencing

44

words, a matter of a few minutes, seemed to carry on for hours. Although it could have taken Miss Gentry an equally short time to don her blue slacks and a thin green blouse, to Harry it seemed equal to a death sentence.

There were smears of grime on her face and arms and cobwebs in her hair. The oval face was severe as she glared at him.

'And what the devil, constable, are you doing snooping so disgustingly on private property?'

'I'm terribly sorry, Miss, I was too startled to move. Tallent gave me permission to mooch around and didn't mention you.' He was startled to find his face flushing.

Her eyes fell and something like a grin appeared at the corner of her mouth. 'Oh, well, I don't wear much more on the beach, I guess, but somehow, in there...'

'I'm very sorry, Miss,' lied Harry.

'I don't believe you are,' her voice was gentle again. 'But I'm still puzzled as to why you are here.'

'Well,' said Harry, 'you know we never did find the source of the tainted food that killed Sir Guy, so it's an open file and it happened that I'm checking around.'

'I doubt whether you'll find a clue two hundred miles from where he died, poor fellow,' she said tartly.

'Just general background,' he said lamely.

'Do you mind coming in the house while I wash this grime off?'

He followed her while she unlocked a back door.

The kitchen was large and bare, save for the sinks in one corner. She shut the door behind him. He strolled about while she took a towel from the side of the sink and washed. When he turned she was busy with a comb and lipstick.

He thought when she had finished that even the grime had not impaired her beauty and nearly said so.

'I think I'd better see your warrant card, Mr. James.' Her voice had turned cold again and he noticed that near her foot was an old iron bar, impedimenta from an old kitchen range, he guessed.

'Just toss it over.' She stooped effortlessly and straightened up with the bar in her hands.

He flipped the card over at her feet.

She looked down at it for a long minute.

'Hm. You see, when I passed Howard, the local policeman, on my way here he told me there was no P.C. James at Bradshaw and he ought to know, he's been here years.'

'Transferred from Manchester four days ago,' said Harry.

'Perhaps you'll just stand aside.'

He went to one corner of the room. 'I must remind you, Miss, that assault's a serious offence and you'd have to marry me.' One part of his mind stood aghast at his levity.

'We'll see whether you'll laugh in a couple of minutes. And remember that if I yell, Tallent will hear.'

She opened the door to what had evidently been the butler's pantry. He saw a telephone on a ledge and listened to the dial click.

'Hallo,' she said, 'East Bradshaw Police Station? Have you a P.C. James? You have? Was he transferred from Manchester? No, it doesn't matter, thanks.'

'Well,' she said, in her small voice. 'I seem to have made a fool of myself again.'

She tossed the bar under the sink and produced a key from a pocket. As she reached down and unlocked the door Harry said, 'And I didn't hear you lock the door on me.'

'You weren't meant to,' she said absently. 'The locks in the house are all well oiled.'

She opened the door, but he stood looking at her from his slight advantage of height. 'You know,' he found himself saying, 'I still think you should marry me.'

She turned, blocking the door. 'You know, you're a very queer sort of policeman, a very queer sort of policeman. In fact....' He saw her eyes narrow.

'Is there anywhere around here where one can sit down?' asked Harry. 'I'm just out of hospital, and these hot days....' He bent slightly with nausea.

'I'm sorry,' she said with quick concern. 'There's only the gardener's cottage. Wait a minute.' Her hand caught his wrist and they walked past the stables. Harry saw a number of hay trusses stacked against the wall and sank down on one. She sat beside him and asked if she should get him water.

He shook his head. Mercifully they were in shadow and presently he felt better.

'I'm sorry I'm such a rotten policeman,' he said contritely.

'I'm afraid I don't *much* like policemen, any policemen.'

'Unlike my landlady who does.'

'Your landlady likes you?'

'Too much. In fact her habit of drinking gin on top of stout has contributed to my feeling lousy.'

'Oh, just a hang-over, and I've given you sympathy.'

'No, it's not just hangover.'

'Anyway, your landlady sounds a pet.'

'Yes, a Miss Fanny Walsh, ex fan and belly dancer, so she says.'

She gave a start. 'That's odd. You see Guy Tavisham ...'

'I know, she told me. He left her the house and furthermore used to keep her back in the '20's when she must have been a howler.'

'He did?' She gave a little squeal of enjoyment. 'I'm glad. Poor old Guy didn't have much pleasure. I pity people who never have any fun.' There was an intensity in her voice that puzzled him a little.

'I should explain,' she added, 'that Guy left me £500—although for different reasons—plus some furniture I'd always liked, and made me one of the three executors. Everything's settled except this whitish elephant. I've taken the job of seeing that the structure is kept sound.'

'I'm sure the haylofts are the best kept in the county,' murmured Harry.

She gave him a brief, measured side glance. When she spoke he was conscious that their brief intimacy had passed.

'Yesterday I had a nagging feeling I'd seen you before,' she said, 'and it came to me in the bath. In London, just after ten, last Saturday.'

'I'm glad you remembered. I couldn't summon up courage to speak to you.'

'Thank you.' A little smile touched her lips and vanished as abruptly. 'A much travelled P.C. London, Bradshaw and Manchester, like a railway train.'

'I went up to see a doctor,' he replied rather stiffly.

'What's the matter with you?'

He felt an urge to impress her. 'Three men, six heavy shoes and an iron bar.' He reproached himself for having said it.

She was silent. 'I hate violence,' she said.

'Don't we all.'

'No,' she said slowly. 'I'm afraid all of us don't.'

He changed the subject. 'I know that the bulk of Tavisham's money went to cancer research. I suppose the servants were looked after?'

'Guy virtually inhabited four rooms plus the kitchen and bathroom. There was the butler and his wife who were well pensioned in the will, and of course, Tallent, who could retire but prefers to keep on. The land was let to the neighbouring farmer and once every six months a drove of chars came in to clean the part of the house he kept closed.'

'I find it difficult to visualise Tavisham,' said Harry.

She picked up a piece of straw and nibbled the end. 'My father was at Oxford with him and when he died Tavisham was executor. In fact he was abroad and his solicitor did what work was to be done. Until I came here five years ago I had met him only two or three times. He introduced me to a few people, found me my cottage at the Strand, helped me get a mortgage on it and found me a job. Not a bad effort. He was very kind, very formal and personally pretty efficient.'

'And a recluse,' he pressed.

'In an odd way. He shied away from people generally. I used to come here once a month and have a simple midday meal with him. He could be a charming, erudite talker and had travelled a lot. That's why I said I was glad he'd had some fun once. He had everything, most people would say, and yet he had so little.'

'What did you think about his manner of death?' He felt he was in the police groove again.

She shrugged. 'Guy was notoriously indifferent to food. I said he was efficient and so he was. But I can imagine him leaving an open tin in the sun for a few days and then quite absent-mindedly eating the contents.'

'Did you ever go to his cottage?'

'No.' She got lithely to her feet. 'And that's enough questions, I think.' She gave him a long stare. 'And I think my opinion of policemen is unchanged.'

He gave her stare for stare and suddenly found his arms round her waist and his mouth over hers. For a moment he thought she had responded. He was short of breath and dry in mouth as he said, 'And Miss Holland, if you care to report me there will be one policeman less.'

Her face was unreadable. Finally she said, 'Oh, I shan't report you. It's just...' and to Harry's horror she sat down on a hay truss and started to cry.

He bent down. 'I'm sorry,' he said, 'please don't....'

'Oh go away,' she said through racking sobs. 'Oh, go away.'

To his great relief the gardener was not in sight as he walked down the drive.

CHAPTER THREE

Going back to the police station he resolutely tried to push Rhonda Gentry to the back of his mind. And his own behaviour: he sweated when the memory crept past his barriers. So, manlike, he cursed Hawker, the Force and his own fate.

The Desk Sergeant gave him a brotherly wink. 'Got a window breaking job for you later,' he said. 'Jeweller, some watches pinched.'

The Inspector was out, so Harry was able to use his telephone in privacy. He called Hawker who listened without comment.

The old man finally said, 'I think there's something there. I smell somebody blackmailing somebody. Keep as close as you can to la Gentry. You can stay two weeks if you think it's worth it. And I forgot to tell you, the Super's pretty hot stuff even if he doesn't look it.'

Harry held the line and had a clerk dig out the file on Marcus and read back the summary pasted to the last page of the file. He typed his shorthand note back on a beaten-up typewriter in the communal office. An Inspector unknown to him, named Merry, had handled the case—

John Redfern Marcus, b. Bristol Sept 8, 1903. Parents Underwood Marcus, retd. Engineer and Ursula nee Barrett. No known relatives, unmarried. Junior partner in Bourne and Coming, Cripplegate, London, from 1934. Elected Member for Bradshaw East 1937. Applied for Chiltern Hundreds July 3rd, 1939, granted July 10th, grounds ill-health. On the morning of July 16th, Marcus left his house, *Imberbrook*, The Strand, East Bradshaw, presumably to catch the 7.30 express to London, as was his habit. Later that day he called his secretary to say he would not be in, telephoned his club to ask if there was mail for him and also telephoned a fellow M.P. about a minor matter. The last call was at 5 p.m. No further trace. He possessed assets estimated at £4,300 plus an unexpired four years' lease upon his residence. Staff, one elderly housekeeper and young maid. No indication of worry, office accounts o.k. by audit. No medical evidence: deceased apparently had no regular doctor.

There followed a line of code letters indicating that Merry had checked hospitals, mortuaries, unidentified bodies. Harry noted that Marcus had not possessed a passport in the tight insular little England of his day.

Merry concluded:

Marcus' origins seem obscure and he did not talk of them. In fact he seems to have been very reticent about any personal affair. Active in politics since his late 'teens and a very competent speaker and hard worker which brought him to the notice of the party whips.

There was a short addendum:

File passed to M.I.5, returned without action

He went down and asked the Sergeant if there was a bicycle he could use and that amiable man showed him two heavy horrors parked in the yard at the back. After testing both, he decided to hire one at a shop nearby.

He collected the window breaking complaint, hired his bicycle, the lightest he could choose, and caught some lunch at an ABC. It was years since he had ridden one and his calves soon ached, but it sweated something out of him and he was quite light-hearted when he reached the small jeweller's with its gaping window. The glass had been bashed in crudely with a stone.

The card in his pocket notified him that the breaking had occurred around six that morning and that four watches, worth £45 retail, had been taken. The card also had the notation that the usual iron shutter had been found inoperable the night before and so all stock had been removed except for four watches that had somehow been overlooked.

The proprietor was unhelpful and wanted advice on the insurance position, which Harry couldn't give.

He shrugged and closed his notebook. It was a matter of giving the description to local pawnbrokers: ten to one there would never be any arrest. The hour was unusual and on a sudden impulse he found the nearest bus stop and studied the time-table. He went back to the jeweller and borrowed his telephone.

The bus depot was quite helpful. He had to phone back as each early morning shift checked in and spoke to the conductors.

Finally he struck oil, and more. A conductor had picked up a fare a quarter of a mile from the shop with a hand bleeding badly, wrapped in the flap of his coat. He had set him down at Tom's Corner.

'Thanks, sorry to have troubled you,' said Harry, and then something prompted a last shot, 'Didn't recognise him, did you?'

'By sight. Cheeky young bastard, red hair and pimples, lives in one of the houses near the sweet shop a few doors from the stop.'

When he got to the Station he saw the Inspector and this time got a car with a driver. Tom's Corner was seven miles out, with a sweet shop, cum grocer, cum post-office and a sprawl of decaying bungalows dating from the '20's.

They found Mr. John Hill, aged seventeen, with red hair and a nasty-looking hand, in his bedroom resting.

'I tol' him,' said his mum, 'that he should 'ave his hand looked at. After all, it's free, but since he got sacked from the gas works, he's been a different boy. Proper nasty set he's got into.'

It was wearisome, routine police work. Hill's bluster didn't last long. His girl friend's parents had been at Blackpool and there'd been a party. Yes, drink, plenty of that, stout and gin mostly. (Harry winced inwardly).

He'd had to get out about five because the girl friend's neighbour was a prying old bitch. Yes, he was still fair shickered and hadn't his complete fare home so he had to walk a couple of miles. He remembered seeing this window and thinking it would be a joke to smash it with a stone. He'd cut his wrist on the glass. No he didn't know nothing about watches. Well, when he came to about eleven there were some watches in his coat pocket but he didn't know how they got there. He'd got frightened and sneaked down and dropped them down the drain at the corner.

Mum came back to the Station to arrange about bail. The Inspector was pleased.

'That was smart work.'

'Mostly luck and the conductor.'

'Well, it won't do any harm to you as a cover. It'll get around.'

It was four o'clock by then and Harry prevailed on the Sergeant to have a cup of tea at the café next door, leaving a constable at the desk.

'A bit more info' from you, Serge,' he wheedled. 'Who kept house for Marcus?'

'An old trout that died some years ago and a little tweeny-maid who was half-witted.'

'I suppose she's not around?'

'Oh, yes,' the Sergeant swigged his tea. 'She's around. Got married ten years ago, God knows how—she 'ad a snuffle like a bellows. Name's Maitland and she lives in Conan Street down near the station, her 'usband's a shunter, very respectable.'

Harry parked his bike in front of the neat little row house. Mrs. Maitland was plump and given to sniffing, with wispy hair the colour of a faded sack. Harry thought he could see skeletally a gawky, adenoidal parlour maid.

Her kitchen was as neat as one could be that numbered among the effects a baby in a pram and a girl of about eight messing around with crayons.

'Mr. Marcus, sir, well it's long ago since I thought of 'im.' Her voice was thick and heavily accented and Harry had to listen carefully.

'The police come at the time and went through the 'ouse and me and old Mrs. Strong—gone to 'er rest these fifteen years at the age of ninety-two—was questioned. Mrs Strong, though put out by pore Mr. Marcus goin' off without a word, was very mad. "Maudie," she'd say, "questioning us as though we was criminals or pore people if you please".'

'What I'm looking for is any clue, absolutely anything, as to whether Mr. Marcus was worried.' He found himself speaking as if to a deaf person.

' 'Ow, 'e always worried about 'is 'ealth, except for the last few munce. One day he threw away all those bottles of pills 'e kept in the bathroom. Mrs. S. arsked 'im why. 'E said, "I don't need 'em any more!" but Mrs. S. got 'em out the dustbin and took 'em 'erself. Some of 'em was very expensive she reckoned and came from foreign parts.'

'Nothing else?'

She hesitated for a few seconds. 'You must realise, sir, that then I was a slip of a girl, quite innocent like.' She looked at him keenly, as if hinting, between worldly people, at the depravity she had latterly found. 'I was too shy to say anythin' then.'

'Oh, quite, Mrs. Maitland,' said Harry.

'Well, one night, when Mrs. S. 'ad 'ad to go out becorse 'er son 'ad fallen off 'is crane and was poorly, I get a ring. There was Mr. Marcus in 'is study and 'e spoke to me very sharp. "There isn't a glass here, get me one." So I gets one from the dining-room and takes it up and then 'e wants ice. We had a refrigerator,' she said this with pride. 'Well, I brought it up....'

She hesitated. Harry said quickly. 'You know, Mrs Maitland,

anything you say to me will be absolutely secret between us.'

'Like one of them Irish priests?'

'That's it.'

'Maralyn,' she turned to the little girl, 'take your crayings into the front room and do as I say.'

'Oh, mum.'

'Or you'll not 'ave any Lucozade no more.'

Maralyn slowly dragged her impedimenta to the door and through it.

'Little pots 'ave big ears,' said Mrs. Maitland. She glanced at the baby as though estimating his. 'Well, now,' she lowered her voice, 'I was a slip of a girl then and I found my eye at the key 'ole, great big 'un it was. There's the master opening his bookcase and coming out with a bottle of whisky. He 'alf fills the glass I'd got 'im and tops it with ice. Then 'e starts striding up and down the room mutterin' to himself.'

Her round eyes goggled at him. 'And Mr. Marcus was always so against the drink. He fairly trounced Mrs. S. one day when he was messing around in the kitchen straightening things—'e used to drive us mad—and found 'er gin bottle she'd forgot to put away. She said she'd taken it away from 'er son to keep 'im off it and 'ad to pour it down the drain while 'e watched. "Still waters run deep, Maudie, you mark my words," she said to me after.'

'Yes, yes, Mrs. Maitland, now about this muttering business.'

She took the plunge. 'Young like, I found I had me 'ear over the 'ole. Course, he was walking up and down. He kept muttering "Wilks, Wilks, a criminal type if I ever saw one". Then I 'eard Mrs. S. come in and was off downstairs.'

'Wilks?'

'Yes, you know, Wilks.'

'And nothing else?'

Sadly she shook her head, her saga said.

He thanked her warmly and beamed at the baby. Little Maralyn shut the front room door rather too quickly as he left the kitchen and he grinned to himself as he went into the street.

The heat had been growing less during the afternoon, but even so Harry was not attracted by the thought of Miss Walsh's kitchen. He admitted truthfully that he would have liked to have called on Miss Gentry and dutifully put the temptation to one side. Instead he stood himself a dinner of the best which the town could offer and a film afterwards. It was nearly ten when he got out and walked through the streets, the concrete exuding the heat of the day. On impulse he made his way back to the Station, made himself known to a laconic night desk sergeant, changed into the slacks he had left in the locker room and collected his bike. He slid up side streets to avoid the traffic and found himself taking a circuitous route which he hoped would by-pass the traffic arteries and take him somewhere near Tavisham Hall. His riding muscles seemed to have acquiesced to their task and he whistled as he rode along, passing little traffic.

There was a half moon and finally he recognised the outline of the Hall on its hillside. He propped the bike against a tree and lay down upon the stubbly grass, arms under his head, staring at the black sky. It was comfortable and he toyed impractically with the idea of sleeping there until he caught himself cat-napping.

He shook his head and glanced at the luminous face of his watch. It was a little before twelve. Stooping, he stretched himself and felt a warning stiffness in his calf muscles. They would need embrocation tomorrow.

His eyes narrowed. He could have sworn there was a light in one of the Hall's rooms. It had vanished as soon as he had glimpsed it.

The reflection of a passing headlight? He dismissed the thought because of the distance and angle. Perhaps Miss Gentry was at it again.

He cycled down the lane, found it a cul-de-sac, retraced his path and after twenty vexatious minutes came out not far from the open lodge gates. He walked quietly along the gravel, wondering where Tallent's cottage was. Windows gaped at him vacantly from the house. Walking round he gently tried the back door. Locked.

Some aberration of the eye nerves, he guessed, as he glanced over towards the stabling. The doors were firmly closed and pad-locked.

His ear caught the cough of a car starter and he froze. There was a soft whine of gears and the purring of an engine. Whatever it was, he registered, it was an expensive model. The sound seemed to have come from the other side of the house and he trotted towards it.

The moon was overcast and Harry cursed as he barked a shin. He could dimly see that the gravel path extended much further between trees. He sniffed the slight breeze and smelled exhaust fumes. He sweated back to where he had left his bicycle and rode back. The gravel path was narrow, but wide enough for one car.

But it was rutted and he had to steer with care. Where the greenery of the trees did not obscure it, he glimpsed barbed wire and realised that the path steered a course through the farmland attached to the Hall. Half a mile further on was a gate leading on to the road. He used the bicycle light to look at the edge of the path. It was difficult to see but there were the marks of one or more vehicles. He steered his bike through the gap by hand and in the moonlight saw a policeman's helmet twenty yards from him.

'I'm Constable James from East Bradshaw,' he said. The face beneath the helmet was a ferrety one, oddly small for the massive frame that supported it.

'And I'm P.C. Howard, stationed at Eagleham. This is the boundary of Bradshaw. Funny meetin' you. There was a lady yesterday morning enquiring. I said I never 'eard of you, but then I got to thinkin' and phoned my cousin 'oo's desk sergeant at the east station and 'e told me you'd joined the strength.'

He gratefully accepted one of Harry's cigarettes. 'I wish the Guv'ment'd bring 'em down,' he said. 'It's 'ard on night duty, the price they are.'

Harry agreed, conscious of the curiosity in the small grey eyes.

'Cursed business altogether, night duty. The Old Man's troubled about a gang that's going round pinching lead and the like off these disused big houses and told me to make a survey. A hell of a job. That place there looks deserted, now.'

Howard's eyes had softened. 'Ar,' he said, 'lead's a good pinch today at the price. That Tavisham 'All, deserted these twelve munce, no furniture or anything, but there's a gardener in the cottage, old Tallent.'

'No risk there, then.'

'Well,' Howard elongated the word as though savouring it. 'Since 'is master died and 'e's bin 'ere alone, old Jim generally goes to the local of an evening and buys a couple of quarts to take away. No 'arm done, but likes 'is drop, and why not, 'im being pensioned? But they say that after his three or four pints you can 'ear the snortling a 'undred yards away. I wouldn't put my faith in 'im.'

'It's a funny thing,' said Harry, 'I'd have sworn I saw a car turn out of this drive.'

'Ar? Then it must have gone back towards Bradshaw because I was wheeling my bike from Eagleham and nothing passed me for fifteen minutes. It's a rum thing, now, but four days ago when

I was on night, I'm riding towards Bradshaw, about two hundred yards further because Charlie Baker wanted me to keep an eye on 'is daughter's cottage particular as she's in the infirmary and a car passed me without lights, driving fast.'

'Make or number?'

'Too dark, but it was a largish car I thought.'

'Oh well,' said Harry. 'Keep your eyes open and I'd appreciate a phone call if you see anything suspicious.'

'That I will. Good night to you.'

Harry cycled slowly back more or less the way he had come. He took a turn round the Strand, exploring fully its radial system of streets and inevitably found himself pausing for a cigarette opposite Miss Gentry's cottage. It was very black by now so that a faint stain of light against one curtained window, invisible had there been more light outside, was barely visible. Harry realised that the street lighting was particularly bad around here.

Probably reading in bed, he thought, and then suddenly extinguished his cigarette as he heard the slight grating of an opening door which stuck a little against the lintel.

His straining ears found the sound of footsteps. They paused. Opening the gate, Harry thought, and stood frozen.

He waited until the steps had almost died before mounting his machine and switching on the lights. In a few seconds he was abreast of the figure and past it. He had a glimpse of a face swiftly turning to look into the light. It was George Stryver.

He looked at his watch, it was something after four. Wearily he parked the machine in the area of the Walsh house and fumbled for his latch key. It was very dark in the hall and his fingers crept along a large area of sticky paint to locate the switch. A cat mewed faintly once, then again. Harry found himself standing very still. There had been something reminiscent about the sound and he realised that he had once heard himself making it. His fingers flicked down the switch. To the left of the hallway was a door which he gently opened. From the hallway, light flooded over pink carpet and a woman's figure, face downwards, which twitched slightly. He ran for the telephone in the kitchen.

When he returned he bent down and saw that the body sprawling on the carpet was Miss Tweddle. Her face lay sideways and there was a faint ooze of blood into the grey hair over her ear. He found a weak, thready pulse before straightening to his feet. The room was furnished as part sitting-room, part workroom. A battered old sewing machine stood in the corner, flanked by an over-spilling box of cottons and wools. There was an old-fashioned roll-topped desk which had been forced open so that fragments of wood had dropped to the carpet. He went to the window, and pulled back the heavy drapes. It looked on to the blank side of the next house and as he felt it the bottom half of the frame slipped easily upwards.

The ambulance and the police car arrived silently and a young doctor knelt over the woman.

'A vicious crack,' he said, 'we'll get her to the hospital immediately.'

Harry made himself known to the plainclothesman in charge.

'Been a few of them, lately,' was the comment. 'You better get the old lady down.'

He remembered hearing the landlady's heavy steps passing his room and ascending. Using a flash he walked quietly along the floor above. One of the doors was thickly painted in mottled violet and he took a chance on this.

Miss Fanny Walsh's mass of hair sprawled over her face and she snored gently. He had some trouble in arousing her, but she finally said she'd be down in a minute.

The ambulance had departed when he got back. The plainclothesman was dusting for fingerprints.

'Looks like being dozens of 'em,' he said wearily, 'and I'd bet a quid it's everybody but the guy who broke in. Better lock it up and we'll send round tomorrow.'

He jumped at the apparition of Miss Walsh in the doorway, the large face pale and damp from the recent application of water, large body wrapped in a pink gown of astonishing fluffiness.

'You said burglars,' she said accusingly.

'Take a look at the desk,' said Harry, 'just a look to see what's gone.'

She bent over and stared for what seemed a long time.

'I always keep thirty pounds there for emergencies and a couple of old rings, rubies.'

'Worth much?'

'Insured for three-fifty between them, but you couldn't replace 'em for that.'

Her big eyes rolled vacantly around the room. 'Here what's this?' Moving with surprising agility she picked up two knitting needles attached to some large, amorphous garment. 'This is Tweddle's bit of knitting.'

'Better come into the kitchen,' Harry said gently.

Between them they got her into her usual chair and Harry told her.

Fanny Walsh remained silent, with a peculiar expression of concentration. Finally she said, 'I hope that for once you get the bastard.'

'Who is he, do you think,' asked the plainclothesman very quietly.

The bloodshot grey eyes switched momentarily towards him. 'Any bastard that bashes an old woman like Tweddle.'

'Perhaps you'll tell us when you last saw her.'

'Oh, we were all sitting in the kitchen having a bit of a gathering. I remember seeing Tweddle go out at, oh, it was about half past eleven. She didn't come back.'

'You didn't think anything unusual?'

Fanny Walsh shrugged massive shoulders. 'Tweddle and I leave each other alone. Sometimes she just goes off to bed. What happened tonight would be that she ran out of wool for her bit of knitting. She keeps it in the front room.' She levered herself out of the chair, looking very old. 'And now I'd better go to see her.'

'I'll run you there,' said the plainclothesman.

Harry went up to his room, printed 'Do Not Disturb' on an envelope and gummed it outside his door.

When he awoke shortly before noon the house appeared deserted. He was in time for sausage and mash at the little café which catered for the police station.

The Inspector, an old-timer with grey cheeks and a lantern jaw, was assembling the case into a neat file.

'All prints accounted for except half a dozen which probably belong to the men who came last week to clean the carpet,' he told Harry.

'A pro. teevee job, window catch eased up by a tool.'

'Fanny Walsh doesn't hold with the teevee,' said Harry. 'She says in the flesh or not at all.'

The Inspector's face didn't alter. 'Everybody knows old Fanny. She's become a local character in under a year. Everybody knows about her kitchen and the stout and gin and half the neighbourhood there. I've been there myself.'

Harry looked a trifle startled.

'Yes,' said the Inspector, 'everybody knows. That's how they work. Hit a new town and spot the right pub, find some young delinquent who'll give them the run-down of the district for a few quid.'

'How many cases have you had?'

'With this one it's seven in two weeks, they don't stay much longer than that. They got four nice rings from a fish-and-chip shop out Hagley way and three hundred quid from a farmhouse. Gawd's strewth, the gaffer'd drawn the money out to pay the fruit pickers and left it under the kitchen breadboard while he went to watch the play.'

'No clues?'

The Inspector shrugged wearily. 'We got a tip that a thief named Joe Larter is around.'

Harry whistled. 'I nicked Larter two years ago and it didn't stick. He does high-grade jewellery jobs around the posh blocks of flats, works about three times a year.'

His companion was uninterested in professional quirks. 'You work it out, all he wants is a driver for the car: the same man takes the stuff out by a morning train so that Larter's clean. Say the fenced price of what he's got is eleven hundred quid, which'd be about right. That's two hundred for the driver and a bit less for exes. That leaves a snug seven hundred.' He cleared his throat disgustedly. 'Who'd be a mug copper, eh?'

'Who indeed?' Wickstraw had entered the office silently. 'No, no, keep your seats.'

Harry thought the Inspector looked a trifle wary as the Superintendent drew up a chair. 'I was mentioning Joe Larter, sir.'

'Ah, yes. There's a man here who operates a club, quite within the law, but he was at one time in London managing places that were "known", so he keeps in with us. He phoned his contact and said that he was driving in Old Town and was waiting for the lights. A car crossed the intersection, a small shabby Fiat 600, and Larter was beside the driver.'

Harry squinted as he cast back for Larter's record. Educated— a Mayfair Boy they'd have called him years ago—and splendidly athletic, reactions like a cat. Not violent, but there had been a query against that. Larter would perhaps be violent, but only when he could see no alternative.

'Don't like him for this one, eh?' Wickstraw sounded sympathetic. 'The money's good and these big flat jobs—Lady Somebody's family jewels—are getting more difficult to set up.'

'The Inspector could be right.'

'He often is.'

The big policeman bridled with pleasure.

'There were three or four of these organised gangs a couple of years ago—the teevee gangs, kitchen and bedroom stuff. They were smashed, largely due to old Hawker's brains, by the way, but Larter could have resurrected the idea with a minimum of hired help.'

'We're not concentrating on the Larter angle alone,' said the Inspector. He broke off as the telephone rang.

A slight grudging smile touched his mouth when he finished the call. 'That was a lead from a bed-and-breakfast place at Bentleigh. The landlady's pretty sure that it was Joe Larter who moved out this morning after a two weeks' stay. He was alone. I'll get the net out, wanted for questioning.'

'I'll not get in your way,' said Wickstraw and Harry caught his glance and followed the Superintendent out. He realised with a sense of shock that he had not enquired about Miss Tweddle.

'She's conscious,' grunted Wickstraw in response to the question. 'Fractured skull with no complications, but it'll be a week before she can make a statement. Fanny Walsh was with her all night, but is home now.'

He cocked a shrewd look at Harry. 'You might have a word with the old girl. We've got her statement, but ...'

Wickstraw rubbed his nose reflectively. 'When Fanny came here we took a good look at her after the stories started coming in and we found she was just a warm-hearted eccentric old character with a liking for gin. You know Tavisham left her the house?'

Harry nodded.

'Must have been interesting when she was young: Tavisham was a pretty dry old stick from the file. I saw Fanny this morning. There might be something wrong there.' He shook his head. 'Oh, we got a statement, description of the two rings, etcetera, but, I dunno, she looked a bit more scared than I'd have expected from a tough old trooper like her. See what you can do, I'll drop you at the house.'

His landlady was seated in the kitchen surveying a glass of stout, her ordinarily expressive eyes lack lustre.

'I'm glad to know that Miss Tweddle's conscious,' he said, feeling inadequate.

'The good Lord knows what damage is done,' Fanny Walsh said gloomily. 'I can't even relish a drink.'

'It's an uncomplicated fracture,' said Harry, 'and she'll be right as rain.'

She gave a gusty sigh. 'Old Tweddle—people wonder about her. There was a time when a girl caught fire in the wings, the silly cow had broken the rules to have a smoke. It was one of those gauzy panto costumes and she panicked. It was Tweddle who threw her down and got the flames out, burning her hands.'

'I see,' said Harry, not seeing.

'I was the silly cow,' said Fanny Walsh, shortly. 'Here, get yourself a bottle of stout.'

'You'd better eat.' He made a plate of cheese sandwiches.

'Funny how you don't think of food,' said Fanny. 'You know, we've had fun here, old Tweddle and me. Now I wish I'd never come here.'

Harry swallowed his mouthful. 'If you're alarmed,' he said, 'I might be able to fix for a policeman to keep an eye on the house during the day.'

She shook her head with something of her usual spirit. 'I've had to get in a woman to take care of the house, didn't you hear her?'

Harry vaguely recalled various bangings as he had come into the hall.

'Nine until seven,' said the landlady, 'and costs a fortune. But she's fifteen stone of muscle and worth four policemen, even full grown ones.' He was pleased to see her grin again.

'I don't envy your bill for breakages,' he said, but she had grown solemn again.

'I'm not a fanciful woman, Lord, if I had been I shouldn't be sitting here today. But Guy Tavisham was afraid towards the end and, by God, so am I.'

'Afraid of what, my dear?' He reached forward to touch her shoulder. He saw her lips purse and saw that the big grey eyes could be very cold. She shrugged her massive shoulders.

'I'm getting old. No. I can't eat these sandwiches, you finish 'em. I'll go and get some sleep.'

She walked slowly out of the kitchen.

Presently he went to his own room and to clarify his thoughts as much as for duty he wrote a report to Hawker. When he had finished he read it carefully. The last paragraph read:

'I think that the late Guy Tavisham could have been an accomplished blackmailer, quite apart from whether he was a murderer or not. When he died somebody might have acquired his papers. Can you suggest any way we can verify his sources of income?'

The desk sergeant, invaluable repository of miscellaneous information, had told him that Marcus' local party chairman still survived in that capacity and after phoning through Harry climbed the narrow stairs leading to the office of 'H. Rufus. Coal Agent'.

Rufus was a hard, swollen old man of seventy something. Harry was conscious of the imbalance of the two adjectives, but although the flesh over the bones had turned to soft jelly the man exuded an aura of ruthlessness reflected and conveyed by his flat amber-and-red eyes.

'Old times, officer. Marcus would have been fifty-eight this year, a good speaker, persuasive, good back bencher, maybe an under-secretary eventually, although I doubted it.'

Fascinated, Harry watched the old gentleman methodically pick his nose, oblivious of any convention to the contrary.

Rufus put his handkerchief neatly away in a side pocket. 'Fact is, the man who had the seat with a majority of 1,000 died. They were dicey times then and it wasn't a safe seat. Marcus had impressed Them in London so he got the nomination. There was a turn of the tide, and a population shift—he might have been shrewder than we thought—and he got in by over three thou'.'

Harry did a piece of mental arithmetic. The flabby years would have been shrunk by twenty and Rufus would have been under sixty.

'Looking back, what did you think of him?'

The massive shoulders jerked.

'Haven't thought of him for years. Slight dark man, horn-rimmed glasses.'

'Socially, I meant.'

'T.T. Gets in the baptists and some of the wesleyans. Mind you, it's not an unmitigated asset. Lot of Irish around and they don't trust a T.T.'

The purplish cheeks brooded over the blotter.

'I never quite trusted him over the drink. A look in his eye. They won't stand for hypocrisy.'

'Women?' said Harry, aghast at the professionalism and thinking of the leader in his morning's *Telegraph*.

'It's twenty years ago, Mr., er. You're sure you aren't M.I.5?'

'Sir, I assure you I'm just an ordinary C.I.D. sergeant.'

The old blue eyes reflected. 'Might just draw me up a little memo to that effect, eh?'

Harry got out his fountain pen and wrote a couple of lines, under-scoring 'on political background known to me'.

Rufus looked at the slip absently. 'They didn't mind about women in those days. That was before the Russians got like they are. The Germans ran 'ores, so they said, but no 'arm was done. They had their measure, and a lot of men got their 'oggins at cut rate if they were in prominent positions—subsidies they call it now.'

It was evidently an old quip because Rufus didn't even trouble to smile.

'This included Marcus?'

The big head gave a negative shake. 'I took him out to dinner when he came up asking for the seat. He didn't drink, which makes it difficult, but I thought he wasn't at all over-strung and I can spot a man that is. You don't want them for a candidate.'

'Boys?'

Rufus smiled wearily. 'That was when the *News of the World* called it a "certain offence" and half the electorate couldn't guess what it was. 'Ow do you spot them? It's a nightmare today.'

'Effeminacy?' Harry felt inadequate.

Rufus snorted: 'Six foot four and looking like a full forward! They had one near here, not my party, thank God. He was nearly adopted until he tried to tickle one of the committee. Thank Christ the bloke we've got now is respectable.' He glared at Harry. 'Can you deny it?'

Harry assured Mr. Rufus that the sitting member was a pillar of rectitude, and the old man nodded. 'Bit too much so,' grinning a little. 'If the whips told 'im to go without trousers, he would. But a good, safe man over the bomb and doesn't stir up issues that nobody should stir. And a very fair speaker.' He appeared lost in thought.

Harry coughed. 'So Marcus had no intimates?'

Rufus frowned at the phrase and Harry hurried on. 'No close friends, nobody that knew him well earlier on?'

The blue-rimmed eyelids went down like shutters.

'Strange,' said Rufus, ''ow at my age I can remember what happened years ago clearer than what went on yesterday at the committee. Let's see. When They sent him down he had already been vetted, career et cetera. But I remember twice, there was a man. Let's see.... Funny name. Spendthrift. No. I've got it now, Spenderfield. That was all right. Marcus took him around. They like to see the M.P. with schoolmasters.'

He closed his eyes again. 'I remember he talked a lot—educational reform—3d. on the rate,' he made a kind of gurgling noise, and jabbed a finger at Harry. 'It's all right for Them to talk. But then you get higher rates and They like that, don't They, in a marginal seat like this has always been?'

'Can you remember anything more about Spenderfield?'

'Looked after Marcus when he was a lad. He had no kith. The schoolmaster had just moved Bristol way. All right, Sergeant 'um, I've given you enough of me time.'

Harry telephoned Hawker. 'Thorough lad,' grunted the Chief Inspector. 'But it's worth a penny. I'll ask Bristol to send you a report. Don't forget to stick to Miss Holland!'

At six-thirty he was knocking at Miss Holland's door. She looked at him coolly as she opened the door.

'Unofficial, nuisance value only,' he said.

'Oh, come on in, I suppose, but it will have to be tea, I can't afford to buy policemen beer.'

'The country's deteriorating. It used to be cooks in the basement area.'

'I'm not a good cook.'

'That I do not believe.' He looked around the living-room.

'No time,' she said. 'Would you settle for some rather horrible soft drink that the charlady insists on giving me?'

It tasted of rhubarb and sugar.

'She says it's very good for you,' said Elizabeth, 'particularly around the kidneys.'

Harry did not doubt it. He watched her, perched on the edge of a settee, devoid of make-up.

'I wanted to apologise about yesterday,' he said.

'And I don't think we should refer to it.'

He thought she was a very poised lass.

'In any case I suppose we might take an evening off to sample the joys of East Bradshaw. I saw a notice that the Ladies' Pleasant Hour are putting on London Assurance.'

'Small towns aren't that unsophisticated, sergeant,' she said, emphasising his rank.

'I'll ask the Inspector to call round. He's got warts.'

She laughed and took a cigarette from the packet on the coffee table.

'My charlady takes two Sunday papers. I asked her about you and she brought the edition along.' Her amber eyes mocked him.

'At great personal peril Sergeant James....'

He remained silent.

'But you went up in my estimation,' she added. 'I'm sorry, am I irritating you?'

'Elizabeth,' he said her name without quite knowing how he would complete the sentence. The door bell saved him the effort. She excused herself.

The man who entered was around six feet four, heavy chested and flat stomached, a very well preserved sixtyish, Harry judged, professionally, although to the lay eye he could have passed for an athletic fifty.

'Mr. and Mrs. Monck.' Elizabeth Holland introduced them.

The woman was tall, but dwarfed by her husband, seemingly flat chested and broad-hipped. Her inexpressive grey eyes looked clinically at Harry from out of a broad white flabby face.

'We got our London business over exceptionally early,' said Monck, 'and it's just that odd evening when the pool's ideal. So I dropped into George Stryver's and telephoned a few people. What about you, Elizabeth?' He had a virile baritone voice to match his appearance.

'Thank you. Mr. and Mrs. Monck are a local god-send, Sergeant, with a heavenly swimming pool and most generous natures.'

'Sergeant?' Mrs. Monck's voice was a fruity, well-groomed contralto. Harry wondered momentarily whether she had been an actress as he automatically responded, 'Police, just posted here.'

'In this climate we're god-sends for about three weeks every year,' said Monck, while Harry was painfully conscious of the woman's measuring appraisal. He felt sorry for Monck, doubting whether an Inspector's epidermis would have been acceptable for aquatic hospitality. However, Monck took the leap.

'We've got the car outside,' he said, 'and we can rustle up a costume to fit you.'

'A little runt like you,' corrected Harry, mentally, and then reproved himself.

He would have made an excuse if he had not caught a mischievous glint in the girl's eyes. 'That would be very pleasant,' he said.

'I'll get my things,' Elizabeth Holland said.

'Rather a dull spot this for police work,' said Monck, with the air of a man making conversation.

'It's dullish all over,' said Harry. 'Drunken driving, window smashing, that sort of thing.'

He relaxed next to Elizabeth Holland in the leather-scented comfort of Monck's Humber. The drive took about six minutes to a house on the outskirts of The Strand, a point where the odd, old-fashioned atmosphere of the place had grown perceptibly less and the streets beyond became neatly planned suburbia.

Monck drove in and stopped in front of the garage built into one wing of the house.

'Perhaps you'll show Sergeant James the way, Elizabeth,' he said, 'we'll be down as soon as we've stowed the cases away.'

The girl led him round the side of the house. Harry saw that instead of being what he had surmised to be a large bungalow, the structure became on two levels at the back. She led the way on to a long but narrow balcony with large windows opening out from the house. Glancing in he saw a long imposing living-room.

'Quite spectacular!' Elizabeth gestured.

Below was a drop of about fifty feet, culminating at a large kidney-shaped swimming-pool, blue tiled and inviting. Flanking it was a grey tiled building which he took to be dressing-rooms. Beyond and around the pool the land curved upwards, a mass of climbing geraniums and flowering shrubs until it met the back fences of a row of small houses.

'My,' said Harry, 'this is a wonderful set-up.'

'It used to be an old clay-pit,' she said leaning over the low parapet so that the evening sun turned her hair to red gold. 'The Moncks took it before the war and built the pool.'

She crossed the balcony to where a flight of steps led down to the pool.

'An expensive luxury,' he suggested.

She shrugged. 'The Moncks have been around here for centuries. I guess Lester owned the land. It's quite self-contained. You can reach the stairs from the other side without going across the balcony. In case you're invited again, I must tell you it's rather formal. You go down and use the pool and the Moncks may come down or may not. But you don't call at the house except by special invitation.'

The pool was deserted except for two youngish men swimming. Elizabeth called a brief introduction and vanished into one of the dressing-rooms.

Presently Monck trotted easily down the long flight of stairs, wearing a blue dressing-gown.

'Unless I've lost my eye this should fit you.' He handed Harry a cellophane packet. 'That's the men's changing room at the right. There's a towel with the trunks.'

By the time he had changed, the number of visitors had increased to a dozen. Monck himself, mahogany brown, was diving from the high board at one end of the pool, and Harry was glad of his own tan as he slid into the water. Mrs. Monck flashed past him, muscular arms and legs pushing her powerfully through the water.

Harry swam for ten minutes or so, until one leg began to ache. He towelled himself and relaxed in one of the chairs by the side of the pool, his eyes seeking Elizabeth Holland.

'Warm enough?' She spoke from beside him. He felt himself blush as he started. Elizabeth was wearing a rather conservative costume which if anything enhanced the bold curves of her body. Harry was conscious that he was staring and saw embarrassment in her eyes.

'Sorry,' he said, 'my thoughts were far away. Do sit down. I'm afraid it's difficult to introduce oneself around at a swimming party.'

She nodded towards the various people swimming and mentioned names. Apart from the two men he had seen earlier, no one looked less than in their middle fifties.

'Shortage of youth, hereabouts?' he ventured.

'It's a neighbourhood for retired people,' she said, rather shortly, and he didn't pursue the topic.

'You have a wonderful tan, sergeant.' It was Mrs. Monck who in spite of her bulk managed to look severely patrician in her costume. He got to his feet and drew up a chair for her.

'Not a London tan,' he explained, 'I've just spent a month in France, St. Jean-de-Luz.'

He sensed that her opinion of him had edged up a notch. She proved a fluent conversationalist and he was glad that his father had seen to it that his French accent was good. Under her skilled probing he found that in an old friend of his family, a shipper of claret, they had a mutual acquaintance.

'We heard a rumour of a terrible happening in East Bradshaw, sergeant.' She abruptly switched the subject.

'Ah, yes,' he said, 'I suppose that would be Miss Tweddle, an old lady who was coshed by a burglar, in the house I live in by the way. The landlady's Miss Fanny Walsh.'

'A strange character, I believe.' Her voice was disapproving.

'A genial, superannuated fan dancer,' he said and sensed that she was regally unamused.

'There seems to be much more crime in this district than there ever was,' Mrs. Monck was delivering a judgment. 'I trust that it will not spread further.'

'It's difficult,' said Harry, wishing he dared to smoke in her awful presence. 'People huddle round the television and the sneak thieves take the opportunity. In this case the old lady surprised the thief and got knocked over the head.'

'Has there been no arrest?'

He shrugged. 'Not that I know of, although,' he said in justification, 'we have some idea of who it might be.'

'There should be more policemen.' Mrs. Monck got to her feet with an accusing glance and walked determinedly to the diving board.

Elizabeth Holland was having difficulty in suppressing her laughter. 'You mustn't mind Gladys Monck, Sergeant. Her husband was in the diplomatic for many years and Gladys sort of got into the habit of addressing Lesser Breeds.'

'Including policemen,' he said half-resentfully.

'Including the perlice,' she mocked.

With an odd sense of shock he noticed the old man with the birth mark on his cheek emerge from the pool at the opposite side. The short legs still carried heavy muscle and over the paunch the white haired chest was taut and powerful.

'Who's that?'

She hesitated slightly. 'That's old George Stryver, one of the nicer residents.'

'I'd like to meet him.' He turned to look directly at her but she had averted her face.

'Oh, George!' she waved and the old man came round the edge of the pool with his purposeful walk.

'George, this is Sergeant James, an addition to our law enforcement. Sergeant, this is Mr. Stryver.'

Stryver's eyes were sharp and rather hard as he shook Harry's hand.

'We need it from what I heard today. How is the poor old woman?'

'She should recover. Do you know her?'

Stryver shook his head abruptly. 'Are you stationed here permanently?'

68

'They shift us around quite a lot,' said Harry and knew that he was not deceiving Stryver.

The old man hesitated and Harry was conscious that the shrewd eyes were looking at somebody over his shoulder.

'Well, I'd better change before I get pneumonia,' and Stryver stumped abruptly away.

Harry looked round and found that Elizabeth Holland was talking to a group of people a few yards away. He went to change, said goodbye to the Moncks, who casually hoped they would see him again and walked home. The big old house was unaccustomedly silent as he went up to his room.

CHAPTER FOUR

NEXT MORNING MRS. Walsh had recovered her equilibrium sufficiently to invite Harry to breakfast with her off scrambled eggs and finnan haddock. She told him that Miss Tweddle had spent a peaceful night.

At eight-thirty the telephone rang and the landlady jumped and spilled her tea.

'I'll take it,' said Harry reassuringly. It was a call from the Yard. He should catch the first available train: they would inform East Bradshaw of the fact. Yes, he would be returning, but probably not for two weeks.

He explained matters and managed to catch the nine-twenty by the skin of his teeth.

'Sorry to drag you back,' said Hawker, 'but the fraud squad are up to their necks, what with holidays and sickness, so tomorrow you'll report to them. They sent round an s.o.s. for anybody who could count.'

He took Harry's reports from a drawer and frowned down at them.

'Looks as though we've strayed away from the Tavisham angle,' mused Hawker. 'I'd have sworn he was the lynch pin. Regarding your enquiry about his money, it only took me a few phone calls to establish that the family originally got rich brewing and then stashed the fortune away in Australian grazing companies.

'Tavisham inherited an estate worth £300,000 in 1927. He left rather less than people expected, so he might have been blackmailed. He got good money when he was working, lived in what he would call a modest style but which would be ruddy luxury to me.'

He butted his cigarette stump. 'Then there's Marcus. You can bet that old Wickstraw didn't plant that thought on to you for nothing. Cautious old devil, doesn't want to carry that baby himself.' He screwed up his eyes. 'I can't seem to see Marcus from your report.'

'Fairly colourless,' said Harry, 'no strong light and shade. Always trying to set a good example like a head prefect, keeping his Scotch locked away, things like that. Quite incorruptible I would have imagined.'

'In other words a perfect subject for blackmail, like all fanatically respectable types. I haven't been completely idle. Tavisham was in France during the June and July of '39, but he was hopping back between Paris and London. It was some kind of fairly minor Government mission about ammunition. 'Mm, we're clutching at straws, maybe, but we'll keep going. The evidence of Marcus' ex-maid was interesting, but there's no Wilks on file any place that would fit your bill,' said Hawker. 'There's a Wilkins who used to knock off sub-post offices around that area in the 'thirties, but he's dead now and I can't see he'd ever know an M.P.' He sent for another cup of tea.

'Let's stick to the fact that Marcus was a politician and that this Wilks was probably somebody he met politically. Now there's an Inspector Briggs, Special Branch, retired, who lives at Surbiton. I'll phone Briggsy up and ask if you can come and see him.'

Briggs was in and Harry waited while Hawker exchanged professional banter.

'It's okay,' Hawker nodded. 'You are hereby authorised to hire yourself a cab at H.M's. expense. Lor', if the Queen knew I was treating sergeants to hackney carriages!'

'Old clown!' thought Harry and blushed when Hawker's disconcerting eyes met his.

'Thank your stars you're not attached to me permanently,' said Hawker, thought reading.

'I didn't...' stammered Harry.

'Dry up and listen. Briggsy was a sergeant in '39. In fact he might not have risen any further but for the war although he's a fine chap. He couldn't organise at all well and as for the paper work!' he shrugged. 'Old Briggs is reputed to have written one report: "Sir, the man is a bastard. He is a law-abiding citizen." But Briggs had the best memory for names and faces in the Force. Astounding! That's why he was Special Branch, that and the fact he had a couple of foreign languages. He was a good artist, too, with pencil or crayon. Off you go.'

Ex-inspector Briggs lived in the comfortable semi-detached oldish house that Harry associated with retired officers. There was the familiar fairly musty smell, the substantial mahogany furniture and the presentation clock with its brass plate brightly polished.

A heavy old man, Briggs welcomed him warmly between puffs at his pipe. 'Wilks, now,' he said. 'Just let me think.'

He pushed himself out of his chair and fetched a tantalus of whisky from the sideboard. He poured a measure and reached for another. Harry, briefly reviewing an inspector's retirement pay in terms of Scotch, declined.

'No, laddy, I've always a drop for people from the old shop, and besides it helps the brains.'

Briggs sat and savoured his Scotch. 'Let's see, a crook with political leanings. Not too many of them, if you discount the House, of course. Wilkes, Wilkie, Wilkins, could be any of them, eh?'

'It's a pretty long shot, sir.'

'Um,' the old man peered under shaggy eyebrows like a child doing a conjuring trick. 'Now would Whelks,' he spelled it, 'be of use to you?'

'Suppose I listen.' Harry smiled affectionately at him.

'Dunno why they called him Whelks,' said Briggs. 'Five feet ten medium build, light brown hair, dark eyes, but a great greasy olive-skinned face with pimples on it. Once seen, never forgotten. Here.'

He took a notebook and pencil from his pocket and sketched. 'This might help you.'

Harry considered it a remarkable effort. The face was youngish, but Briggs' broad pencil strokes conveyed the suspicion of bloat which accentuated the thin nose, with a twisted end which seemed too small for the large, wide set eyes and heavy mouth.

'Wonderful, sir, and how old was he then?'

'That was how he looked in '39, when he was around twenty-seven, which puts him at the half century mark now. I'll tell you the history. I think, in fact I'm pretty sure, his name was Mudd with two d's. But everybody called him Whelks or Whelkie. He lodged near Old Crompton Street.'

Whelks, or Mudd, had been fairly well-known around the criminal fringe and, listening to Briggs, Harry recognised a fairly familiar pattern. He had been a come-on man for the fake auctioneers and for a year a salesman for a much-travelled firm of radio retailers.

'They'd open for a few months and skip,' said Briggs. 'Seaside resorts mostly. The usual thing, defrauding the hire-purchase outfits with duplicate policies, flogging cheap radios in classy-looking cabinets, and a couple of times stock fire. In the end the principal got eight years and a couple of others went down, too.'

'But not Mudd.'

'He left well before the lid came off and there was no evidence to prove he wasn't a paid servant. In fact he was rather that. The heads knew he wasn't the man to get himself really involved. He was always peering behind him. At one time he used to run errands for Big Jack, an Australian who was around then—the con game and a bit of blackmail if the opportunity was there. And books, banned books, he seemed to know most of the regular dealers.'

'How did he come to your notice?'

'He spoke French perfectly, with just a touch of a Breton accent. Somebody tipped off the Aliens Department and they checked thoroughly, but he was born in London of English parents all right. So they sent a chit to us, a wrong 'un who could pass as French.'

He refilled his pipe.

'The old man's memory seems all right!' He chuckled. 'I had a feeling about Whelks which never was justified. That's why so much stuff has stuck in my mind.'

'Was he educated?'

'Not in the formal sense. Left school at fourteen, I guess, usual south London accent. Quick witted, but what higher education he had must have come from reading his dirty books.'

'And that was all, seems queer about the French.'

'I asked him once. He said he lived with a Frenchwoman.' Briggs' brow sagged into deep wrinkles. 'Come to think of it, I didn't check on that. He was a natural born mimic, could imitate anybody, so he probably could pick up a language quickly.'

'And about the political part?' prompted Harry.

'Oh, yes, there was a cranky little bunch called European Freedom. As usual they had no idea what the ordinary man thinks of as freedom. Toadies to Hitler mostly, but a few coms.—they weren't as far apart as people thought. I recall there were a couple who we knew were employees of the Reich Government and one very dubious fellow who said he was Hungarian. I concluded that Whelks was doing a little fishing in those waters, just to see if there was money to be picked up. In fact I'd have washed him off, but he used to visit France several times a year.'

He glanced at Harry. 'In those days, sonny, it was unusual for a lower class Englishman to cross the Channel in his lifetime except when there was a war on. Anyway he was probably a messenger boy from the dirty book trade, the stuff used to be printed there.'

Harry felt that the old Inspector was trying to justify himself a little. 'And that was the end of the matter?'

'Well,' said Briggs, 'one week I noticed Whelks wasn't around any more. The best anybody could tell me was that he'd gone north, which usually meant Birmingham then. I dunno whether we didn't dismiss him rather lightly, but after all his name and description were on the lists. He went a few months before war broke out and by God, every manjack of us had sufficient work for ten. I guess I got thirty hours sleep a week.'

It was sufficient, Harry thought, if Whelks were indeed the man that had been in Bradshaw he would either be inside or on record. The pattern was all too familiar, sooner or later Whelks would have been drawn a little deeper into some racket and then he or some partner would slip. Then the little overcrowded cell.

He spent another half an hour on shop talk, listening to Briggs' stories of men who had met the hangman long ago, before taking his departure.

Rather confidently, he asked records for the list of Mudds. Half an hour later he discovered no Mudd of suitable age group was on record. So he ordered the bulky file giving the resumés of known frauds between 1932 and 1937 and was lucky enough to pinpoint the case in which Whelks had been involved at the fourth stab. Under "associates" was typed 'Kitchener Mudd (Whelks), born 2, 2, 1911, salesman.'

'Routine, routine, the mills of God,' mused Harry, settling down at a telephone. After an hour he had established that there was no record of Mr. Mudd having died as a civilian or in military forces, neither did he have a valid British passport. Double check to emigration: no Mr. C. E. Mudd had transferred to Empire outposts after 1945.

'Um,' said Harry and drank tea before establishing that Whelks was not a licensed victualler, nor a member of the Commercial Travellers' Association, the latter being a long-shot. He called it a day.

It was good to plunge into purely routine work. He spent hours calling back figures from the accounts of a dubious investment society and the next forty-eight hours passed quickly. On the Thursday he found himself in the vicinity of Cripplegate and remembered that Marcus' old firm had been there. He consulted

74

a phone book and found that Bourne and Cuming still operated under the same name. First he telephoned a friend.

'Bourne and Cuming? Yes they're all right. They went down a good deal after the war, but are now perking up. The senior partner's name is Trice.'

Bourne and Cuming occupied a floor of a conservative old building. Glancing round the general office Harry guessed it to be a nice, smallish business.

Trice was a sunburned man who looked like the popular conception of a sailor.

'Marcus, that's very old stuff, isn't it?'

'The file was never closed, sir, so periodically it's given to somebody to look into as long as the person concerned might be alive.'

'I see. The long arm, etcetera. You'll appreciate that no firm likes that kind of publicity.'

'He hasn't been with you these twenty-five years.'

'What do you want to know?'

'Oh, a bit of general stuff might be useful, sir.'

Trice doodled on his working pad. 'This firm had two partners, one my grandad. They were getting old and took a third, Marcus.'

'Did he put money into the firm?'

'He'd worked here for five years, becoming manager. Then he bought a partnership.' The blue eyes defied Harry to ask at what price.

'What was he like?'

'I joined the firm in 1937, just after he became an M.P. Shortly before he disappeared I had been called up by the R.N.V.R. You'll bear in mind I was a junior in those days, but I never liked him personally.' His eyes measured Harry. 'I was never comfortable around him. Nobody these days likes the phrase "not quite a gentleman", but the man was uneasy, trying too hard.'

'I see—and professionally?'

'He had an encyclopaedic knowledge of the profession and particularly of municipal taxation. If you wanted to know a point you'd go in to see Marcus and come out stuffed with enough facts for a lifetime. Very impressive.'

'I suppose he got on well with clients?'

'Yes. The old gentlemen were terribly nice, everybody liked them. But they were getting along in years. On balance they thought it a good thing when Marcus got into Parliament. You know the thing, "Just a minute, here is our partner, Mr. Marcus M.P.," and Marcus would rattle away like a machine gun. We got a steady increase in clients, particularly businesses looking into new sites.'

'One thing,' said Harry, 'and I know you either might know it or not wish to talk about it, but I'd like to know how his estate was divided.'

'There's no particular secret. He died intestate and no heirs came forward. After seven years the court declared him dead. It didn't create more than a couple of lines in my morning paper, everybody had forgotten poor old Marcus, I guess. Oh, we had inconvenience. There was his equity in the firm and there was quite a flap with Somerset House about the valuation. However, we got over it.'

'Do you have your business records for '39?'

'Well,' Trice considered, 'we'd keep the master files. A proportion of old records went up in the blitz. We were in a building near here which was badly hit.'

'Could I examine what remains?'

Trice sighed. 'You know we consider our last job at least as confidential as a lawyer's.'

Diplomatically Harry mentioned his civilian experience and Trice looked suitably impressed at the name of the firm.

'Well, as long as you appreciate the position I suppose no harm would be done.'

A junior, whose curiosity Harry firmly repressed, took him to a couple of cell-like, dimly lit rooms in the basement.

The 1935-9 shelves were tightly stacked with files. Harry started taking them out. In those days the firm had apparently worked on a registry system and each file had been booked in-and-out, with the name of the person noted on the cover.

Harry started in January, 1938, noting the files Marcus had consulted, taking a few minutes to glance at their contents. It was faintly odd to look at the typed signature 'J. R. Marcus'.

It took him a couple of hours, including his hypothetical lunch hour, to note the files Marcus had consulted.

Nobody asked him for an explanation of his lateness when he regained the large, partitioned office he had been working in for a week and he was soon enlightened as to the reason. An official of the company being investigated had decided that his bounden duty was to law and order. He was a bland, round-faced man and he had brought two solicitors and his duplicate set of books.

Police work, thought Harry. Ten days of labour, foot-slogging, a nice case being built up out of sweat, and then somebody confesses!

Over the partition he heard the mellifluous voice of one of the solicitors explaining the involved, but professional and civic, reasons for his client having come forward at this date. He half-heartedly started to dissect cash deposits for 1961 and realised that he wouldn't be wanted on this particular job after he had finished for the day.

He had seized the opportunity to take an early evening meal in the canteen. A colleague joined him. When they reached the coffee the man remembered something.

'You were in East Bradshaw when they sent that enquiry down about Joe Larter, weren't you, Harry?'

'Did you pull him in?'

'Joe wasn't at home. But, you'll never guess it, an Interpol Report came on my desk this morning. Joe's in Teneriffe, living like a ruddy millionaire. He flew there a day after we got the Bradshaw call.'

'Having a ball, is he?'

'And how! The local *seguradad* report that he's paid a deposit on a nice little estate and that he's placed a sizeable foreign, non-sterling, remittance in a local bank.'

Harry raised his eyebrows.

'He was broke before,' said his informant. 'Hadn't touched for six or seven months. You know that he's cautious, we heard he'd turned a couple of jobs down because of the risk. No, the lucky devil must have found a nice black-market hoard, stuff that couldn't be reported, dollars, maybe. Well, if he's staying there it'll be one worry less.'

Back at his cubicle he found that the solicitors were still talking. Awaiting him, from Hawker, was a bulky packet resulting from Bristol enquiries of Marcus' old schoolmaster. He put into his brief case and signed off, painfully conscious that nobody cared about his going.

His flat was hot and airless and he opened all the windows before sitting in his old club chair and opening the case. As it happened the Bristol sergeant, who had collected the assignment, had been on two courses with Harry who had found a kindred soul. The written report was brief, that the sergeant had interviewed Mr. and Mrs. Spenderfield with inconclusive results, but, attached, was a manila folder personally addressed to Harry.

A note read:

'Dear Sourpuss. I'd like to fix *you* up a chore like this. The Spenderfield male is a retired schoolmaster, tiny, full of good works. She makes two of him physically, also full of good works. Kind, civic minded people at 120 words per minute, rather over my shorthand speed now. When Marcus' parents died—influenza—he was fifteen. The solicitor (local bank manager) arranged for Marcus to board with the Spenderfields, who had been close friends of the parents. Make no mistake, there was no father-son relationship. A reserved youngster, was Marcus, I think. The Spenderfields like boys *en masse*, he was one of them. At 17, with their blessing, he went to London to study. However, old Spenderfield's house is a mine of filing cabinets and iced tea, for God's sake. He gave me this file which comprises everything Marcus ever wrote to them and carbons of the replies. Rather fancy he took it from a file marked "Boys, dead, presumed". Marcus seems to have had a warmish, fish-like regard for them both: Spenderfield proudish because Marcus was "never in trouble", and got an M.P. after his name. In 1939 they decided that he must be "on secret service" and the war plus a couple of thousand other boys embalmed Marcus as another statistic.

Yours as aye.'

The file contained some four hundred letters, the last fifty type-written, and the painstaking carbons of the replies, each beginning 'My dear Boy'.

Harry sat down with a quart of light ale. It was midnight when he finished. Nothing there. He had got out of the bath and was putting on his pyjamas when the maddening mental itch started to develop, like an insect bite. Wearily he went, not towards the bedroom, but to his living-room, stopping to open another bottle on the way.

He spent Sunday with friends, playing golf in the afternoon and manfully resisting the impulse to phone Elizabeth Holland. Monday morning found him feeling sour.

In his 'in' basket was a yellow sheet requesting him, Harry found, to attend the weekly progress Committee 'A', the one dealing with unnatural death. He made a discreet enquiry as to the Chairman. It was a Commander popularly known as the Vice-

Precedent because of his habit of quoting ancient parallels from cases long since forgotten by anybody else.

It was highly unusual for a sergeant to appear at such an august gathering and Harry was suitably awed.

'Ah, James, at Bradshaw,' said the Chairman, glancing through the report with his habitual expression of distaste. 'Think there's anything there? It's pretty tenuous, eh?'

'I think that Tavisham was involved in blackmail and that the M.P. who disappeared, Marcus, might have been murdered.'

'Yes,' said the Vice-Precedent, looking round the table. 'There was a parliamentary candidate in Sydney, Australia, some years ago who disappeared and it was almost certainly murder. But, sergeant, Marcus was an ex-M.P. Keep that firmly in your head. We don't want headlines about missing M.P.'s and if you do find any leads, emphasise that it's a routine investigation of an open file,' he cleared his throat, 'thereby creating the impression (a) that we never abandon a case (b) that you are not merely a policeman without sufficient work to occupy himself.

'Very well, tomorrow go to East Bradshaw for another week. Two headings, Tavisham and Blackmail, and Marcus, Disappearance of.'

Unexpectedly the Chairman smiled, 'And incidentally two investigations for the price of one look better in the accounts. Good luck.'

As he turned for the door, Harry heard the telephone ring.

'Sergeant!'

He turned. The Chairman was listening intently and gestured for Harry to remain. After a few minutes he put down the handset.

'That, gentlemen, was Superintendent Wickstraw, speaking from East Bradshaw, informing me that a Mr. George Stryver vanished from his home, at the Strand, East Bradshaw, some time yesterday morning. He thinks we shall be called in by the Chief Constable, but not for forty-eight hours. However, they would be glad if Sergeant James returned forthwith. A trifle irregular perhaps, but understandable.'

He looked sharply at Harry. 'Officially you're still on Tavisham and Marcus until a superior officer arrives, when you'll report to him. We'd better send you by car.'

It was a luxury for a sergeant and Harry took the opportunity to stretch out on the unoccupied back seat.

Wickstraw had taken possession of the only decent office in the

East Bradshaw station. Cigarette butts smouldered in the ashtray on his desk. His eyes had the bloodshot look of a man who had not slept.

'Glad to have you back. The running reports are over there. First of all I should tell you that Stryver is a very important man, a first rank Scottish industrialist until he retired. We're conducting the most complete local search that we've ever made here.'

Harry found a battered chair and started to read.

The disappearance had been reported by Stryver's cook at five o'clock on Sunday night. At his home the Lodge he maintained three indoor and two outdoor staff. He was a man of fixed habits and on Sundays invariably dined at two o'clock in the afternoon, that being the main meal of the day.

On Sunday morning there had been a tennis gathering, a usual happening at the Lodge in summer. The guests had departed between one and one-fifteen and Stryver had last been seen entering the shed where garden chairs and tennis gear were kept.

The other reports were negative. Nobody had seen Stryver around the Strand that day. He had not booked a railway or long distance bus ticket and both cars were in his garage.

In spite of himself Harry felt a little prickle of horror down his back.

'A swine of a thing, eh?' grunted Wickstraw massaging his eyeballs with finger and thumb. 'We haven't approached the B.B.C. yet and the press aren't on to it. I'll have to arrange a broadcast tomorrow.'

'The people at the tennis party have no clues?'

'A routine party, everybody shook hands with George and tootled off. There were no mysterious callers and the cook swears that Stryver didn't come in by the kitchen entrance nor did he walk round the front of the house, because that way goes right past the kitchen window. So he's still on that bloody tennis court. Prowl around, sergeant, and see if you can come up with any good idea.'

He cycled to the Lodge, noting with dissatisfaction that a sallow youth with pencils protruding from the top pocket of his sports jacket was lingering at the gate.

'I don't suppose you are calling on Mr. Stryver?' The youth addressed him.

'Not particularly,' said Harry. 'I understand he keeps a staff. I'm here to measure up for his new boiler.'

'Ah,' the youth shifted a wad of chewing gum around in his

mouth. 'I'm the *Weekly Gazette*. One of the printers had a story that the old gent had disappeared. The woman who answered the door said that he's ill in bed. I didn't like her manner, or his. . . .'

The pointing finger was directed at a man digging round the rose bushes. Harry creased his brow and then remembered sharing a bench with the man at the little pub. It seemed ages ago.

He opened the gate.

'I'll be here when you come out if you find out anything,' said the youth suggestively.

It wouldn't be long, thought Harry, before it hit the papers.

The gardener looked up in puzzled recognition.

'Keep your voice low,' said Harry, 'I'm from the police and there's a reporter hanging around outside the gate.'

'I gave him a flea in his ear,' the man muttered. 'He's got no right here.'

'If you abuse him, you'll just make things worse,' Harry warned. 'Just be polite and know nothing.'

The man nodded.

Harry walked down a path leading by the side of the house. He found himself looking in the kitchen window as he passed it. Behind the house was a spacious lawn intersected by flower-beds and lined with flowering shrubs on one side. To his left was a path leading to the wire-caged tennis court. There were tables and chairs arranged under a large awning and near to the house a small shed with the door open. Beyond the court the six foot retaining wall continued with honeysuckle trained along it.

He grunted and knocked at the back door. A florid, dumpy woman glared at him.

'I'm police,' said Harry and her manner altered abruptly as she invited him inside and into the kitchen.

'I'm Mrs. Gates, the cook, and don't hesitate about asking any question because we're all worried to death.'

He listened for a few minutes to an eulogy on the virtues of Mr. Stryver.

'Nothing unusual in his manner?'

'I said no yesterday when the Inspector came round.'

'I'm sorry. . . .'

'No, it's not that. I said "no", meaning that he hadn't been depressed or excited. But on thinking it over I should have said that he looked extra cheerful these last few days.'

'Extra cheerful?'

'Yes, he was a dour one usually. Scotch you know. Often you wouldn't know whether he was serious or making a joke. But when he was happy he used to do a little jig, like this.' She made an incongruous motion with her fat little legs. 'Skippy, like. Last time I saw him do it was when he backed the Derby and Oaks double two years ago. But Saturday, when I went in to discuss his evening meal, there he was doing it.'

'Was he looking at anything?'

'No, he was staring out the window.'

'No doubt in the direction of Elizabeth Holland's house,' thought Harry hollowly.

He felt in his pocket for his warrant. 'Take a look at this. If anybody comes round saying there are police, ask for it. I've known some reporters not above hinting they were police. And now I'll take a bit of a look around.'

The house had been considerably remodelled, he saw, resulting in a dining-room, four reception rooms and six bedrooms, each with its bathroom. There was a servant's wing with three bedrooms and one bath. The reports indicated that the house had been searched so it was idle for him to pry in the closets. The place generally was redolent of solid comfort, a trifle unconventional in parts as though its owner knew what he wanted and wasn't concerned with what other people thought. The big master bedroom was lined with books on one wall. Harry glanced through them ... all of John Buchan and, more modernly, Hammond Innes, volumes of books about sea voyages and exploration, a section of what looked like valuable books concerning mutiny and piracy.

He smiled at what a rather grim industrialist should use as his private reading. A bathroom led off one side and at the far end was a large work room. He admired three shot guns and a collection of salmon rods. At one end was a substantial, old-fashioned desk. It was strictly against the rules to touch it, but Harry found himself trying a drawer. It slipped open. He tried the others and found several unlocked. He wondered how the searchers had missed that particular indication. A dour man like Stryver would scarcely leave his desk unlocked if he intended being away for any length of time.

He went back to the kitchen. 'Did any of the tennis guests come into the house?'

'No reason for them to. They never did. Anyway I'd have heard them. They've got their own lavatory out there.'

'What about refreshment?'

'There's the fridge and serving bench out there. I put in two jugs of orange juice and two plates of canapés before they came. Mr. Stryver used to take the hard stuff out himself.'

'Did you clear up the refreshments?'

'Usually I got the Master settled down to his dinner and cleared away while he was eating. When he didn't turn up I went out and did it.'

'Same as usual?'

'The shed looked a bit of a mess so I called Bob Johnson and asked him to clean it up a bit.'

'A mess, how's that?'

'Untidy, things out of place, didn't look neat like the master always wanted things.'

'Johnson is the gardener?'

'Yes. He's a widower and would rather potter around than be home. On Sundays he cleans the cars and puts the tennis net up and finishes off with a bit on the garden. I give him a bottle of beer and some sandwiches about two and then he goes home.'

'Where does he eat?'

'In winter he comes in the kitchen, but yesterday he knocked at the door and I gave him the tray to take outdoors.'

'Where was he after the tennis party had broken up?'

'He was down in the kitchen garden. That's right at the far end.'

'Could you get him for me? There's a reporter hanging around outside the gate and I don't want to put him wise to anything.'

Johnson told Harry that he'd arrived pretty early, around seven, washed the cars, put the net up, and then retired to his seedling beds.

'Did you see anything?'

'I came through the gate into the garden about 1.15 to get some grub from Mrs. G. I saw the young lady, Miss Holland, come running back from the front of the house and almost immediately afterwards one of the gentlemen, Mr. Burke, followed. They only stayed a few seconds and then went off together. When I went back with my food I saw the master going into the shed.'

He dismissed the man and thanked the cook, asking, as he left, how many servants had been in the house other than herself.

'Two. Ivy generally has Sunday off.'

He found the *Weekly Gazette* representative leaning over the gate. 'Did you see Mr. Stryver?'

He thought of lying, but it didn't do to put the Press' back up, even the *Weekly Gazette*.

'They didn't say anything,' he said vaguely. 'I just got on with the job.'

'New boiler, eh?' said the youth. 'Who do you work for?'

Harry registered the lesson of always providing for contingencies. He rejected the thought of claiming to come from a nearby town because of the bicycle, so he registered righteous indignation.

'You should have something better to do than stand around asking bloody silly questions.' As he rode away he glanced back and saw the reporter gazing at him sceptically. He saw an ancient car parked nearby and thought the youth might quite easily follow him, so he made a quick turn to the right to follow the line of the Lodge's boundary wall. He stopped before the ruined church he had seen a week previously and noted that somebody had painted 'Keep Britain White' in irregular letters on the grimy sandstone portico.

He smoked a cigarette, keeping an eye open for the reporter, but evidently that persistent burr had decided to keep his vigil. From the other direction Harry glimpsed a perspiring face under a policeman's helmet and waved a greeting. It was one of the constables he had met at East Bradshaw.

'Morning,' greeted the man, with the suspicion of a grin, 'so you're back.'

Well, thought Harry resignedly, they would soon know.

'I heard about old Stryver,' he said aloud. 'Funny sort of a business—'

'And hard on the feet. I interviewed sixty householders this morning. None of them saw Stryver yesterday. The old Super's having a house to house check with the old man's photograph. Reckon it'll take a week, but Wickstraw's thorough, I'll grant him that.'

Harry jerked his thumb at the church. 'Did anybody look there?'

'Every vacant building around was gone through as soon as word came in. I was up until one, and then on again at eight. What a life!'

Looking at the church Harry rubbed his nose. 'That was the obvious place. I can't see Stryver walking round a place like The Strand without meeting somebody.'

'Oh, Sunday at two-ish!' grunted the constable. 'Nice bit of beef, yorkshire and two vegies, a hot afternoon, the *News of the World* and two penn'orth of shut-eye. You wouldn't have found a dog in the streets.'

'I suppose you're right,' said Harry.

'That reminds me,' said the constable. 'The wife's got a cold joint of lamb at home and I'm hungry as a wolf. I'd phone into the sergeant and pack it in only for this.'

From the pocket of his uniform he produced an old-fashioned key.

'It's for that place,' he said. 'Nobody admits owning it, so the key's kept at the fire station. I don't suppose...?'

'Sure, I'll drop it back,' said Harry, extending his hand. 'I think I'll have a glance in first.'

'I'd better show you the way,' said the constable. 'Dark as hell inside.'

They opened the rusty lock and the sergeant flashed a torch down a short flight of marble stairs. 'Queer place,' he said, 'Old Squire Monck, they were the old family hereabouts, quarrelled with the bishop and built his own church. I don't think it was ever consecrated.' He flashed his torch over the roof. 'All the windows went during the war and were boarded up. He gingerly trod between the rotting pews. 'He spent a lot of money on it.'

The torch beam picked out faded, damp scarred frescoes on the wall. They were religious in character, but very fleshy in execution.

'Queer old bird,' said Harry.

'That he was. And look here.'

Before the altar was a tomb, its cover beside it, the rotting remains of a thick blue velvet cloth covering the top, weighted down with a board.

'He always said this was to be his burial place. See the inscription...?'

'Randolph Walter Sebastian Christobel Monck. Christian. Born January 17th, 1842. Passed to the Greater Life...'

'And in the end,' the constable said, 'he wasn't buried here anyway.'

'Hell, there's a stink around here,' said Harry, a sick feeling in his stomach.

'I've got one of these summer colds,' said the constable.

Harry tugged away the board and felt the blue velvet unpleasantly in his hand as he tugged it away. They looked down into the swollen, purplish face of George Stryver.

The constable's face assumed a greenish tinge round the mouth as he bent forward into the rays of the torch. He tried to grin, 'There goes any hope of food.'

'Only if you hang around,' said Harry. 'Give me the torch and phone up Wickstraw. Then catch a bite and some sleep.'

Left alone he bent over the tomb with a handkerchief tied over his mouth. The place was like an oven in spite of the thickness of its walls. Stryver's eyes goggled sightlessly upwards. He was wearing a white shirt, cream trousers and tennis shoes. A scrap of white paper appeared above the breast pocket of the horribly stained shirt and Harry gingerly drew it out by the corner. It was about three inches by one and in blue pencil was printed: 'Urgent meeting in the Old Church at 2.45. Urgent.' The last word was underscored heavily. He went back to the door and stood breathing hungrily until the two police-cars screamed up.

Wickstraw jumped out first. He peered past Harry and then told the Inspector, at his elbow, to arrange for emergency light.

Harry carefully took the paper out of his pocket. 'In the corpse's shirt pocket, sir;' Wickstraw studied it and whistled through clenched teeth.

'Make anything of it?'

'Yes,' said Harry. 'Look at those angles. Written carefully with a ruler. You won't get a handwriting expert to touch that one.'

Wickstraw slipped the paper in a cellophane case. 'No hope of fingerprints, of course.'

The Inspector uncoiled flex behind a spotlight from one of the cars and hurried behind it up the aisle.

Wickstraw looked sombrely at what remained of Stryver.

'I'll bet a thousand to nothing it's not a natural.' He addressed the Inspector, 'Get more lights in here and take everything apart if you want to. The police surgeon should be here in ten minutes.'

'Come on,' he turned to Harry.

'Better close the door right up to the wire,' said Harry.

Wickstraw looked surprised.

'Keep the room temperature level for the surgeon.'

Wickstraw grunted and gave an order to the policeman at the door.

'The time of death should be fairly easy,' said Wickstraw, 'what with known time factors.'

'This heat could complicate it, sir,' said Harry.

'I suppose ...'

Wickstraw broke off as the young reported materialised from behind the shoulder of the uniformed man.

'Ah, Mr. Green,' said Wickstraw, eyeing the poised pencil and notebook as an early Christian would a lion.

'Any statement, Super?'

'Mr. George Stryver has been found dead in that ruined church.'

'Cause of death, Super?'

'You've got your story. Trot away like a good man.'

As they went to one of the police cars Wickstraw made a mock groan. 'That young fellow has many of the attributes of a burr. Unless somebody scrapes him off their shoe one of these days he'll end up on a Sunday paper.'

'You'd better keep the car,' said Wickstraw. 'Drop me at the Station. I've got about three hours' on the blower ahead of me. The position is that the Chief will ask for Yard assistance as soon as I've talked with him. Stryver had his business interests in Glasgow and London and the genesis of this affair could lie there. The Inspector will handle the immediate issues. Meantime see those people at the tennis party. Kid gloves, I always believe in that first time up.'

'If I may suggest it, sir,' said Harry, 'we'd better get full depositions from his cook and gardener. Two of the guests went back for a few minutes after the gathering had broken up—Mr. Burke and Miss Holland.'

'Gawd.' Wickstraw gazed out of the window until they reached the police station. Harry got out from courtesy and then consulted the driver.

The nearest house was that of the Moncks. A maid showed him into the room which he remembered looking into as he had made his way down to the swimming pool. There was an air of elegance which was reflected in Lester Monck himself, cool and relaxed in a white linen suit. An old chow dog at his feet gave a perfunctory snarl.

'Come in, Sergeant,' he sounded a trifle surprised.

Mrs. Monck was seated in a wide leather chair, book on her knee and Harry gave her his politest bow.

Then he told them about George Stryver.

'My God, this is terrible!' Monck's face turned pale under its deep tan.

'Perhaps you had heard he had disappeared from his home?'

'A policeman came round last night. He was pretty vague as to why he was asking about George. I told him that we had seen him in the morning at his tennis court.'

'He appeared all right?'

Monck ran his fingers through his heavy hair. 'I thought he was just the same as ever. He probably wouldn't see seventy again, but he was a fanatic about tennis, and most hospitable of course.'

Harry turned to Mrs. Monck, sitting with set face. The book had slithered down to the carpet.

She said, slowly, 'I thought George was a trifle preoccupied. It's difficult to define, not quite at his usual form. However, it was an exceptionally hot day and he was a heavy man. I don't think any of us felt one hundred per cent in the humidity.'

'I understand these Sunday gatherings were regular occasions during good weather. Who were present?'

'Well,' said Monck, with a faint smile, 'it wasn't exactly a young people's gathering, rather an old fogies' club. Let's see, yesterday, there were ourselves, more or less regulars when we're at home, Colonel Rodgers and his son Tony, who's a London solicitor but comes down most weekends, and Tom Burke, a local stipendiary, and his wife. The only young person besides Tony was Miss Holland, whom you know. Usually there were more of us—old George liked people around—but as my wife said the morning was quite oppressive.'

'I understand Guy Tavisham used to turn up when he was alive.'

'Guy?' Monck's head went back. 'Well, he was something of a recluse, but if I remember rightly he did turn up a couple of times each month. It became about the only call he ever did make towards the end, but he had been a tiger in his youth, Wimbledon Class.'

'I understood that Tavisham and Mr. Stryver were intimates,' said Harry.

'Can there be any connection between these two deaths?' Despite her rather preposterous voice, Harry thought that perhaps Mrs. Monck was shrewder than she seemed.

He smiled placatingly at her. 'At this stage, madam, it's more or less random questioning. Later we become more precise. But as you have evidently realised, when two friends die violently within the space of a year, we have to check on any connection.'

Monck lounged back in his chair and frowned a little in thought. 'I wouldn't have associated the word "intimate" with Guy. He was a valued acquaintance of mine and more recently of

Stryver. I was in the Foreign Office for some years, until last year in fact. Guy started in the Diplomatic and resigned, a pity because he was a first-class man. Are you sure you won't take a drink, because we do at this hour?'

Harry declined and watched Monck fill two sherry glasses. He spoke over his shoulder, 'Afterwards Tavisham used to do random jobs for the F.O.; very useful man in an emergency to stand-in. During the war, of course, he came back full time. He had no financial worries—a wealthy man in fact—and no professional ambition.'

'I would have imagined his dislike of meeting people was a handicap,' said Harry.

'Oh, he could be most charming socially when necessary. It was just that in his private life he became progressively more withdrawn. A pity, because a lot of people would have liked to have seen more of Guy.'

'I see. Now when did you and Mrs. Monck leave the tennis court?'

'I went at one and my wife left at noon. The couple who do for us insist on Sundays off, and so she has to prepare our meal.'

'Nothing unusual during the tennis?'

'Oh, no. George was dour, you know. Even if there had been anything seriously worrying him, I doubt if you would have known it.'

'Of the people present, were there any particular friends of Mr. Stryver?'

'We've known George for maybe seven years and I suppose we were pretty close to him. Colonel Rodgers used to play chess a lot with him. And Miss Holland would drop in to see him any time she cared. I think the Burkes mostly only called for tennis—he's a very busy chap these days.'

'No enemies you know of?'

Monck smiled ruefully. 'I wouldn't have thought old George had an enemy in the world. I always thought a lot of lame dogs owed a fair bit to George. Of course, his career was based in Scotland. I'd say, at a venture, that he was a man that would not tolerate what he called "funny business".'

'Foony business, he pronounced it,' said Mrs. Monck. 'Old George was dead straight and he loathed anything crooked. I was told once he never had a strike on his hands when he was in business.'

'What was his particular interest?'

'Processed food,' said Monck. 'George inherited a moderate sized canning company from his father and proved a genius at it. I suppose he would be a millionaire.'

'He seemed to live fairly quietly for one.'

'Oh,' said Monck, 'he didn't like the south. He told me once that when he retired a younger brother took over and he deliberately moved away from his business. He didn't like London or southern England, but he fell in love with this place, between both worlds as it were.'

'Thank you very much, sir,' said Harry and left, the asthmatic chow following his heels to the door.

He found Burke, the stipendiary, at work in his office.

'Yes,' Burke said, 'I know, the Super 'phoned. What a dreadful business!'

'I gather that the Sunday parties were semi-regular.'

'Old George, God rest him, was a hospitable man, he liked people around.'

Burke had a leonine, Irish face and a powerful frame, stooped a little from desk work. 'Yes, old George was one of the people who made life possible here for my wife and me. It's a dull place, taken by and large.'

He gave Harry a shrewd glance from his blue eyes. 'Wickstraw said you're Yard?'

'I happened to be up here on something else, so I'm doubling until the brass arrive.'

'And doubling well, so the Super said. You'll want to know about Stryver. He was an extremely wealthy retired industrialist, with enough money to do what he wanted, which was fairly modest in character. He rented a bit of shooting and fishing, both of them prime, in Scotland, belonged to several golf clubs, hired a yacht when he wanted, which wasn't often. Altogether he lived fairly quietly, for a man of his means.'

'Women?'

'Burke's heavy eyebrows met. 'His wife died shortly before he retired at sixty-five, maybe a contributary reason why he came here. They had no children, by the way. But mistresses, I don't know. He was a very conventional man, close-mouthed in many ways. If he had one, or more, I never suspected it, neither,' he smiled 'did my wife, which is more to the point.'

'No enemies?'

Burke shrugged. 'Not to my knowledge, although I'd hazard that he was a tough nut in his time and nobody's fool. However, what enemies he had wouldn't be in Bradshaw. He contributed largely to charity and was quite the reverse of a hard man.'

'Now, this tennis party, what happened?'

'The usual. We played easy sets. I usually took on Stryver. I'm a mug at the game which evened things up and I must admit I never tried to make him run too much. Colonel Rodgers played Mrs. Burke. Miss Holland went to sets with young Tony Rodgers and after she and Tony played doubles against the Moncks.'

'What was drunk?'

'Drunk? During the game I think we all had plenty of iced orange juice, except young Rodgers who had a pale ale on one occasion. Afterwards we all had a ritual Scotch before departing, plus the usual plates of savouries.'

'What was the order of leaving?'

Burke considered. 'Mrs. Monck left first as she always did because of domestic commitments. Her husband took her to the gate and then returned. The party broke up between one and one-fifteen. My wife walked out with Colonel Rodgers and I went to the gate with Tony Rodgers. In fact I returned and so did Miss Holland.'

Harry was conscious of his eyebrows jerking upwards.

'We'd driven half a mile and then I remembered I had something to tell Stryver so I drove back.' Burke filled his pipe. 'I didn't see Stryver as much as I'd have liked to. We exchanged dinners about every month but,' he gestured to the documents on the desk—'I don't get much time for social activities. But I'd seen him a month previously and he asked me a question—you know how people attribute wisdom to a magistrate. I told him I'd have to look it up.'

'What was the question?'

'He asked me a hypothetical question,' Burke smiled faintly, 'as everybody does. It concerned an irrevocable trust of long standing administered by professional trustees. He wanted to know how one found out the original source, in this case complicated by the fact that he rather thought the provenance was Switzerland.' He puffed at his pipe. 'I don't for the life of me know why he didn't consult his own solicitors. However I liked old George and didn't want to snub him, so I said I'd look into it. In fact I asked a friend of mine who does trust work. George didn't make it sound urgent, so what I nipped back to tell him was that he hadn't a hope in Hades unless he had some legal claim against the trust.'

Harry stared down at his pot-hooks. 'And there was Miss Holland, also returning?'

Burke stroked his fleshy nose. 'Yes, I saw her disappearing round the edge of the house wall as I opened the gate. She was maybe a second ahead of me.'

'What did you see when you caught up with her?'

Burke said, 'I was hurrying, we were late for a luncheon date. She'd not have been more than two yards ahead when I caught up. George was seated at one of the little tables with a large Scotch and ice. That was his custom. As the last guest went he'd pour himself a large Scotch on the rocks, raise the glass and say, "The Host's Privilege" and settle down with it.'

'How was he dressed?'

'Conservative white shirt, cream bags and tennis shoes. Oh, and his old canvas hat, a fishing sort of thing, was on the table near the glass.'

'What did Miss Holland say?'

'She'd forgotten her lipstick. She went in to the wash place and came out and she and I went back together. I drove off and she walked home, or so I presumed.'

'She saw you coming?'

'No, George did. He looked up and said, "Oh. Hallo, Tim," and Miss Holland glanced round.'

'I just want to get a mental picture,' said Harry. 'There was Stryver, sitting at a table sipping his Scotch. Was the bottle and water on the table?'

'No. Stryver always poured the drinks in the little bar and he was meticulous in taking the used glasses back. He always took a new glass for each drink: he was rather a fanatic about hygiene. No, he was at the table with his glass. There was his old hat, his tobacco pouch and pipe....' He paused and said, 'Oh, and his capsule.'

'Capsule?'

Burke half smiled. 'George had various strongly held theories, one of which concerned vitamins. After any exertion he took a gelatine capsule containing various vitamins, a little glucose and salt. He used to have them made up specially.'

'What was the capsule in size?'

Burke shrugged. 'I suppose it was the normal sort of capsule, maybe bigger than most. George always took it with a shot of Scotch. I once said jokingly that I thought the Scotch would neutralise the contents and he was so worried he consulted the local doctor.'

'When Miss Holland went to the wash house she passed between you and the table?'

Burke nodded, drumming one set of fingers on his desk. 'This looks ugly, Sergeant. Was Stryver poisoned?'

Harry shrugged. 'I didn't like his skin colour, that bluish drowned look. It remains for the post-mortem, of course.'

Burke shook his head. 'I can't understand it.'

'Look here, sir, frankly I wouldn't ask this question of a layman. Off the record, was there the slightest indication that Holland was his mistress?'

Burke blew a cloud of smoke. He hesitated:

'I've always found Miss Holland a charming young woman. My wife likes her. She is stand-offish and we've both wondered why an attractive woman of her age should immure herself among a retired area like the Strand. I suppose it's possible. All I can say is that I have not seen any evidence of it at all.'

'Mm,' Harry looked down at his notes.

'How long did Miss Holland take in the lavatory.'

'Well,' said Burke. 'We didn't stay long. It was merely a matter of a few sentences, maybe a couple of minutes. She proably put some lipstick on when she'd found it, women being women.'

'Was Stryver anxious to get the advice you gave him?'

'He didn't seem so,' said Burke. 'He mentioned the matter when he came to dinner, on the Tuesday of last week. I should warn you that George wasn't a man who wore his thoughts on his sleeve.'

'And you had no opportunity of telling him your advice during the morning?'

Harry was glad that he was dealing with a professional and therefore had no need to excuse any apparent irrelevance.

Burke hesitated. 'I naturally had a mental note to tell George, but the opportunity didn't somehow arise and then it passed from my mind.'

'So he didn't ask you?'

'That's odd,' the Stipendiary said, 'now you bring it out. Stryver was a man of vast business experience, with all the verbal skills that can entail. Come to think of it perhaps he didn't want to discuss it.'

'That's just an impression?'

'Once, soon after we'd arrived, I started to say something, but somewhere along the line the conversation was switched and I think it might have been George who did that '

'Thanks,' Harry snapped his notebook shut. 'Probably nothing to the information part, but perhaps you'd avoid talking about it for the time being.'

'Of course,' Burke nodded.

It was after six-thirty and Harry and his driver took a beer and a sandwich before going on to the Rodgers' house which was out in the direction of Eaglesham.

Colonel Rodgers was an upright old gentleman with glittering glasses and a wide moustache who talked in a series of peremptory honks.

'Stunned by it,' he said, 'stunned by it. The Moncks phoned me. Have you got the man?'

'We only found the corpse a few hours ago.'

'You may think I'm an old fogey, sir, but nowadays there is more of this brutal violence than there ever was when I was a young man.'

'Oh, God,' thought Harry who had once read a history of crime. 'It'll be the lash, at any minute.'

'Not that I believe in capital punishment,' said the Colonel. 'I believe the educational process has failed.' He gave a short, piercing laugh. 'You've got me typed as a dug-out, Sergeant. Believe me, that type of officer died around 1920. We're not so stupid these days. Have a Scotch?'

'Not on duty, sir.'

The Colonel solemnly filled two small glasses. 'Sergeant, it takes a wise man to know when he should take a small Scotch, so let me be the judge.'

Harry relaxed and sipped while Rodgers surveyed him with his little blue eyes. 'I was Intelligence for the last twenty years, Sergeant, so I have a little knowledge of policework.'

'That's a relief, sir,' said Harry. 'I *was* expecting a dug-out.'

'You get to look like it,' said the Colonel. 'People rather expect it with colonels. Now, about your problem. Firstly, the tennis party was normal except that usually there might be two or three more people. Mostly elderly folks having a bit of a knock-up, a leisurely two hours with plenty of orange juice and gossip. A good Sunday morning, in fact.

'Second, Stryver. He was an admirable resident. I'm on the committee of this and that and Stryver was always good for a cheque. Not a mug, you had to convince him that the cause was

94

good; but when you did he was forthcoming in princely fashion. Good background.'

'The party was absolutely normal?'

'Yes.'

'As I understand it the drinks were kept in the refrigerator in the shed?'

'Yes,' said Rodgers. 'Orange juice mostly, but my son—he works in London, by the way, so you'll have to contact him there—drank one bottle, I think, of pale ale. We all had one final nip of whisky when the tennis had finished.'

'Straight?'

'For me, yes. My son had water and so did Monck. I think the Burkes took it straight, but Miss Holland and Mrs. Monck split a bottle of ginger ale. George used a splash of soda as he always did.'

'How does Miss Holland impress you?'

The shaggy eyebrows lifted a fraction. 'Impress? As a very pleasant person. Keeps to herself, rarely goes out, so gossip has it, rather impersonal in conversation.'

'I see.' Harry snapped his notebook shut.

'One thing,' said Rodgers, 'you know how these little communities are, always a certain amount of backbiting and the villagers as uncharitable as villagers are. The last year there has been a funny undertone about the place.'

He fiddled with his glass and glared. 'I'm not imaginative, but I had a job where you develop a sense of atmosphere and it struck me only the other day that there was something funny going on somewhere.'

'Can you be precise, sir?' Harry stood looking down at Rodgers, seated ramrod erect in his windsor chair.

'I don't want to start up hares, Sergeant, and it's hard to put my finger on it. I'll have to think about it and perhaps talk to you later.'

Harry glanced at the rat-trap set of the Colonel's mouth and shrugged. 'I suppose you knew Tavisham?'

'Guy? Yes, of course. In fact I had a bit to do with him during the war.'

'He was in Intelligence?'

'No harm admitting that after all these years, I suppose. Yes, he operated in Portugal and Spain, the former mostly, a superb linguist you know. He was a very shy, reserved man and seemed to get more that way as the years passed by.'

Harry thanked him and sat in the car pretending to read his notes, putting off the final interview. Finally, with an inward groan, he gave the address.

Elizabeth Holland was cooking and her hands were floury as she peered round the door at him.

'Well, Sergeant,' she said, 'you appear at inconvenient moments.' He followed her into the living-room. She was wearing tinted glasses and her cheeks looked hollow.

'Sit down, Miss Holland. I'm afraid I'm here quite officially. You don't look well, by the way, and if you wish we could postpone things until tomorrow.'

'No, I'm all right.'

'Now this'll be a shock. George Stryver's body was discovered in the ruined church. It may not be natural death.'

Her teeth grasped her lower lip and she cringed back against the chair.

'Oh, God, when?'

'Three hours ago was when he was found. You knew he was missing?'

'Mrs. Gates, his cook, came round pretty upset.'

'Any particular reason?'

'I knew her well, she's a kind person and hasn't got many friends down here. Later a constable made a house to house check.'

'Did he seem normal during the tennis party?'

'Very cheerful,' she said. 'I knew him enough to spot his moods.'

'You went back afterwards. Did he speak to you?'

'I just said that I'd left my lipstick and went and fetched it. When I came out Mr. Burke had appeared and was telling him something about a trust. We left together.'

'That was the last time you saw him?'

She gave a dry sob. 'Yes.'

'Miss Holland, I want you to listen very carefully. First, were you in the habit of meeting him in London?'

'You saw us that day. Yes, I met him there probably a dozen times over eight months.'

'What did you do?'

'I don't care to discuss a purely personal matter.'

'Secondly,' said Harry, 'if you know anything that can possibly bear on his death, it is your duty to tell me.'

She merely shook her head.

'All right. Now, I'll be unofficial.' He touched her shoulder lightly. 'For God's sake think carefully, my dear. And keep your door and windows locked tonight. If there's a killer around, well, you never know.'

She sat there, apparently too absorbed in her own thoughts to hear his farewell.

Back at the station he found Wickstraw talking to a police surgeon, a lean weary man. The Superintendent introduced him.

'I've been telling the Super that the heat in that mausoleum played merry hell with things. It was in the high nineties when I measured it, but the difficulty is to calculate how much it would have dropped during the night. If the heat factor wasn't there, you'd have said he died three days ago.' He gave a barking laugh. 'As it is the best I can do for you is to suggest in the region of four yesterday afternoon.'

'What was the cause?'

The surgeon shrugged. 'There was a bruise on the side of his head, but he almost certainly died of poison. I've sent the cadaver to the police laboratory in Manchester.'

'When shall we know?' said Wickstraw.

'If it was arsenic, which I doubt, or antimony, maybe half an hour after they start testing, but if it's anything fancy it might entail a thousand or so tests. Maybe a week.'

'This is just a hunch,' said Harry, 'could you have them test for hyoscine immediately?'

'Don't get many cases of that, laddy,' the surgeon said, 'but I'll give them a ring later tonight.'

When they were alone, Wickstraw looked at Harry sharply.

'What's this about hyoscine?'

'Purely a very remote hunch.'

'His family will be here tomorrow, and the Chief 'phoned the Yard. They're sending Chief Inspector Richman and he'll be here in an hour so you'd better get your reports out.'

Harry typed away at his questions and answers and had just handed the carbon copies to Wickstraw when Richman came in. He would have been a matinee idol apart from his protruberant grey eyes. His reputation was one of attention to meticulous detail and the Prosecutor's Department were reputed to welcome any case sent up from him.

The formalities over, Richman sat opposite Wickstraw with the original report. The Chief Inspector read quickly and finished ahead of the Superintendent.

Neither man commented and Wickstraw produced a plan and a stack of full plate photographs which he spread on a long table in the corner of the room. His stubby index finger stabbed at a photograph of a boarded-up window and identified it on the plan.

'That's at the very back of the Church and not overlooked. It's four feet by four and the same from the ground. It leads into what was the vestry. The board hangs from one nail and swings to the side. This other photograph shows how the dust has been disturbed.'

'He looks quite a big fellow,' said Richman in his quiet voice. 'If the supposition is that somebody moved the body it would seem to me to involve two persons.'

'Unless, of course, he was murdered inside,' said Wickstraw. 'The surgeon says he weighed around twelve and a half stone dressed. One person could drag that weight over the top of that tomb. Even a strong woman,' he added.

Richman peered at the photographs. 'What about the floor? I can't see much.'

'It's a devil,' said Wickstraw. 'The plaster inside the roof, plus a couple of beams crashed down in the spring, so the floor is actually not covered with smooth dust, just jagged bits of stone and plaster.

'And a couple of weeks ago the Borough Surveyor's department took their six monthly look inside, so you couldn't put any faith in that kind of evidence.'

'Apart from the note, two handkerchiefs and his reading glasses, the only thing on the body was a small bunch of keys, one fitting the front door. Here!' Wickstraw slid them over.

Richman grunted as he took them. 'If he died around four somebody should have seen him going in, or being carried in.'

'It was a very oppressive afternoon, sir,' said Harry, 'and I don't think there were many people around.'

'One report mentions a householder having seen a big blue Ford "hanging around",' said the Super, 'I've got men on it.'

'Well,' said Richman, 'anybody in the house?'

'The servants; the relatives come tomorrow.'

'Well, I'd better take Sergeant James and have a look see, Superintendent.'

After they had seen the Church they pushed their way through the mob of sightseers into the driveway of the Lodge, but not before half a dozen flash bulbs winked. Harry recognised a couple of London reporters.

They shut themselves in Stryver's workshop. Richman looked at Harry over the rolltop desk.

'I digested your reports to Hawker,' said Richman. 'A messy, nebulous sort of business. Hawker's stuff often turns out that way. Perhaps you didn't know that I was his glorified messenger boy for four years. Lord, the capers he used to send me on.'

Richman had not the reputation for conviviality, but he sat back in the big chair and seemed disposed to talk.

'If you have any spare time, of course you'll continue your Hawkerian researches, but,' he paused significantly, 'keep the mess well away from this case. This is a nice straight murder and on form we'll tie it up nice in a couple of weeks. Okay,' he said 'there are twelve drawers, we'll share them out.'

'Some aren't locked,' said Harry.

The Chief Inspector tried them methodically. 'Three are unlocked.' He grimaced. 'In keeping with Stryver's character?'

'Definitely not.'

The first drawer yielded two thick files marked, 'Bank, current'. Richman pushed them over. 'Your alley, I think,' and Harry felt pleased.

After an hour Harry looked up. 'Household cheques indicate that he spent around £80 a week so he lived well. Rest are wages and charitable bequests. No inexplicable outgoings. However, Miss Elizabeth Holland was paying him £18 each month.'

'Paying *him*!' Richman looked startled.

'A loan, I would imagine,' Harry said, a trifle stiffly.

'Of course,' the bulging eyes looked thoughtful.

'Only other thing,' said Harry, 'is that he paid a man named C. Guy Blucher £350 over the past eighteen months, last payment £60, on the twelfth of last month. I imagine it's our old friend.'

'The old devil *is* doing well. I remember him when he'd climb a wall for five bob.'

C. Guy Blucher operated as a private detective under several different trade names. Years ago he had been a C.I.D. sergeant and it had been touch and go whether he was allowed to resign or not. As an investigator he had prospered and his name was known in certain quarters as a man who could, for a fee, get results. Had any licensing system for private investigators been in operation, Blucher would have lost his authorisation years ago.

'We'll shake him down right smartly,' said Richman, making a note.

They shared out the business letters. Stryver's business approach was wary and tough, Harry found.

'It appears,' said Richman, 'that when he retired seven years ago Stryver's reckoned assets, including a forty per cent equity in the family business, were a bit over twelve hundred thousand pounds. He put most of it into non-revocable trusts for his three nephews, sons of his brother.' He glanced at the clock. It was 11.45 'If it's all right with you, we'll plough on, Sergeant.'

Harry nodded and filled his pipe. An hour later the phone rang and Richman took it.

He replaced the handset. 'That was Manchester forensic lab.' Harry felt himself tense. 'Nothing on the poison, of course, but the stomach contained a mixture of crab and prawn meat, mushroom and egg. The canapés, I take it. Death occurred some three hours after it was ingested, so I'll make a note to check when the canapés were eaten. And the equivalent of four pretty stiff Scotches. Do you know his drinking habits?'

'I'll see whether the housekeeper is up.'

Mrs. Gates was seated determinedly in her kitchen. 'Can I bring you up anything, sir?' she said.

'If you could,' said Harry, 'a pot of coffee and maybe some sandwiches, if the larder will run to it.'

She nodded and went to the refrigerator.

'By the way,' said Harry, 'could you tell me how much Mr. Stryver drank?'

Apparently his custom was to have two small Scotches before lunch and only water with the meal. At dinner he would take either half a bottle of claret or the equivalent of hock. He disliked all sparkling wines. At bedtime he took one glass of whisky or rum.

'He didn't drink that much,' said Mrs. Gates. 'If he went to his club I think he had a few drinks with friends, but never enough to notice.'

He reported to Richman.

'Could be significant?' said the Superintendent. 'The more I read his letters, the more it is apparent that he was a man of strong convictions who didn't alter his habits easily.'

The cook came in with a tray. 'Ham and cold beef,' she said.

'Mrs. Gates,' said Richman, 'would it surprise you to know that Mr. Stryver had taken four stiff Scotches shortly before his death?'

She shook her head. 'He never took more than two small, not even on Christmas or New Year's Day.' She departed shaking her head.

'This is a life-saver,' said Richman, helping himself to sandwiches.

At half past three only a metal strong-box awaited examination.

Richman extracted a pile of insurance policies, one of them a five thousand life policy. 'Nothing here,' he said, leafing through them.

'And here's a copy of the will.' He studied it.

'Generous man, Stryver,' he commented. 'Everything goes to various hospitals except some family jewellery, which is left to his brother's wife, and legacies totalling £15,000. There's the staff, Colonel Rodgers, down for £500, and, hm, £2,000 to Miss Elizabeth Holland.'

He started to stack the documents back. 'Just a minute.' He drew out a small notebook. It had a worn black cover.

'Some kind of shorthand mostly,' he said, 'and annotations about money. That's to go to the backroom boys. I'll put a receipt in the box.'

They packed everything away. 'Where are you staying, Sergeant?'

'I'm not,' said Harry ruefully. 'At least I can't appear at my last lodgings at this hour. They'll probably have a spare cell at the Station.'

'My pub's got a night porter. He'll find you somewhere,' said Richman, and they stopped at the station to pick up his case. Chief Inspectors did themselves nicely, thought Harry as they pulled up at the best hotel Bradshaw could boast. There was a room available and Richman suggested that they breakfast together at nine.

The thought of a hot bath attracted Harry, but he finally just fell in to bed and was asleep almost immediately.

He didn't wake until the night porter rang through at 8.45, and he took a hurried shower before going down. Richman, however, was himself late.

'Sorry to keep you waiting, but Wickstraw was on the blower. Nothing much new. The big blue Ford turns out to be the property of a man giving his wife driving lessons, poor devil. They noticed nothing. The forensic boys have virtually nothing to report on the note found in Stryver's shirt pocket. Letters drawn with a ruler on cheap paper. One smudged print of deceased's left index finger.'

They ordered bacon and eggs and the morning papers.

'They've done us proud,' said Richman, picking up a tabloid. Harry saw his own undistinguished features besides the Superintendent's handsome profile. 'You'll be pleased to know, Sergeant, that you are one of the Yard's most promising officers promoted to bring new blood to the tired old Murder Squad. And I, let's see,' he chuckled, 'oh, yes, the Adonis of the Yard. My wife always gets a kick out of that.'

Harry turned to the obituary in *The Times* and scanned it rapidly. 'Distinguished old boy,' he said, 'millionaire industrialist, gave largely to charity, founded many industrial scholarships, endowed a department for research into metallurgy, chairman of two hospitals until he retired, a well-known shot, served during the war as an adviser to the Treasury on foreign currency.'

He attacked his bacon and eggs.

'Can't make too much progress until we get the cause of death,' said Richman. 'I'll see the people at the tennis party this morning, but I doubt whether there's any more to wring out there at this stage. I was glad you didn't press too hard, often a mistake first time up. They say something ill considered and then feel themselves obliged to stick by it.'

The Superintendent ate his food rapidly. 'Ah,' he said, 'that's better. I'll have to leave for London at noon. My desk is stacked with stuff. I'll be back this evening. What a life!'

'Any special instructions, sir?'

Richman spooned out marmalade. 'Get me a list of Stryver's movements over the past week and see the relatives. It turns on the medical report, but you can tie up as many ends as possible.' He shook his head, 'poor old boy, dying like that.'

Walter Stryver had a faint facial resemblance to his brother, but whereas George had given the impression of gruffness, his younger brother was bland and unobtrusive.

'My wife was too upset to come, so I decided to come with one of my sons, Sergeant. I saw the Superintendent briefly when I arrived.'

'I realise this is a painful business, sir, but there's really only one question. Do you know any one likely to have murdered your brother?'

For a moment Walter looked as though he would faint. 'No, sergeant, I can honestly say I don't. I have given it careful thought. In business, particularly a very large business, you just cannot avoid causing resentment at times. The only real enemy George ever had was a man who tried to do him down and George hit back, but the fellow's been dead thirty years.'

'Just for the record, who was he?'

'Fellow named Armstrong. George was pretty young when Dad died and Armstrong tried to get the business off him. He never forgot or forgave.'

'Was there any particular reason why Mr. Stryver retired here?'

'Oh,' said Walter. 'He liked this funny little place. It was central and the house was what he was looking for. You see, when he was sixty-five he decided to retire as Managing Director. We tried to prevail on him to continue his Chairmanship, but he refused. He'd had a very hard time during the war. Besides the works and the procurement nightmare, he had endless conferences at the Treasury. He was fortunately as strong as an ox, but he made up his mind to get out while he was at his top.'

'Did you see much of him?'

'Once a month I'd get a telephone call that he was coming up for a few days. He'd see old friends. One of the reasons he lived here was that back home he knew so many people intimately. He wanted a quiet life. His wife had died and that affected him very much.'

'And he'd relinquished all business?'

'Unfortunately. I nagged him into attending an informal directors' meeting once a year. He'd got one of the best financial brains in the country, and he'd give us his opinion on money policy. That was all.'

'That's about all, except one routine question. Did your brother have any special women friends?'

Walter looked at him blankly. 'George? Oh, I see, the *cherchez la femme* business. George was very happily married for forty years and he never looked at another woman after Martha passed away. My wife used to joke with him a little about it.'

'A quantity of whisky had been consumed by him shortly before his death, sir, which doesn't seem to be in character.'

'That's odd.' Walter dabbed his mouth with a handkerchief. 'He was strictly a two-small-whisky man.'

Going out, Harry saw that the two cars had been rolled out of the garage, a smallish Hillman station wagon and the old Lagonda. The gardener was polishing the latter, in between directing fierce glares at the gate. Something clicked in Harry's mind. What was the man's name? Ah, Johnson, that was it.

'Good morning, Mr. Johnson,' he greeted.

'Morning, Sergeant, I wish you could move that mob of carrion crows along.'

'We'll try to do something later. You can drive a car, I see.'

'Used to drive him sometimes on long trips,' Johnson said. 'Like when he went north.' He shrugged. 'I'll miss those trips.'

'And that spectacular trick of yours—climbing over the front seat when Mr. Stryver got out in a traffic jam.'

Johnson stared at him, breathing heavily down his nose.

'Come in here,' he jerked his hand towards the garage.

'Now,' he said, 'how did you know that?'

'Saw you do it. Nearly gave me a stroke.'

'Well, I never did,' said Johnson. 'We only did it once, the time you must have seen us. I drove most of the way and the governor's fidgetty, not like himself at all. Every now and then he'd glance back. We stopped on the outskirts of London for a cup of tea and some toast. We'd left pretty early and it's a fairish drive. While they were making the toast, the guv'nor gets up and goes and takes a look out the door. When he came back he said, "You know, Johnson, somebody's been following us."'

The gardener mopped his forehead with an old yellow handkerchief.

'It set me back. I just said, "Why would that be, sir?" He gave me a very straight look and said, "Just let me think."'

Johnson cogitated for a few seconds. 'Yes, that's all he said. Then he said that he didn't like people following him and he told me this plan.'

'I see,' said Harry, 'you arranged yourself under the tarpaulin hood in the back, until Mr. Stryver gave the word. Then you crawled out and over and drove on.'

'I was game,' said Johnson, 'though it was hot and sticky under the tarp. And what beat me was nobody took any notice. There was a bus ahead, but I guess they were too busy reading their newspapers. Anyway, it went off clean as a whistle.'

'You didn't see who it was following?'

'I was concentrating on driving.'

'Didn't you think it unusual?'

'It wasn't my business. He was a good guv'nor to me and that's all that mattered. 'Sides there could be reasons, he might have been meeting somebody on the quiet like.'

'A lady perhaps?'

A stubborn look settled on Johnson's face and Harry called it a day, not wishing to offend the man.

'Well, thanks a lot anyway.'

He reported back to Richman, who was seated at the Inspector's desk. The Chief Inspector's voice was heavy: 'The report came in from the Manchester lab. Old Stryver had enough hyoscine in his vitals to kill a regiment. Here's my note.'

Harry studied it and asked, 'Nothing else?'

'What else should we want? The bruise on the head occurred half an hour before death, give or take five minutes. A healthy body, should have lived for years. Now look at these.'

The Chief Inspector spilled the contents of a large tin on his blotter. There were abnormally large capsules.

'These were George's patent pills,' said Richman, 'made up for him by a Glasgow chemist in 500s. A tin lasted him about a year. The surgeon, a sceptical man, says the only useful drugs are morphine and epsom salts, but that these are harmless, might do some good and that the glucose would give one a lift.'

'Damned hard to swallow,' muttered Harry.

'Practice,' said Richman. 'The old gentleman could slide one of these boluses down his throat with a small slug of Scotch. They're an old-fashioned size. The Glasgow people say that they've been using an old batch going back thirty years or so and when they ran out, in two years time at the rate he was going, they would have to have them made specially or persuade Stryver to take three small ones for a dose.

'Now, assuming the capsule was switched, the problem of the original arises. I've never known a case of poisoning where the poisoner does not get rid of the poison or container at the earliest possible moment. He realised that if there is a slip-up he can't argue that away. Here, the original, harmless capsule is the equivalent. Take one sample with you. Wickstraw's got two brawny coppers waiting for you at the Lodge. Try everywhere you can think.'

'What about the lavatory flush?'

'Ah, the only person who went in there before they left was Miss Holland, looking for her lipstick. Anyway, have a go.'

The two constables were gossiping to the gardener. Harry beckoned to the three of them, and displayed the capsule.

'Each of you have a look at this.' They handled it gingerly.

'That looks like one of the old guv'nor's pills,' said Johnson. 'I used to see him swallowing them.'

Harry put the capsule in an envelope and signed his name in pencil across the sealed flap. 'Add your name, would you constable? This is just to make quite sure that if we stumble on one of these capsules we can prove it is not this one.'

He stowed the envelope away and walked to the area beside the tennis court. There were four flower beds containing geraniums of various colours.

'Do these get much water?'

'They don't need that much,' said Johnson. 'The day the Guv'nor died I hadn't watered there for maybe a week. The other beds are sprinkled daily.'

'In that case,' Harry said, 'somebody pushing down with a finger would be unlikely to penetrate more than an inch, so if Mr. Johnson will supply a sieve, check the earth down to two inches, but be careful not to harm the plants.'

'Oh, curse the plants,' said Johnson.

Harry smiled at him. 'And if you can rustle up a couple of stiff brooms we'll check the lawn.'

Johnson and he were only halfway through their task when one of the constables came up with a negative report. Harry straightened an aching back.

'All right, proceed the same way with the beds against the side wall beyond the court.'

The lawn yielded a sixpenny coin, found by Johnson, and a pile of match-sticks.

'That'd be the guv'nor's pipe,' said Johnson sadly.

'Now we'll take the path round by the house,' said Harry. The gravel was packed down hard. To conceal anything some kind of instrument would be needed, and for the time being Harry was content to rule the possibility out.

They passed the kitchen window, from which Mrs. Gates was looking out, and turned the corner. Here the wall was covered with some kind of creeper with showers of green blooms.

'We'd better poke about behind these.' He eyed the thick stems as they went into the earth.

'There's an old drain somewhere here,' Johnson bent and peered. 'Ar, 'ere he is.'

Squatting down, Harry glimpsed a rusty iron grating.

'It's part of the old drain system,' said Johnson. 'When the guv'nor bought the place he had a new lot put in, but

I reckon they didn't disturb this trap because of the creeper.'

'We'll have to disturb it now,' muttered Harry. 'Could you get a suitable saw?'

'I'm more used to this than you,' said Johnson when he returned. Expertly he sawed through a couple of stems. 'Ah, now we can get at him.'

The iron grill was thick with rust. Johnson fixed his powerful hands on the side bars and wrenched. With a grinding noise the grill came off so abruptly that Harry caught him as he reeled backwards. On his knees, he pointed a pocket flash into the hole.

'Leaf mould and gravel, mostly,' he told Johnson. 'We'll have to scoop it out in a tin.'

Johnson produced a tin and newspaper. 'I'll dig it out and you spread the stuff flat on the paper,' he suggested.

After five minutes, Harry tapped Johnson on the back. He pointed. Recognisable under a patina of fine leaf-mould was a capsule. He picked it up carefully and placed it in another envelope which he marked, 'Found in gully trap' and passed to Johnson to countersign.

'Tell the other fellows to knock it off. I'll phone the Boss.'

Richman didn't seem surprised. 'These things always follow a pattern, Sergeant. Keep everybody there, I'm coming out.'

He told the constables to wait.

'We found this,' one of them displayed a small white button. 'It was on top of the earth by the honeysuckle.'

Harry stowed it away.

Richman took possession of the envelopes with the capsules when he arrived.

'Good work,' he said.

Harry produced the button.

'Mm,' mused Richman. 'The old gentleman's shirt according to the inventory, left sleeve.

'Now, Mr. Johnson, after the tennis party the housekeeper complained that the shed was in a mess. Could you please recreate that mess, putting things around to the best of your recollection?'

They watched Johnson work. A pile of folding gardening chairs stacked neatly against the wall were spread around the floor.

The gardener scratched his head. 'It was mostly the contents of that box.'

It was about three feet each way, without a lid. Johnson upended it. Twenty or so old tennis balls rolled out and he kicked them into the far corner of the room. The rest of the contents, iron brackets and a small winch, he let lie in an untidy heap.

'Like that,' he said.

Richman picked the box up. 'Stoutly made,' he said as he turned it. 'Look at those earth marks.' He nodded his head towards faint smears at two edges.

'That's right, sir,' said Johnson. 'It was lying against the wall underneath the honeysuckle.'

The Chief Inspector put the box down very slowly and looked away for a few seconds.

'Did you think that was normal?'

'I thought it was the dratted boy. I took Saturday off, but the boy came in the morning. I'd given him his tasks. The wind tore that honeysuckle something cruel, so I told him to make a careful check of the supports. I thought that, being too lazy to get the ladder, he'd used the box.'

'You've just spoilt a nice piece of deduction. Oh, never mind,' Richman added as Johnson gaped at him. 'Suppose you put the box where you found it?'

Johnson walked along carefully. 'I reckon it was here, give or take a foot.'

'Make a note of it, please. Now you, constable,' he addressed the shorter of the two men, 'get on the box and see how you go at getting over the wall.'

The constable made it effortlessly, except that as he slid down the other side his head and shoulders still remained above the wall.

'Big pile of rubble the other side, sir,' he reported before he climbed back.

'Thank you, gentlemen,' said Richman. 'Mr. James and I'd better go about our business.'

'The reconstruction seems pretty clear,' he said to Harry later. 'After everybody had finally departed, old Stryver sits drinking an unaccustomed allowance of whisky. He's excited because somebody dropped that note for him to find.'

'Might not he have found it earlier or received it by post?'

'He was always up in time to collect the post personally, according to Mrs. Gates,' said Richman, 'but in that case I don't think he would have carried it with him. And the fact of the breast pocket is significant. If you are seated and somebody drops a piece of paper, you can lean sideways, put it in your palm and glance at it, but if you then start fumbling to put it in a trouser pocket you might attract attention. It's much less obtrusive to slip it into a breast pocket.'

'It seems logical,' Harry nodded.

'So we have the old gentleman sitting there thinking of a plan of campaign. Holland and Burke come back for a few minutes. After they've gone he makes a decision. He'll conceal himself in that old tomb and overhear this meeting. Did you see his library, filled with spy stuff?'

Harry nodded. 'It's in character.'

'And he's had more whisky than normal. The question is how to get in to the place unobserved. He knows about the window and if he's quick he can get over the wall and in through it. He goes into the shed and first examines the folding chairs—no good for his purpose. Then he thinks of the box. The poisoned capsule is well and truly in his stomach. The analyst's report is that taken after food something like forty-five minutes elapses before the thing dissolves and releases its contents.

'Stryver is lying in his box when that happens. After one hour he's unconscious. His head falls sideways and cracks against the side of the tomb and inside forty minutes he's dead, poor devil.'

'We'd have to establish he was familiar with that church,' said Harry in his role of devil's advocate.

'I spent a couple of hours going into the question of the church,' said Richman. 'Since the Monck family sold it, successive owners of the Lodge and its grounds, originally four times as extensive as they are today, have flatly denied liability or ownership.

'Mad Squire Monck built for posterity. The walls are three feet thick, solid stone blocks and the roof would need an engineering feat to remove. No contractor will give a firm quote. As it's classified as a religious building, they aren't rated, so they can't establish ownership that way.

'The Council does a minimal amount of work on it. The desiccated old Town Clerk whickered at me that any major effort might be taken as admission of liability. The main danger is from pieces of stone falling off that horrible ornamented façade.

'Four months ago, when the inside plastering crashed down, the Borough Surveyor took a thorough look-see. He knew Stryver and the old chap walked round with him. The Surveyor pointed out what a valuable piece of land it would be to Stryver. Richman chuckled. 'He hadn't much of a hope with that astute old trout. Nevertheless Stryver looked at every inch of the place, including that window with the loose board.'

'I wondered why there hadn't been a court determination of ownership,' mused Harry.

'It nearly came to that a few years ago, but the Council took a look at Stryver and his money. They knew he'd get the best lawyers and fight to the last ditch—he was like that—and the aldermen were frightened of the cost if they got caught.'

'There's a nasty mind at work there,' said Harry. 'Making a man pick his own tomb! I think I heard that you had no imagination!'

'Imagination, nothing,' said Richman. 'A good, reasonable working hypothesis. I never could see people carrying a corpse in broad daylight. And we must remember that but for a lucky break it might not have been found for months.'

'I'm having the people who attended the tennis assemble there tomorrow,' said Richman. 'It's difficult for young Rodgers and Burke to make it before. We'll fiddle about and get as precise a time table as we can. Meantime suppose you get out to Miss Holland's place of work and enquire about hyoscine. They make veterinary compounds on a large scale. I'm told they'd be unlikely to use hyoscine these days, but you never know.'

The laboratories were a one storey assembly with large glass windows ten minutes out of town, surrounded by lawn and neat flower beds. Harry got in to see the General Manager, an affable Lancashire man.

'Hyoscine,' he said. 'Well, we haven't used that for some years. Veterinary medicine has changed about as rapidly as anything in the drug world. It used to be compounded for a tranquillising effect, horses mostly. I'll get the ledger on dangerous poisons.' He gave an order to his secretary.

'Here we are. Heroin, ah, hyoscine. Yes, we bought in several jars in 1946, discontinuing using it in 1953. In 1961 I decided that it wasn't worth hanging on to some of the old drugs we carried just in case some old-fashioned veterinarian should take it into his head to prescribe them, so I issued instructions to destroy. There's the minute.'

Harry looked at the page of figures giving usage. The last total was 75 grains and underneath was the neat notation, 'destroyed, 4-5-61. E. Holland.'

He felt himself slump a little in his seat as he made

a shorthand note. He went back and reported to Richman.

'We'll let it lie for the time,' the Chief Inspector said, 'and now I'll catch my train.'

He had finished his notes when Wickstraw called him on the inter-com.

'There's Mr. C. Guy Blucher at the desk,' the Super said. 'I thought you'd better take him, so you can use my office. I've got to go to headquarters anyway.'

C. Guy Blucher was a large overflowing man who culminated in a disproportionately small head. Habitually he wore a kind expression as if his body was a kind of cornucopaeia from which inner blessings flowed. His accent was unadulterated cockney and he wore American-cut clothes.

'Don't think I know you, sern't.' His voice conveyed grave concern at his own social error.

Harry formally introduced himself. Blucher edged his chair nearer to the desk and blinked his small violet eyes.

'It's about the late George Stryver with whom I might have had business dealings. I was in Manchester on a bit of business when I see his death in the papers, so I dropped off here.' Blucher's voice had the dry huskiness associated with people who have talked too long and too loudly.

Harry remained silent until he saw the man fidget.

'I dessay you know my 'istory and therefore that I am at all times glad to help and co-operate,' said Blucher caressing his small ginger moustache.

'In all Stryver paid you £350. You came fishing to see if we knew that.'

The violet eyes closed momentarily. 'O' course, sern't, we're in the area of solicitors before divulging his private affairs.'

Harry yawned elaborately. 'The heir is as tough a nut as his brother. There's no hush money about, Blucher.'

Blucher's benevolent smile didn't change, but he said nothing.

'I'll subpoena you for the inquest and you can answer the coroner. I can promise you that his questions will be in a form that won't do you any good.'

'O' course,' said Blucher after a few seconds of thought, 'it is my duty to co-operate, reely.'

'That'll save us the trouble of taking a close look at your current business.'

Blucher apparently did not hear.

'Well, Mr. Stryver called at my office a year ago.'

'Which one?' asked Harry brutally.

'The Gray's Inn Road one. I happened to see him personally.'

'Had he an appointment?'

'Well,' said Blucher, 'he had written as the result of my advertisements.'

'And you had checked his credit rating.'

Pity mixed with the benevolence on Blucher's face.

'Business is business, sern't. As I said, I happened to see the client personally, a very secretive man, he was, wouldn't open up at all.' Blucher drummed his fingers on the desk top. 'I'm not at all keen, sern't, on clients who don't disclose a motive. You can find yourself in trouble on that score.'

'I've read your file,' said Harry grimly.

'A man has to make a living,' said Blucher. 'Today I can pick and choose but I've seen my 'ard times, sern't, and I 'ope you don't see yours.' The tiny flicker of malignancy in the small eyes vanished as quickly as it came.

'Well, there didn't seem any 'arm in what he wanted. First, there's an office in Shoreditch held on a forty year lease by "Metal Auxiliaries". All he had been able to find out was that the lease was purchased under the name of "J. T. Robinson" in 1938. We were able to find out that "Metal Auxiliaries" had an account at a local bank. At one time it was a very active account, but hasn't been operated upon for eight years. With charges the current account is now reduced to £120. When the account was opened the instructions came from Zurich, Switzerland, on behalf of a Liechenstein registered company operating there.'

'That was pretty smart,' said Harry. 'We'd have had to get a court order to find out all that.'

The tiny mouth firmly closed and the violet eyes turned to the ceiling.

'Just admiration,' said Harry. 'Did you find out who staffed the office?'

'One of my operatives got the porter to let him in on pass-key. A desk, one chair, and empty filing cabinet and a typewriter, all thick with dust. We couldn't find anybody who could remember a thing about "Metal Auxiliaries".'

'What about the bank?'

'The authorised signature was "J. T. Robinson", but most of the ingoings came by draft from Zurich and the outgoings in the form of cheques drawn in favour of third parties. Mind you, after ten years...'

'You must have formed some conclusion.'

'Stryver was a retired businessman. My guess is that somebody tried to flog the remains of a business and that he was approached. The Liechenstein registration is the usual tax angle.'

Harry wondered exactly how much Blucher was holding back. It would be ingrained second nature in the man for him never to reveal all he knew.

'You said there was another matter.'

'Six months ago the client asked us to keep a Miss Elizabeth Holland, a near neighbour of his, under surveillance. He specifically asked us to note anybody hanging round her house at night from the time she got home.'

'Didn't you consider this an odd request?'

Blucher wrinkled his mouth into an ugly O. 'Well, sern't, the first case was the one which worried me. We make it a rule to get a solid reason on file as to why a client wants commercial information. If Metal Auxiliaries hadn't been moribund, I wouldn't have touched the case. But watching people, why, sern't, that's eighty per cent of our business.

'With men, it's usually sex, but a small percentage of employers want to check on their staff. Cases involving women are h'invariably sexual in one way or another.'

'Did you ask him?'

Blucher snickered. 'I guess you never saw the old bird. I'd have soon asked him about his bank account than his sex life. Mind you he was pretty old, and she was a sexy young piece according to the reports. It was a difficult assignment. She lives...'

'I know,' said Harry.

'Then I don't have to tell you the difficulties of a neighbourhood like that. It cost plenty, a fresh car or van every night and two men on the job with infra-red camera equipment. For two nights we faked a broken down truck. Even so the local copper spotted something was up and my men had to convince him they were on divorce work.'

'How long did this go on for?'

'Well, he said he wanted a fourteen day check, but after a week I got a phone call from him to pack it in.'

'What was his reason?'

Blucher twitched his shoulders.

'From memory, sern't, he just told me that circumstances had altered. Maybe they'd made it up.'

'M'm,' said Harry with Blucher's heavy after-shave lotion cloying his nostrils, 'and what exactly did you report to him?'

'She had two visitors during the seven days, both women. One of them worked at the same place that she did, so the operative reported. I just put the report and the two photos in an envelope with an account. The cheque came on the first of the following month.'

Harry thanked him for his assistance and watched Blucher lumber out.

He transcribed his shorthand note on the typewriter and saw the sergeant who had been checking possible sources of hyoscine.

'No go,' the man said. 'We checked the chemists and a wholesaler in Bentleigh. What hyoscine there is, and it's not much, checks with the registers to the grain.'

Harry added that to the report for Richman. The Chief-Inspector arrived back at seven, his usual immaculate appearance crumpled by the heat.

'H'm,' Richman said, 'so the old gentleman had the Holland girl watched. Jealousy, I suppose.'

Harry said nothing.

'I hope it isn't what at first glance it looks,' said Richman. 'Women prisoners are the very devil, headlines, crack counsel engaged for 'em by a newspaper, the police officers concerned ridden to death. So we'll go very cautiously as far as that young lady is concerned.'

'Any news about Stryver's notebook?' Harry changed the subject.

'No problem there. It was an old-fashioned shorthand system, covering the movement of money back to the 'thirties, too cryptic to mean much to us. I got a call from Glasgow, by the way. George had the whim at one time of having large sums in cash.'

'Carrying it?'

'No, no, he kept it in the best safe obtainable. He used to back people occasionally who spotted a good thing and hadn't the money. Usually it was a matter of urgency and a quick turnover. The figures might refer to that and there's the alternative that he might have parted with a large sum of cash recently to somebody who killed him rather than return it. Anyway the Glasgow police are doing a thorough job at their end. As a long shot I'll see his bank manager and anybody in business that he knew here. As for you, better call it a day.'

CHAPTER FIVE

EXCEPT THE BURKES, who were five minutes late, the tennis party reassembled by the appointed hour of eleven next day.

'Sorry we're late,' said Burke, 'but there was a case that dragged on.'

'Please all of you be seated,' said Richman. 'Now the purpose of this meeting is to give us a clear idea of what happened at Mr. Stryver's last tennis party. And I may say how very grateful I am for your co-operation.'

Everybody looked ill-at-ease reflected Harry from his corner seat. It was Mrs. Monck, square and competent in a linen suit, who spoke first in her usual precise and authoritative tones.

'There's a rumour that Mr. Stryver was poisoned. Is this so?'

Richman bowed slightly. 'Mr. Stryver died of poison. As the inquest tomorrow morning will reveal the fact, I may as well tell you that he had somehow taken a massive dose of hyoscine.'

To Harry, watching, Elizabeth Holland's face was mask-like.

'And may we take it,' said Mrs. Monck, 'that you suspect *us.*'

'Oh, nonsense, dear,' said Monck, looking down at her from his great height.

'No, it's quite a reasonable question,' said the Chief-Inspector blandly. 'At the moment we have no area of suspicion. I just want to get a clear picture of everything that Mr. Stryver did that morning, hence this little reconstruction.'

Mrs. Monck looked sullen. There was a ghost of a grin on the face of Tony Rodgers. He was a chunky young man, handsome in a rugged way. Harry thought he looked more like a professional athlete than a young solicitor.

Finally everybody sat down uncomfortably.

'Mr. Burke,' said Richman, 'I understand you arrived first with Mrs. Burke. Is this how the tables and chairs were arranged?'

'Yes,' said Burke, 'except that one,' he indicated an unoccupied table with four chairs round it, 'was a foot or two nearer the shed.'

Richman had the two attendant constables move it.

'Stryver was seated there as we arrived. We sat down and chatted briefly, and then Mr. and Mrs. Monck came and joined us. I brought over an additional chair from there,' he pointed.

'Then Colonel Rodgers arrived with Tony, with Miss Holland on their heels. I would say the time was then 10.15.'

'Is everybody in agreement?'

There was a general rustle of agreement, except from Mrs. Monck. 'I am so sorry to interrupt,' she said. 'As far as I can remember that seems correct, but I don't want to go on record as having committed myself irrevocably to anything.'

Harry grinned down at his notebook.

'What my wife means,' he heard Monck's clipped tones state, 'is that she dislikes swearing to anything of which she is not absolutely certain.'

'I should have stressed that this is purely informal,' said Richman. 'Nobody's on oath and I assure you I know better than most men how small details can become mixed in one's mind.'

Mollified, Mrs. Monck allowed her weight to sink back in the canvas chair.

'Then George and I got up and played a set,' said Burke. 'The poor old lad was having trouble with his backhand.'

Richman glanced over to Tony Rodgers. 'While they played, Dad got up and went over to have his usual talk about politics with Mr. Monck, and Mrs. Monck joined Elizabeth and I.'

'When we'd finished,' said Burke, 'George and I came back to the same seats and he went and brought two glasses of iced orange juice.'

'Just a minute,' interposed Richman, 'there was in fact nothing on the table.'

Burke thought for a few minutes. 'Trouble is that these parties were fairly regular things and it's difficult to pick one from another. Yes, George's spectacle case was in front of them. He sometimes used them for close work.'

'And then?'

Elizabeth Holland spoke. 'I partnered Mr. Monck against Tony and Mrs. Monck.'

Richman looked at Burke. 'I got up and stretched my legs with George. There was a lot of moving around as we watched the play.'

Mrs. Burke spoke for the first time, a pretty little brunette with a soft Irish voice. 'We were all in one group mostly. George was discussing television with my husband, I remember.'

'That's right,' said Burke. 'When the set had finished, George brought out orange juice for them, except Tony who opted for a

116

pale ale. Then Colonel Rodgers went on the court with Mrs. Burke.'

'How was the grouping then?'

Tony Rodgers said that he and Elizabeth Holland joined Stryver, and the Burkes sat with the Moncks.

The first clear impressions were getting slightly blurred, thought Harry. After the Colonel and Mrs. Burke had finished, there were a series of short knock-ups, Burke against Monck, Stryver against Elizabeth Holland, and Mrs. Burke against Tony Rodgers.

'When were the canapés produced?' asked Richman.

'At twelve, on the dot as usual,' said Burke. 'I was on the court with Monck and I saw George bringing the tray out, so I called to Monck to knock off.'

'How long did the refreshments last?'

'As usual there were plenty of them,' said Burke, 'I suppose about twenty-past twelve we'd all eaten as much as we cared, and George took the plates back into the shed.'

'I helped him,' said Elizabeth Holland.

'Then,' said Burke, 'there was general chatter about nothing in particular, relaxed Sunday morning kind of stuff. Elizabeth played Stryver for about five minutes and I went out with Monck for about the same time.'

'Now about leaving times?'

'I left at noon,' said Mrs. Monck.

'Alone?'

She said, at her most precise, 'My husband accompanied me to the gate. I walked the fifteen minutes home.'

'Mrs. Burke and I were the next,' said Colonel Rodgers. 'At ten to one, Stryver produced the farewell Glenlivet. Mrs. Burke and I were on our way by five past the hour.'

'A few minutes after,' said Elizabeth, 'I walked out with Mr. Monck.'

'I was in the lavatory,' said Burke. 'Then I gathered up the racquets, walked out with Tony, and I suppose we were starting the car not later than 1.15.'

'Fine, a great help to me all that,' said Richman, smiling around. People were starting to get up.

'Just one small thing.' Like a conjurer he held up a capsule. 'Did you see one of those near Mr. Stryver's glasses?'

'I certainly didn't when I said goodbye,' said Mrs. Monck, pouncing on a concrete fact.

Richman stood there like a genial auctioneer

Tony Rodgers said, very seriously, 'We all knew about George's capsules. I think,' he smiled, 'it was one of his personal tragedies that he couldn't persuade anybody to try them. I'm fairly sure I saw him take it out of the spectacle case, fiddle with it, and rest it against the case soon after he poured out the whisky. We were all standing around, but, as was his custom, George sat down, looking around like Mr. Punch.'

'I don't know,' Colonel Rodgers said doubtfully. 'He always carried one of the things wedged down in his spectacle case. But I couldn't definitely say that I saw it that particular day.'

The poll resulted in Elizabeth Holland, Tony and Burke thinking that they saw a capsule and the rest negative.

'And just for the record, how many of you had occasion to enter the lavatory?'

Harry admired the choice of words, but even so he saw outrage on Mrs. Monck's broad face.

It transpired that Elizabeth Holland, Mrs. Monck and Mrs. Burke each had had occasion to go there, and of the men Burke and Stryver.

'Can you recall when Mr. Stryver paid that visit?'

Colonel Rodgers honked that it was during the mixed doubles. He was sure of it as he was looking around for George.

'That's all, and thanks very much,' said Richman, 'except that I'd appreciate it if Mr. Burke and Miss Holland remained for a few minutes. Mrs. Burke, you can make yourself comfortable while we tie the ends up.'

Harry ushered the party as far as the gate. He felt a touch on his arm.

It was Colonel Rodgers. 'Any progress?' Harry would not have imagined before that he could whisper.

'Very little, it's dogged as does it, sir.'

'I know,' said the Colonel. 'I'm afraid I was a bit cryptic the other day. Perhaps I'm getting old, imagining tension where it isn't. Yet you know, George Stryver was watching people.'

'Watching?'

'In my old game you were taught to spot it. I've seen George talking casually and felt that inside his brain was working away at something else. Sometimes he used to stare pretty thoughtfully at people when they were looking the other way.'

Harry walked slowly back. The Chief Inspector had seated himself at a table with a glass in front of him and a spectacle case next to it.

'Where did you see the capsule?' he was asking Burke.

The big Irishman wrinkled his heavy forehead, and after a moment placed a stubby finger on the table, about four inches away from the glass.

'This concrete is slightly uneven,' said Richman, 'so the capsule must have rolled.' He gazed down in concentration. 'As it was, Stryver was slewed slightly in the opposite direction so that it was not directly in his range of vision. Now, Mr. Burke, you saw Miss Holland before she actually turned the corner of the house?'

'I was right behind,' said Burke. 'As I turned the corner perhaps a second later she was a yard or so from the table.'

'She was talking?'

'Saying something. I called out, she looked round and nodded, and went on into the lavatory.'

'Is that your recollection, Miss Holland?'

The girl nodded. 'I had the thought that maybe Mr. Burke might want to talk confidentially.'

'Just an impression?'

'Something about his attitude,' said Elizabeth. Her skin looked blotched under the sunlight.

'How did you walk past?'

'Like this.'

They watched and Burke said, 'I think you went in front of him, Elizabeth, not behind.'

Her spine drooped. 'I'm not sure, I can't remember.'

'Never mind,' said Richman, his face betraying no emotion. 'And you remained for how long in the lavatory?'

She coloured momentarily and then looked irritated with herself. 'Probably a couple of minutes,' said Burke, soothingly. 'I heard the lavatory flush, and George looked annoyed as he always did. He was always having the plumber in to try to silence its gurglings.'

The girl looked at Burke gratefully and Richman suavely thanked both of them for their assistance.

When they were alone Richman got up and stretched his long spine. 'I got the family's consent to stage this reconstruction, facsimile. So, Sergeant, if you go to the refrigerator you will find the housekeeper's canapés and orange juice, and, for the sake of verisimilitude, a bottle of the deceased's Glenlivet. I suggest you leave the orange juice where it is.'

Richman bit into a chicken canapé and poured whisky. 'Very few ha'pence in our job, Sergeant, so,' he drank Scotch, 'let us be grateful for small mercies. Lord, I'd like to spend this afternoon here.'

They finished the food.

'Did himself well, old Stryver,' said Richman, pouring a second drink. 'And somebody murdered him at his own table.'

'According to the evidence of the capsule,' said Harry. 'You've realised, sir, that somebody could have substituted the capsule on some other occasion and planted the harmless one in that drain?'

'Crime's usually not that ingenious,' said the Chief Inspector. 'If Burke is right, Stryver was seated as I am, half turned away from his spectacle case and the capsule. Here, take my place!'

The Inspector placed a penny next to the spectacle case as Harry sat down.

'Now, just keep on looking at where you were seated before and where Burke was standing.'

Harry was conscious of a tall shadow passing. He looked down and saw that a shilling had been substituted for the penny.

Richman grinned down at him sardonically. 'I'll admit I served my time on the short change and ringing-in boys, but, even so, a month of practice....'

'Wouldn't have Burke seen it?'

'They were both at an angle to the capsule. The girl's hand could swing and make the substitution. If either of them saw anything, she'd stumble, upset the table, and retrieve the plant— the old short-change technique.'

He took Harry's look of consternation for flattery.

'Just one hypothesis, Sergeant,' he said, kindly.

'It seems to me,' said Harry, 'that the greatest opportunity fell to Burke—an unsubstantiated story about an enquiry, a few minutes alone with Stryver....'

'Except his profession,' said Richman, dryly. 'There's rarely a scandal in the judiciary, for the very simple reason that their profession takes a long and unremitting look at its members.

'John Patrick Burke, fifty-two, a junior with all the paper work he could handle, had a vocation to be a stipendiary magistrate when he was forty. Lives strictly within his income, no investments outside of gilt-edged, wife ten years younger and no shadow of scandal. Motive?'

The Chief Inspector brushed crumbs from his lap and stared at Harry.

'Have you considered suicide, sir?'

'Go on, you interest me,' said Richman.

Harry ticked points off on his fingers. 'According to Rodgers senior, and for that matter to the gardener, the old man was behaving strangely, staring at people, thinking he was being followed. Now, he was a romantic from his choice of reading and it might be in character for him to choose a bewildering form of suicide. As to the poison, it's one of the most painless ways.'

'And where would he get the hyoscine?'

Harry shrugged. 'He might have been the kind of person who liked having poison around and could have acquired it ten years ago for that matter. When I was in uniform I had a case of a seventeen year old kid who had assembled enough toxic stuff to wipe out the whole town—he couldn't explain why.'

'You're painting pictures,' grunted Richman. 'Last night Wickstraw took me to his club and introduced me to a few of the local businessmen. There was a meeting two weeks ago to discuss methods of attracting new industry here. A couple of Ministry fellows came up for it, and Stryver was invited. George was more than impressive and as sharp as a razor. In fact he ended by running the meeting. I spoke to four people who were there and they were unanimous that no man looked more firmly *on* his rocker than George.'

He smiled suddenly at Harry. 'Yes, I had considered his sanity and between ourselves he might have been growing eccentric in his old age, but suicide, no! I have no doubt that defence counsel might take that line, but I don't think any British jury would swallow it.'

Richman took a typewritten sheet from his wallet and passed it over.

'One of Wickstraw's men saw the Holland char.,' he said. 'A loyal old party, but very partial to a glass of port and brandy.' Richman grimaced. 'After the third Wickstraw's man was well in her confidence. Stryver used to call in on Holland occasionally, but he stopped doing it about a year ago, at any rate as far as the char. knows. It might be significant. Then about London. The char. reckons time in terms of football fixtures and the Derby, but the pattern looks as if Holland usually took an early Saturday train to London on the third Saturday of every month.'

'From what I've seen of the joys of this place,' said Harry, 'a lot of residents must do that.'

'Precisely,' said Richman. 'Pity we can't ask her straight out what she did there, but it wouldn't be proper, I think, at this stage. The char. thinks she occasionally stayed overnight, but

Wickstraw's man doesn't think much of her general accuracy. There is one thing. Stryver had the same habit, except that he drove.'

'Third Saturdays?'

The Chief Inspector nodded. 'Heard of McCreedy's Club? Stryver was a member.'

Harry shook his head in astonishment. 'I wouldn't have placed him there.'

Richman chuckled. 'The late George Stryver was evidently difficult to type. Yes, McCreedy's—a lot of advertising people, some actors, very modern decor. It seems that one of George's friends was in advertising, a man in his early sixties whom George helped to get started. They used to lunch fairly regularly on the third Saturday of each month. I telephoned the agency. George's friend was deeply shocked etcetera and said that as far as he knew George hadn't an enemy in the world.'

Harry watched the Chief Inspector rub the tips of his fingers along the table top, deep in thought. 'You know, James, I just can't see the Burkes, the Moncks, or the Rodgers committing this thing. They all have impeccable backgrounds and are well fixed for money. That leaves the Holland woman. She's pretty well broke, mainly due to that nice home of hers, but there's only an area of suspicion at the moment. I don't feel that there's anything helpful at the Glasgow end. Now, we assume that somebody switched capsules during the tennis. That's borne out by the harmless capsule you found in the drain, the note in his pocket and where he died. However, I can't altogether rule out the possibility that somebody not present at the tennis party made the switch.'

Harry looked about. 'It's as near to a locked room mystery as ever occurs in life.'

'Somebody could have got over the wall from the church,' said Richman. 'Stryver was in the shed for some time by the evidence. An agile man, say a cat burglar, could swarm up and down that wall.'

'It's far-fetched,' said Harry reluctantly.

Richman wagged his head. 'Maybe, but not when a skilful counsel puts it to a jury. There might be a London angle. You'd better get a list of all his London acquaintances from the brother and see what you can dig up, and if you can find anything on what he and the Holland girl did up there, so much the better. You'd better have a couple of detective constables to help, I'll telephone about it. I suppose forty-eight hours would be enough.'

'Can you cope, sir?'

Richman nodded. 'Wickstraw's got a couple of pretty smart men available. The inquest is tomorrow at eleven—it'll be a simple adjournment. Anyway, get back as quickly as you can and telephone me if anything breaks.'

Stryver had indeed possessed many London friends and acquaintances and Harry groaned to himself in the train as he read through a list of two hundred names annotated to show the degree of intimacy. He was given a pokey little room with three telephones in it and with two assistants started checking. They worked on until ten, and then concentrated upon reports from various police stations who had sent men to call upon those on the list who for some reason could not be reached by telephone.

At midnight he was staring wearily at the work sheets. Twelve people could not be located as they were out of the country. Of the remainder, none had any suggestion as to Stryver's death except one evidently ancient man who blamed communism. Thirty had seen or spoken to Stryver within the past twelve months and Harry divided up the list, keeping the ten most promising to himself, before going home.

Stryver's advertising friend was a small gnomelike man with an extrovert energy that seemed to glitter through his gold-rimmed glasses. Harry caught him between conferences tip-toeing over his office carpet which was strewn with drawings. In spite of his frail appearance the two-handed grip which greeted Harry felt strong enough.

'I told the Inspector—Richman's his name?—that I could think of no reason why anyone should have murdered George.'

'Yet he either was murdered or killed himself, sir.'

'Find yourself a chair, Sergeant, don't tread on the artwork too hard.'

Harry found a chair and stared down at a photograph of a man with a billiard ball on the bridge of his nose. The gnome balanced, small feet swinging, on the edge of the inlaid desk.

'Either is inconceivable, but, I am absolutely sure, Sergeant, George Stryver would never have taken his life under any circumstance.'

'That leaves murder,' said Harry.

'In which case your murderer is a maniac,' announced the gnome.

Harry produced his wallet and a photograph of Elizabeth

Holland. Bending forward gingerly over the artwork he handed it to the gnome.

'Did you ever see this lady?'

'Striking face.' The little man's brow wrinkled.

'You know,' he said, 'I don't fancy old George's name being dragged into anything.'

'How do you mean?' Harry asked.

'The dead can't defend themselves. I knew George—he was good, honest and intelligent. I wouldn't want a K.C. to draw him as decadent.'

'You know that's nonsense,' said Harry. 'Oh, no, I don't want to argue with you about what a K.C. might or not say about Stryver. If you have information the police require it's your duty to give it. In those terms it's simple.'

The gnome slid off the desk end and carefully walked round to his chair. Harry guessed that some ingenious optical engineering had gone into furnishing the room, because the man appeared much taller seated behind his desk.

'All right,' he said. 'Firstly Stryver wasn't a womaniser. In fact he took all his pleasures within reason, and I knew him for thirty-five years. Six months ago I'd had a whole day with a client.' His small hands made a circular gesture and Harry could see whole acres of lay-outs covering expensive carpet. 'I was walking home about eight, it was a Saturday, and I just mooched along in the light fog, not even trying to flag a cab. Like that, Sergeant, in a kind of tirc 'trance. My steps led me into an unfashionable area at the side of Regent Street, and suddenly I felt very hungry.'

The man paused like the showman he was, mouth slightly open, his eyes uplifted to the ceiling.

'Twenty years ago there used to be a fashionable little restaurant there, just two rooms, one leading off the other. Unlicensed, but you could get good wine brought in from the local pub. I remembered it well and turned the corner. Sure enough, there it was, the same dirty-green swinging door and the sign you couldn't read further than a yard away.

'I went in. It was as though I was in a dream. What looked to be the same cadaverous splay-footed waiter was at the front of the house, the walls had the same shade of yellow paint. There were perhaps half a dozen people in the front room and the light was worse than I remembered it. But in the corner George Stryver was seated with this woman.'

'Are you sure it was them? You mentioned the bad lighting.'

The man shook his head. 'George was distinctive and as for her, I can remember the shape of her face and those eyes—it's part of my job. No, George saw me, nothing wrong with his eyes except for reading.'

'What happened then?' Harry prompted after a long pause.

'George nodded, but it was the kind of nod you give when you don't want to be interrupted. Supposing you're holed up in a bar with an important client and your best friend comes in. You give him the sign, "Glad to see you, old fellow, but don't butt in".' The little man mimed it vividly.

'So you didn't go near him?'

'It's difficult to find the words, although I play with them all the time, but, do you know, for an instant when George saw me I thought he looked not only startled but suspicious. Me!' He gave a sad little laugh. 'So I went into the inner room, incidentally passing close enough to George to see that he was finishing some fish. I had something to eat, they still do a good pepper steak, still feeling this dream-like quality about the whole thing. I took my time and when I came out and caught a cab—the fog had become pea soup—they'd gone.'

'Did you mention the encounter to Mr. Stryver?'

'We'd had a lunch date that very day, but I'd phoned him and cancelled it because of this deal I had going. It was four weeks before I saw him again and somehow I didn't mention it. George was a great friend, but,' he hesitated, 'he had great personal dignity, not the kind of man you nudge and ask "who was that cutie I saw you with?"'

'He seems to have been a complex kind of man.'

'Oh, George inherited a rickety business young and plunged into it. He had a sense of humour and a sense of fun, but forty-five years in a cut-throat business on top of a calvinist upbringing is a bit of a straight jacket. In a lot of little ways he was a rebel. You know he gave me my real start?'

'I heard something,' said Harry.

'Fifteen years ago. I was in a small way and I saw that unless I had the capital to expand—research department, teevee, and god-knows-what the advertisers want today—I might as well sell out and take a salaried job. I wanted a lot of money and, plainly I only had my own genius for security.' He grinned impishly over the desk and immediately grew serious.

'I'd known George for six years, we'd met during the war when I was helping to get people to collect old rags—God knows what happened to the stuff, but no matter. George gave me the money.' He held up his hand, palm upwards. 'Get it out of your head that George was the Cheeryble Brothers. He wasn't. I made a proposition and he called me in for two days. At the end of that time I knew more about my own business than I had before and my accountant, who was with me, was sweating like an African bride. Then, suddenly George grunted, "I've heard enough," and while I'm groping for my hat he fishes in his drawer and pulls out a cheque.'

The little man got up and paced delicately between the lay-outs on the floor. 'Think better on my feet,' he grunted. 'It was a certified cheque, and the accountant starts babbling about agreements and solicitors. George produces a bit of paper with six lines on it and handed it to me. "This what we've agreed?" I said, "Yes". "Then what the hell do we need solicitors for?" Mind you,' he chuckled, 'I think George enjoyed a dramatic moment. Anyway, I did well, and George did well from his investment. I finally bought him out, as agreed, ten years later.'

'He must have been a judge of character,' said Harry.

'He was.' The gnome hesitated. 'I guess George had his losses, but I'd bet they were small in comparison to the gains. Look, Sergeant, I hate this business. What are suspicions and where do they end if you indulge in 'em?' He hesitated for a long moment. 'Here I go, I guess. I was talking about the time he backed me. I was pretty close to him, don't you think he was the kind who lends money and then spreads the fact around. But he'd backed a youngster, a son of a neighbour—the name was Rodgers—and the money wasn't being repaid as per agreement. George didn't like that, not because of the money, but because of principle. It sounds priggish, but George was a stickler. If anybody fell behind it would have to be explained, not lightly dismissed, which I gathered was the case.'

Harry saw that the man was glancing at his watch.

'Nothing else?' he asked, rising.

'Afraid not. Don't take too much notice of what I told you about Rodgers, George was more in sorrow than in anger.'

Harry interviewed six other people without tangible result and looked up Tony Rodgers' business address.

When he was connected Harry found the answering voice more ingratiating than he had noticed it at Richman's reconstruction of the tennis party. Tony was up to his eyes in work, had an appointment immediately after work, but could Harry come round to his Chelsea flat about eight. Harry agreed to do this, and went and had a meal.

Young Rodgers' apartment produced a tiny creak of envy in Harry's heart. He wondered which of the cars in the parking area went with it.

Tony Rodger's face looked different to him than it had on the tennis court. He thought there was a slight weakness in it, a rather too practised charm.

He followed Rodgers into the sitting-room. 'Okay, Sergeant James,' said Rodgers easily. 'I'm yours to interrogate. What about a drink first?'

Harry declined Scotch but accepted sherry.

'Briefly, sir, did you owe Stryver money? We're trying to round up his financial affairs.'

For a moment Rodgers' expression flickered. 'Oh, yes, Sergeant, I owe him four thousand pounds, the balance of a loan made three years ago.'

Rodgers would be around thirty-two, Harry decided, as he sipped his drink.

'You see,' said Rodgers, 'three years ago I had the chance of buying a partnership in the firm I'm with. I had some money of my own but not enough.'

He fiddled with his Scotch and smiled at Harry. 'The business is an up-and-coming one, but, well, we act for some people who my dad wouldn't approve of. Times change. The dad would like to see me set up in a nice conservative country partnership, conveying for the gentry, with a room full of japanned deed boxes labelled "the estate of the late Dowager Emily", that sort of stuff. I could hardly ask him for the balance, so I went to George, produced my little sheet of figures, and got what I needed.'

Rodgers poured himself another small Scotch and added ice.

'There was an occasion when you failed to meet the repayment?'

'Oh, dear, oh dear,' said Rodgers, the open smile still on his face. 'That isn't quite the case. I'd had to buy a new car and various other things came up, all together as they always do, so I said to George, "I'll have to renege for a couple of months if it's okay with you". It was okay.'

'You paid eventually?'

'In fact,' said Rodgers quietly, 'I paid it into his London account a month later.'

'Was that the way you generally made repayment?'

Rodgers hesitated. 'Sometimes, not generally. The fact was that I was probably too casual with Stryver. He was young at heart, but of a very different generation. He grunted, in his gruff way, that it was all right but I sensed he didn't approve, and, well, I managed to get together the money by a month later—switched the car to hire purchase among other things.'

'Did you have an agreement with Stryver?'

Rodgers showed white teeth in a smile and slapped his hand on his forehead in mock consternation. 'Damned if I know what my colleagues would say, but I didn't. Old George was like that, that's why I thought maybe I had offended him in delaying that one payment.'

'So there's no record of the transaction?'

'Record? George would have made a note somewhere. I certainly owe his estate around £4,000. If I don't hear from the executors I shall, of course, inform them. I presume there's a record otherwise you would not have known of the matter.'

Rodgers' manner was stiff, smile all gone.

'Surely, surely.' Harry avoided the implied question. 'I suppose the loan was at interest.'

'As a matter of fact it wasn't,' said Rodgers. 'I wanted it to be, in fact I pressed him to accept at any rate two and a half per cent, but he said no, he'd retired from business and was a friend of Dad.'

'Just let me get this straight,' said Harry. 'He knew that the Colonel did not approve of the firm.'

'I told him,' said Rodgers. 'He just grunted and said that I had my own life to lead.'

'And, of course, there was no security for the loan.'

Rodgers flushed and for a moment his face set in ugly lines. 'I've not touched criminal work yet,' he said, 'but I know you have to ask such questions. Firstly, there was my partnership itself. It would fetch more today than I paid, although I would have to wait until I found a buyer acceptable to my partners. Secondly, you've met my father. I'm his only son, and though he wasn't rich by George's standards, he's far from being poor, and he's not the man to let a friend down.'

'That about wraps it up,' said Harry. Rodgers refilled his own glass and extended the sherry decanter.

'Only one thing, I take it Stryver did not tell your father about the loan. That was clear between you?'

'Oh, George got that point, never fear. He was a man you

didn't have to labour a point with, like some counsel,' Rodgers gave his disarming grin. 'Don't misunderstand me. I have no doubt that Dad would have advanced me the money, but there's always been a delightful relationship between us, and I didn't want to force an issue.'

'But he knew you purchased a partnership?'

'Oh, yes, I told him, of course. He accepted the fact without comment. I presume that he thought I had used my mother's money.'

Harry put away his notebook. 'Thanks very much Mr. Rodgers. Nothing else that occurs to you?'

'No.' The way in which it was said encouraged Harry to linger and say, 'You sound a little hesitant.'

'Well,' there was an ocean of men-of-the-world matiness in Rodgers' voice. 'I did get to wondering if old George might have been a little, ah, peculiar.'

'You mean, mad?' Harry did not feel disposed to swap fancy verbal footwork.

The bright smile stayed on Rodgers' face. 'In both our professions, old man, we see people with their conventional faces down, so to speak, because they're worried. I sensed that, well that old Stryver might have been a little out of contact with realities.'

Harry gave him a long stare and Rodgers hurried on, 'I know that he was still on the ball as far as business is concerned. Perhaps I am not making myself clear, but I have encountered, professionally, men that can drive a rigorous professional deal to a conclusion but when they come to sign the contract one wouldn't be surprised if they signed their name Joan of Arc or Napoleon Bonaparte. Different areas, if you follow.'

'I suppose that what you are suggesting is that Stryver suicided in a very bizarre way.'

'That was what I had in mind.' Rodgers' voice was flat and his manner lame.

'I'll bear that in mind,' said Harry as he left. He walked out of the front gates and glanced up at the fourth floor windows of the flat. In the dying light he thought he could see a face looking down.

Next morning he found that one of the detective-constables had drawn in effect a complete blank. The other had interviewed a retired wool-broker who had seen Stryver on two occasions getting out of a taxi in the City. 'Looked very preoccupied' had been the comment.

Harry found that the expert upon firms of solicitors was a man named Pelman in Room 109. He was properly thankful that the building either contained or had access to experts on practically any subject, up and down from the forgery of obscure autographs. By some quirk of numbering it was on a top floor, in a wing which got gloomier as one traversed its corked-floored corridor. The room itself was dingy and had somehow been jammed at the angle of two walls in a fashion which precluded the entrance of much air. Pelman had a pool of light on his desk top from a swivelled reading lamp, and around him were shelves of musty-looking books. Harry found himself sniffing and fancied he could smell the foxy odour of old, dampish paper. Pelman himself looked out of place, lacking the aura of police; no bustling serge-encased personality this, thought Harry. He was bald, with a long upper-lip and dressed like the fussier type of clerk twenty years previously. There was a pair of agate cuff-links visible below his coat sleeves.

He examined with an air of dubiety the slip of paper Harry handed him, but was brisk enough when he spoke, which was with a slightly clerical air.

'I don't know too much about this man Rodgers professionally. Privately I gather that he's on the gay side, goes to the best places, but that might go with the job. The firm are thrusters.' He pursed his lips disapprovingly. 'Not that times aren't changing,' he added judicially, 'but they are rather near the limit, I think. The founder and senior partner had a bad name at one time.'

'Companies?'

'Not then. He could think up all kinds of ingenious ways of getting people out of houses—nuisance was his speciality, and he wasn't too particular how he got the evidence, at least,' the long upper lip descended as a kind of check, 'so it was alleged. Anyway he made a lot of money and got out before the thing became a scandal. His next step was acting for property companies on the financial-legal side. He found three young men who have proved about the best in the business. That was ten years ago and he took them in as full partners after a few years.'

'I understand Rodgers bought a partnership three years ago,' said Harry.

Pelman bobbed his bald skull. 'Did he? However way he became partner, I can tell you that he wouldn't have got there if he hadn't been damned good.'

'What would be the chance of him embezzling?'

Pelman registered distaste, but reached out a long arm and pulled down a fat book with a well-worn look about it.

'No,' he said, 'the firm doesn't carry any long range trust funds.'

'Surely they'd handle some money,' said Harry.

'Certainly,' agreed Pelman, 'and I imagine extremely large sums, but only for a very short time in the case of property dealings.' He pushed his back into the swivel chair and stared over the desk like a schoolmaster. 'There would be no point in anyone stealing such sums, unless they tried to run immediately. Embezzlement always takes place where the firm carries large trust accounts over long periods. Usually a robbing Peter to pay Paul technique is used, but improved regulations make that increasingly difficult.'

'I'd be grateful, sir,' said Harry, 'if you'd give it some thought. I want to ascertain if Rodgers could be in such financial straits as to be desperate.'

'One moment.' A bony wrist reached for the handset. After fifteen minutes, Pelman sighed and hung up. 'Anthony Rodgers has a fair credit rating. Not a good payer, but an eventual payer. He currently owes £850 on his car and £500 on general hire purchase, but it is considered that these debts are well within his capacity. No other debts have been registered against him, so...'

'If you could turn up anything,' Harry urged.

'I'll enquire around,' said Pelman discouragingly, 'but it seems to me to be the usual bright young executive picture, ulcers, perhaps, but no crime.'

Harry made the last of his calls. 'Sounds a bit cagey,' had been the terse comment of the constable who had telephoned Miss Ethel Brown. Harry's notes described her as an ex personal secretary to Stryver for fifteen years. A year before her employer retired, Miss Brown had been impelled to move south, but George still kept in touch—a handsome Christmas gift and, very occasionally a lunch.

He found her, by appointment, in a towering, faceless city block, in a pastel-walled room with copies of *Fortune* on a glass-topped table. Miss Brown was a largish, comfortable woman with neatly coiffured curly grey hair and large pansy-blue eyes.

'I'd be glad to help you Sergeant,' she said with a faint background of Irish brogue in her voice, 'but as you may know I saw very little of Mr. Stryver after I left him to come down here.'

'Was he a man with enemies?'

She shook her head. 'Not that I knew and I believe that I would have.'

'Everybody says he was a nice man.'

A slight, reminiscent smile touched her eyes. 'I should not have stayed all those years with him if he hadn't been. Of course, none of us is perfect, at least to our secretaries. George Stryver was an impatient man who often demanded the unreasonable from his staff and generally got it. He was impatient of fools and gave a lot of people sore backs in his time. He could be cutting when he wished. But enemies, in the sense of people wishing to kill him, I just can't see that.'

'I understand he helped a lot of people, advanced them money for deals, that sort of thing.'

'Yes,' she said. 'I kept his personal ledger when I was with him. So he did. You see, he inherited his business. I know that he doubled and redoubled it, but I think he always wished he had started selling newspapers on a windy corner. Somehow this made him susceptible to backing people with no capital. And, being George Stryver, he made some money for himself.'

'I understand he was casual about such agreements.'

She raised her eyebrows a little. 'Mr. Stryver used to preach that business should be founded on trust. It's true that a lot of his personal dealings were done by perhaps a few lines in the form of a memorandum, but don't get the idea he was a soft touch. It had to be a hard proposition and he had to know exactly what went on.'

'And none of these dealings resulted in hard feelings?'

'Not that I knew. A few resulted in his losing money, but overall he had reason to be satisfied.'

'What was he like with women?'

He saw the large eyes open fractionally for a split second and she hesitated.

'He was devoted to his wife in every way,' she said quietly.

'Miss Brown,' said Harry, 'Stryver was most probably cruelly murdered. You know what your duty is if you have the slightest thing in mind that could help us.'

'Please give me a cigarette,' she said, 'I don't normally smoke during the day.'

She puffed, rather amateurishly, for a few seconds and he was content to wait.

'When you've worked so closely with someone for many

years ...' She looked at him for reassurance and found none. 'All right, I'll state the plain fact. Some months ago, on March 23rd to be exact, I had cause to take a letter by hand to Grey's Hotel, Paddington. A client, not an important one, was staying there and was very anxious to receive some data. It's on my way home so I volunteered to drop it in.'

She didn't appear to be enjoying her cigarette, Harry noticed, as she paused to search for words.

'You may not know the hotel. It's a fairly large old-fashioned relic, almost with rubber plants in the foyer but not quite. It's cheap and suits people waiting overnight for a connection: definitely not for prosperous people. I got off my bus, and went in to reception. I was about to go when, outside the lift, I saw Mr. Stryver and a girl.'

'What did she look like?'

'She was facing me. Mr. Stryver was talking to a page boy. There were two suit cases beside him. She was tall, with copper-coloured hair and very remarkable eyes, tawny coloured. Very good-looking and, in fact, she looked rather nice, not coarse or flamboyant.'

'Did Mr. Stryver see you?'

She shook her head. 'I hurried out. The lift's recessed and I would have been out of his sight in a couple of steps.'

'What were your conclusions, Miss Brown?'

Her lips curled slightly. 'I don't think I want to labour that point. I dismissed it from my mind, after all he was a widower, his life was his own. You know, I think it was mainly the place that shocked me, definitely second rate. I should have felt happier if it had been the Dorchester, somehow.'

'You are sure of the date?'

'When your colleague telephoned me last night, I said, quite truly, that I did not think I had anything of relevance. However, afterwards I looked up the date of the client's visit on the appointment log. I was debating all evening whether it could be relevant or not. I hope it's not.'

The sunlight dazled his eyes as he walked along the busy street. Damn the bitch, he thought, damn all copper-haired women, and anyway she's a case, a soiled notebook with a lot of sordid shorthand notes and maybe a couple of old gentlemen in full bottomed wigs droning away. He concentrated on other things dimly noticing that he was a block away from the premises of Marcus's former firm. Abruptly something clicked in his mind.

Harry was not unused to it. Feed in enough varied information into the cerebral computor and sometimes, just sometimes, an unexpected card came down the chute into the consciousness. Except that the wires can have got crossed.

On impulse, he changed direction.

The senior partner wasn't in, exactly as Harry had hoped, and the clerk he had seen before had no hesitation in conducting him down to the records room and with the imminence of his lunch token to actuality soon departed.

The basement room was dank and Harry felt the perspiration dry clammily on his spine. The two 25. watt bulbs swinging nakedly on wires, seemed dimmer than on the previous occasion.

He ran his finger across the files and selected one. It was fattish and he decided on the sheep or lamb principle to write a receipt, incorporating 'no responsible party from whom to request permission', and stuck it back in the empty space. He placed the file under his coat, top end sticking in to his armpit, and walked out, locking the door after him.

A dismal teenage girl, doing mysterious things over a one-burner gas-ring, took the key without comment after he had walked up the two flights of stairs.

Outside he walked deep in thought until the sweat heated clammily around his kidneys. He was suddenly very aware of the people, hundreds of them, walking both ways along the narrow street. There was a feeling of nausea in his stomach and he found that his flattened hand was resting against a faintly sticky red paint festooning a dim window within which reposed dusty saucers bearing herbal remedies. He stared at the bladderwort almost incomprehendingly for a long minute and then looked in to the face of a grey man whose progress he was impeding.

'Excuse me, sir,' said Harry, 'where is the nearest doctor?'

The grey man's alarmed expression persisted for a second and switched off and on again, meditating involvement, cost of taxis, inquests and minding one's own business.

'Ah,' he said, relieved. 'I remember. Hundred yards down there.' He jerked his finger at a side street leading off the opposite side of the road a hundred yards to the left.

Jostled and scowled at, Harry remained leaning against the window for five minutes, wondering in his mind whether he had the strength to make his way to the traffic lights. The concrete underfoot, bouncing heat, seemed suddenly much nearer to his head. Eventually he made it on rubber legs.

The doctor was large, young, Australian and with a smear of tomato sauce on his lower lip.

'Sorry, I eat early. Are you one of Dr. Parks' patients, because I'm his locum—south of France, lucky man.'

'No,' said Harry, sitting down, 'I just feel queer.'

He gave his case history and found himself on the soft couch while the cold cap of a stethoscope probed.

'H'm,' said the Australian. 'Nothing wrong with you but what's been wrong, if you follow me. That is, physically. Nerves, I'm afraid.'

'I'm not nervous,' said Harry.

'Various symptoms,' grunted the doctor, 'funny things. Probably they discharged you from hospital too early. D'you find your job worrying you?'

Harry shrugged: 'It never did consciously.'

The doctor's eyes were shrewd, 'Past tense, therefore unpalatable. Change jobs, take tranquillizers, or better still take a job with a pick and shovel. Usually people take the second choice.'

'I'll get through it,' said Harry, 'now I know it's nothing organic.'

'Do you drink?'

'Average.'

'Then you might have a medicinal sherry,' said the doctor. 'Got to keep in with the police.' He grinned. 'My surgery starts at one.'

Harry took the sherry. 'Busy practice?'

The doctor shrugged. 'It surprised me. I'm going for F.R.C.P.S. and I thought this was a piece of cake. You wouldn't think there were so many people who had their troubles looked at here. But we've got the offices—people cutting themselves with penknives and the nightwatchmen and their families—a good practice in a way, practically no maternity.'

'How long has Dr. Parks been here?'

The large man shrugged. 'He bought it cheap in '45 and cashed in on the national health. It was an old, run-down practice then. Parks has done well, and if I had the cash I wouldn't mind going in with him. That is, if I could put up with the bloody climate.'

More to make conversation than anything else, Harry asked. 'What about the records for 1939?'

'Records?'

'A James Marcus who worked near here disappeared that year.'

'Might be,' said the doctor, renewing the sherry. 'And this is the end of the prescription. U'm, '39, a bit ancient! Parks bought from an old guy named Frogman, or sounds like it. The boss mumbles through his pipe, ar, gug, ar, but it comes out like Frogaman. Anyway, he was around 90 when he keeled over walking up the stairs and he had a fifty years' lease to go. Parks bought the practice only, but there's plenty of room here and a lot of the old file cards are dumped around. I had a case a few weeks ago—Army Pension, wanted to know whether the applicant had signs of T.B. before they called him up, mean bastards.'

Parks was evidently a bachelor and the apartment behind the consulting room was dusty and sparsely furnished. The doctor caught his eye and grinned: 'If you know a muscular woman who likes cleaning...'

He unlocked a room filled with cardboard boxes, their sides split with overloading. He bent and pulled out six of them.

'These were the old, panel system days. Private patient?'

'Almost certainly,' said Harry.

The doctor had replaced all but one of the boxes. 'Patients, private, 1939. Alphabetically, unless they've been mixed up.' He rummaged.

'Marcus, John Alfred, January 7th, 1939. New patient. Oh,' he whistled through his teeth.

'These dusty ones,' he said surprisingly.

'Eh?'

'Have another sherry.' They went back to the consulting room.

'Maybe, when I'm eighty years old,' said the doctor, 'this won't mean anything, but I don't like reading death warrants.'

He sipped his sherry while Harry waited in silence.

The Australian peered at the card. 'Frogman, you can't get it straight from the writing, recorded in medical shorthand that a James Marcus came in off the street after a fainting fit. Lesions in the legs, shortness of breath, anaemic condition evident. He queried 'cancer of the blood', what we call now leukaemia. He telephoned to Sir Shelly Brown in Wimpole Street for a consultation next day. No further note.'

'Sir Shelly still going?'

The Australian shrugged. 'He was a text-book name when I was at the Shop. Seemed to me he was pretty old. You could try.'

They finished the sherry and Harry took a cab for Wimpole Street. The address had a neat brass plate with the name of 'Mr.

Sanders', who proved to be an affable wizened man with an evident load on his shoulders. He didn't waste words.

'Brown died in 1944. I never met him, having succeeded his
successor. We might have records and if so my receptionist will
find them. And now, forgive me....'

The receptionist was middle aged but attractive. It took her
half an hour to produce a grey card. Harry waved it away. 'Could
you translate?'

Her lined forehead puckered. 'There were three visits. Sir
Shelly diagnosed leukaemia and it was confirmed by path. Prog-
nosis was twelve months. There wasn't much then that could be
done. The annotation reads that he told the patient at the latter's
insistence.'

'The man disappeared,' said Harry. 'He was fairly important,
there were enquiries, with no result.'

She said, quietly: 'My aunt worked for Sir Shelly. In the May
of 1939 he went to the U.S.A., for the Government, in connection
with the supply of drugs should war break out. He was there until
he died before the war ended.'

'To hell with expense,' he told himself and flagged down
another cab to take him to Grey's Hotel. He thought it was all
that Miss Brown had said it was, and more. Sheer hunger drove
him into the large dining-room, dominated by a vast and rather
sinister sideboard upon which stood a line of shabby cruets. The
chops were mainly fat and gristle and the peas undeniably
tinned. He forwent the waiter's suggestion of ice-cream or
rhubarb pie and went to see the manager, a man as depressed as
his hotel, who, however, was used to people looking at his
register.

'Divorce, I suppose, Sergeant,' he said sadly.

Harry did not disabuse him of the notion that the C.I.D. investigated extra-marital matters.

It was as Miss Brown had said it. Miss E. Holland had
occupied Room 441 and Mr. G. Stryver Room 228, the latter
being a double.

'One gentleman and a double room,' remarked Harry.

The manager raised his eyebrows and spread out his hands.
'You can't stop it, Sergeant.'

Harry took a bus back to the office and collected his suitcase,
pausing to drop into Hawker's office. He found the Superintendent chewing cheese sandwiches and working on a chess
problem.

137

'Sit down, laddy.'

'I've got to dash, sir. I just thought I'd tell you what I found out about Marcus, the missing M.P. fellow.'

Hawker listened and sighed. 'I suppose that he decided to make an end of it. It was careless police work, though, supposing that he would only go to a Bradshaw doctor.'

'He was a hypochondriac,' said Harry, 'a great man for pills. When he knew the truth he chucked the pills away and prepared to wind up his affairs. He was a strong swimmer. My guess would be that he went somewhere he knew and swam out to sea. A couple of months later there were plenty of dead bodies being washed up all over England.'

'But not in civilian suits, laddie,' said the Superintendent. 'Don't forget his clothes were never found.'

'Did you ever actually see a clothed body a couple of months after it had been in the sea, sir?' Harry enquired smoothly.

Hawker had the grace to look slightly sheepish. 'Come to think of it I never did.'

'I have, sir, on three occasions and you couldn't tell what they had been wearing, nor what they looked like. The skin becomes plastic and ...'

'Not with my sandwiches, please. Okay, young man, I won't enquire whether it was luck,' he paused and glared, 'or deduction, but I'll see the A.C. hears of it. Get the file annotated some time and tell old Wickstraw that he can rest quiet.'

Harry was opening the door when the Superintendent's voice blared again. 'And by the way, James, how do you account for the fact that he left loose ends in his business capacity, as your reports state? Think that over while you're going to East Bentleigh.'

'Damn the old devil,' Harry fumed to himself, 'he should know that you can't wrap these things up like a quire of paper, and after all these years, too.'

His sense of irritation persisted as he made his report to Richman in Wickstraw's presence. He left the Marcus incident until such time as he could get Wickstraw alone.

'It'll probably come to putting men on checking all the London hotels on the dates that Stryver was in London,' said Richman. 'If he was having an affair with Miss Holland, it's very relevant.'

Harry started to speak, but something in their faces convinced him to hold his tongue.

'How do you assess young Rodgers, Super?' asked Richman.

'Well,' said the Superintendent, 'it's outside of police work but I think the old man is worth four of him. Colonel Rodgers comes of an old army family hereabouts. He married late in life, a pale anaemic girl who became a semi-invalid after the boy was born. She died when he was eighteen. The colonel, captain as he was then, was abroad a lot and it was out of the question for her to travel. So she spoiled young Tony, wouldn't send him to Rodgers' old school, but put him into the local grammar school—a good one, too. My wife's got a nephew who was contemporary. He says that Tony was a brilliant student, but not very popular—a bit too ingratiating and sly. But he got a scholarship to University and took a first without difficulty before qualifying as a solicitor. He's all right, but I've always thought he was a bit too good to be true. Gets on all right with the old man and spends Saturday night until Monday morning with him usually.'

'Your point, Sergeant,' said Richman with his usual cold precision, 'is that Tony Rodgers might have come to a pass where he couldn't repay Stryver and believed that with the old man dead there would be no record of the transaction.'

He looked, not at Harry, but at Wickstraw. The Superintendent's small black eyes blinked over his pipe for a few seconds.

'Tony's the sort of man you have to know well to dislike,' he said eventually. 'You know the type, smooth, ingratiating, always having had it easy. They can bite when they get in a corner: I've had a few through my hands, nice as pie and can't really understand it when they're marched on to the trap. But,' Wickstraw slapped the desk, 'the Colonel is moderately wealthy. He bought some land when he was out in Australia—thought he might build and take his wife to the warm climate. He didn't and what used to be a few acres of bushland is now in the heart of a new industrial suburb. I've heard him tell the story. I'd say he'd be worth maybe sixty thousand.'

'You know local values,' commented Richman.

'Always found it pays. When you hear a man's in a bad way, then's the time to wonder when his factory catches fire or somebody pinches his wife's diamonds.'

'Well,' said the Chief Inspector, 'Rodgers would seem to be featherbedded. I take it, Super., that you have no doubt that the Colonel would make up any deficiency that Tony landed himself with.'

'Well,' said Wickstraw, 'yes, the family-name business. But I wouldn't care to be in the boy's shoes. Rodgers senior is pretty tough when he wants and loathes crooks. I remember something that might interest you. Young Rodgers is probably something of a moral coward. He was engaged to a girl hereabouts with some money. The story whispered over the tea cups is that he met someone in London with more money, so he took his yearly vacation in Austria and broke it off by letter.' Wickstraw laughed shortly. 'A year later the London girl jilted him!'

'It's all very suppositious, as an old mentor of mine used to say,' said Richman. He thought for a few seconds. 'You say you consulted Pelman, Sergeant. I know he's not impressive, but he's pretty resourceful—knows every managing clerk in London, just about—and if Rodgers is in deep water we'll know it within a matter of hours.'

'He tried fairly hard to convince me that Stryver might have been barmy,' said Harry, 'and I wouldn't bet that he would voluntarily approach the executors about the four thousand.'

'Let's see,' said Richman. 'Tony Rodgers left the tennis party with Burke, our best witness as to what happened. I don't think he would have had the slightest chance to cache that capsule, but perhaps you'll check with Burke, Sergeant.

'And now,' he moved two sheets of paper from his basket on to the green blotter, 'I'll fill you in on hyoscine. I went out to the factory where Miss Holland works—she's decided to take her annual holiday, by the way. The drill was that she took the hyoscine jar together with sixteen other bottles of discarded chemicals. They were all very clearly labelled. She called a youth named Walker who put them in a carton and locked them in a cupboard kept for this particular purpose. He was a particularly trustworthy type of lad selected for that quality.

'Now, once each month the county council sends a special van to collect noxious materials from that and similar factories. It's rendered harmless at a central depot and then disposed of into the sewer. They keep a record of the material received, but not a quantative one. Their list shows various bottles received including one plainly marked hyoscine. So there was nothing to prevent Miss Holland from abstracting the drug.'

'And nothing to prove that she did.'

The Chief Inspector gave him a sharp look from his grey eyes. 'That is so, except that the youth subsequently joined the county police and it was an easy matter to trace him. He's rather an earnest young man, keeps a diary of everything he does. In any case he remembered the occasion without recourse to his diary because it was unusual for such a large amount of stuff to be jettisoned. He says that Miss Holland summoned him to her little cubicle and told him what she wanted. In his words, "I remember thinking that she looked rather flushed. There was a small measure of the type the chemists use on her table. I saw her handbag nearby and I took note of it because it was unusual, elaborate leather work with designs of monkeys embossed on it. I think it was green leather." '

Richman's eyes were glittering slightly. 'It's starting to add up,' he said. 'I telephoned her, partly to check that she wasn't leaving this area, and asked her to come in. She should be waiting downstairs.'

She was wearing a grey suit that Harry thought didn't suit her particularly. As the three men rose to their feet he thought he saw wariness, the caution of a cornered animal, in the tawny eyes as they flickered from one to the other. Wickstraw gallantly seated her in the only comfortable chair.

'Miss, um, Holland,' said Richman, at his smoothest. 'I want you clearly to understand that your presence here is quite voluntary.'

She gave the shortest of nods.

'Although I must tell you that there seems to me certain things upon which you owe yourself an explanation.'

'Such as?'

'Frankly, Miss Holland, you were the only person who had any contact with hyoscine.'

'Obviously somebody else did.'

'Quite. Now about the quantity of hyoscine that was jettisoned at your work. How did you go about this?'

'It was approximately two years ago,' her voice was toneless. 'I got the key to the poisons cupboard from the manager's secretary who keeps it in her safe, got out the jars to be discarded, put them on a tray, relocked the cupboard and took them to my cubicle. I then checked the jars against the manager's memorandum and annotated the ledger.'

'Then you called the boy?'

There was a ridge of concentration between the heavy eyebrows. 'No,' a tiny smile transformed her face, briefly. 'We're a very regimented operation, you have to be in chemicals, procedures for everything. The first thing I did was to return the cupboard key.'

'So during that time the poison was on your desk,' put in Wickstraw paternally, while Richman looked slightly annoyed at the interruption.

'Certainly,' she said, 'but I locked the door of my little office. At least, it is such second nature for me to do so that it would be most improbable that I forgot.'

'You returned and called the boy, he brought a carton and took the drugs away and put them in a small cupboard reserved for waste matter,' stated Richman.

'That is so, except that I followed him and watched him do it. He locked the cupboard and went to return that key as I had returned mine.'

'Were you agitated at all?'

'Agitated?' Suddenly she gave a bitter little laugh. 'Oh, the boy, young Walker. I remember he left to join the police. We missed him because he was so conscientious. Well, Inspector, I don't suppose he would wish to gainsay a superior.'

'Miss Holland, the fact that he is a policeman makes his statement neither more nor less worthy of consideration. He says you were flushed, rather distrait.'

The girl gave a deep breath. 'At that time we were all rather distrait. A machine had broken down, production was behind and I guess the managing director gave the manager hell, because he was passing it on in all directions.'

'I see,' Richman's voice was ice-cold. 'And is it a fact that you had on your desk a small stainless steel measuring scoop and also a green leather handbag with a monkey design on it?'

Momentarily she closed her eyes. 'I had a handbag at one time that could be described as that. As for the scoop, I don't remember. In any case there could be a hundred explanations why something like that should be on my desk. I don't deny that it could have been there.'

'That's perhaps unfortunate.'

'I cannot agree.'

It was even so far, thought Harry. Richman's face betrayed a little irritation.

'Miss Holland,' he said, 'please remember that it gives me no satisfaction to put questions to people, but it is my job.'

'Why the hell don't you say "bounden duty",' thought Harry savagely.

'It is a fact that you knew of the fatal effects and action of this poison in view of your special training?'

She shrugged. 'Hyoscine's one of the poisons people know all about.'

'Oh, Miss Holland,' said Richman, his face impassive, 'all the authorities say it's a very rare one.'

'It was mentioned in the Crippen case before I was born, before you were born. How many people have wallowed in the accounts of that case?'

'Careful,' thought Harry. 'Don't start to argue with him now.'

'That's interesting,' said Richman. 'I hadn't considered that point. I suppose some of the accounts would mention lethal quantities, the time factor, etcetera.'

She merely shrugged.

'Better, much better,' thought Harry.

Richman gracefully abandoned the point. 'Now we come to money, Miss Holland. Would it surprise you to learn that you benefit to the extent of £2,000 in Mr. Stryver's will?'

Her eyes opened wide. 'I didn't expect it, but surprise, well, no. It's the kind of thing old George might well do.'

'And I suppose it will come in very handy.' Richman smiled like some gruesome uncle.

'I'd rather see George back,' she snapped.

'I have some information leading me to believe you have been in some financial difficulties?'

She shrugged. 'I find it hard to make ends meet.'

'So much so that two months ago you saw an agent with a view to selling your house.'

'Chief Inspector,' she said, 'now just you listen to me carefully. I owed £1,500 for the house for which I paid £3,200. It's estimated value now is £4,400, so my equity is just under £3,000. I bought it because I wanted complete seclusion and peace. Now it's becoming a strain. I can't afford much domestic help and the garden is large and takes more time than I can reasonably contribute. In addition, I had the urge to associate with people of my own age. I can get a small flat in a new block towards Eaglesham for £1,800, with enough over maybe for a small car.'

'And then you changed your mind about the sale?'

Her face coloured. 'If that old woman Smith told you I approached him about selling, he should also have told you that he said property was scarce there and he received an average of four enquiries each year. So I told him to wait for one. I object to living in a house with a for sale notice.'

'Well, Miss Holland,' Richman persisted, 'it seems to me at least an unfortunate combination of circumstances.'

She met his eyes squarely. 'You can arrest me, Chief Inspector. Any counsel would laugh your motive out of court.'

'Well,' said Richman, 'I didn't know you were such a legal authority.'

'I had a great friend who was a solicitor. He told me about Judge's Rules.'

She gave him a final steady look, took up her handbag and without another word left the room.

'A termagant,' mused Richman, unruffled. 'She'd make a bad witness in her own defence.' He sighed and reached for one of his rare cigarettes. 'She's got it off pat, but the heart of the case is her association with old Stryver.'

'You're a long way from having a case against her,' said Wickstraw uneasily, tapping out a cold pipe.

'I never like dealing in analogies,' said the Chief Inspector, 'but a young woman somehow involved with an old man, wishing to end the affair and start afresh, plus a money angle, is painfully reminiscent. You did a very good job in London, if I forgot to say so before, Sergeant, and I think that I'll phone through to get some men on the job of checking other hotels.' He gave a short bark of laughter and picked up a briefcase. 'That girl was right, you know, I doubt whether we could get all of that hyoscine story past the judge.'

He rose. 'I think I'll get back to the hotel. They sent me up a pile of bumph to read and annotate and I'll phone from there.'

Harry heard Wickstraw sigh as the door closed.

'Maybe I've got a weakness for pretty women,' said the Super. 'My wife says so at times, but even she admits that Elizabeth Holland is most charming. Pity, if Richman's right. I went out with him to the works this morning and chatted to the manager's secretary while he was inside. Holland is well liked, considered reserved but not stand-offish. Good sense of humour, considerate in her slapping down of the odd male approach. Not many friends. Two women there used to exchange visits with her, but they are both on holiday.'

He started to get up, but Harry took the opportunity to tell him the news of Marcus's fatal illness.

The Superintendent sank back into his chair

'Horrible thing to happen to anybody. One always wonders what one would do. Y' know that old file has always bothered me at the back of my mind. I thought there might be something very nasty about it, dunno why, just instinct. I'm glad you've laid it to rest.'

'How is Miss Tweddle?' Harry asked.

'Tweddle!' Wickstraw looked blank for a moment. 'Oh, yes, the old girl's well off the danger list: should be home next week. There's no further lead on that one, except that Joe Larter is in Teneriffe.'

'I heard.'

Wickstraw relit his pipe. 'The local Interpol man sniffed around. Joe tells the story, with his accustomed guileless charm, that he made a killing on the horses and decided to retire to Teneriffe where there's no temptation to gamble except the lottery. People like him, such a charming fellow.' The Super-intendent snorted.

'No possibility of extradition.'

'Not on the evidence.'

Harry went to Burke's office. The stipendiary had his usual expression of slight harassment.

He explained what he wanted.

'You suspect the capsules were switched?'

Harry nodded.

'It was a shock when the inquest revealed hyoscine,' said Burke. 'Well, I walked with Tony Rodgers to the front gate. He was slightly ahead, on my left and therefore well away from the wall. I am virtually sure that he couldn't have tossed anything into the shrubs climbing up the house wall. He certainly couldn't have concealed anything in a drain without my seeing.'

'You just walked along without stopping?'

'Just wait a minute.' Burke thought hard. 'No, at one point, he bent down and tied a shoe-lace. I stopped behind him.'

'At what point was that?'

Burke shrugged. 'I could see the gate ahead.'

'So you weren't looking down at him.'

'I see what you're getting at. No, I was looking straight ahead at the gate and my car parked at the curb, but if he stretched across towards the wall the movement would have caught my attention.'

'You cannot conceive any reason,' said Harry, 'why Tony could possibly want to murder Stryver?'

Burke's tired eyes squinted down at the papers on the desk top. 'I should say that young Tony is self-centred, but it's difficult to say whether he would ever commit violence. Generally you don't find men of Tony's class in the dock for that type of crime, as you know as well as I do. Embezzlement, yes, drunken driving, yes, but not violence.'

'It's also true that when men of education and comfortable circumstances do murder, they favour poison,' said Harry.

'So do all classes of women,' replied Burke. 'Look here, Sergeant, I've known young Rodgers since I came to this job. He's got a very good legal brain and probably not a very firm standard of morality at the bottom of it, purely as one man's opinion. There are thousands of men like him who gradually mature and end as solid, respected citizens. To my knowledge he's a pleasant young man, largely surface with not much depth, who has never done anybody any great harm.'

Harry thanked him.

At the station there was a note for him to ring Pelman. The dry-as-dust tones came wearily into the receiver.

'About Rodgers, Sergeant. He appears the usual type of young man living up to his income, but I haven't been able to trace any outstanding commitment. He gambles a little, but the book-makers rate him as a good risk. There is one thing. He has been thinking of pulling out of his present partnership.'

'Definite?' asked Harry.

'It's the question of finding the right man to buy him out. He's their taxation man, I understand, and that limits the field.'

'Any particular reason?'

'Well,' said hesitantly, 'my information came from a clerk who recently left the firm. He couldn't advance any definite reason, except that Tony doesn't get on too well with a couple of his partners. I'd hazard a guess that although the money's good the firm are a bit too hot for Master Tony and he wants an out.'

Harry sighed, attended to his paper work and went to his lodging.

Feeling weary, he accepted the offer of a portion of steak-and-kidney pie from his landlady. By one of those curious transitions that never failed to amaze Harry in his observation of women, Miss Walsh seemed to have become ten years' younger. She was whistling when he went into the kitchen and was slapping egg-shell blue paint on to a kitchen chair.

'I can get Tweddle home next week,' she said, 'and make the old girl more comfortable than in hospital, although they're kind enough.'

146

'I've been busy in other ways,' said Harry. 'Did she see who hit her?'

A shadow crossed the landlady's face. 'She saw nothing. Just opened the door and felt for the light and that's all she remembers. The police say it's a man named Joe Larter although they haven't arrested him.'

'It's one thing knowing and another thing proving,' he grunted.

Miss Walsh appeared thoughtful as they ate and Harry was grateful for her comparative silence. He declined a glass of stout and said that he'd read in his room and retire early.

Upstairs, he showered and discovered paint smears along one sleeve. As he unpacked his case, he ruefully reflected that the cheapness of Miss Walsh's hospitality was to an extent offset by dry-cleaning bills. He shook out a light-weight pair of slacks and discovered the file he had taken from the archives of Marcus's accountancy firm. Writing a note to return it, he reflected glumly on the waste of time detection involved. He supposed as much as sixty per cent.

The paper-back he had brought with him seemed extraordinarily dull and the murder of George Stryver kept coming between his eyes and the printed page. He was at the point of going out to a pub when there was a knock at the door.

Fanny Walsh had somehow got egg-shell blue on her forehead and she seemed repressing excitement.

'There's a lady to see you, ducks,' she said, 'at the door. You can go into the front room.' At the bottom of the stairs his landlady proceeded to the kitchen with ponderous discretion.

Harry felt no surprise to find Elizabeth Holland standing in the hallway. Her great eyes stared gravely at him as he invited her into the room.

Miss Fanny Walsh's sitting-room chairs were surprisingly comfortable. Outside it was nearly dusk, but Harry did not switch on the light.

He waited for Elizabeth to speak. 'Can I call you Harry?' she asked.

'You could have called me Harry all along, since I first saw you,' he said, gently, rather surprised at his own words.

'I've got the talent for making an absolute bloody fool of myself,' she said.

He threw up his palm.

'No,' she said, 'some people get into messes and I'm one of them. I'd like to talk to you.'

'All right,' he fumbled for his pipe and put it, unlit, between his teeth.

'In the first place,' she said, 'I met George Stryver through Guy Tavisham. For the last few years I think George was about the only man that Guy felt at all close to. I've been considering how to put this for hours. Old George, bless him, was a romantic at heart. He used to read adventure books and one day he told me that as a boy he had always dreamed of being the great secret serviceman.'

'I've seen his library,' said Harry, 'pirate stuff included.'

'That was George. In business he was a great realist, but I think his daydreams didn't concern money.

'Then Guy died that horrible death,' her voice broke and trembled. 'And I was one of the executors, the two others being London solicitors. So it fell to me to supervise the crating of the furniture, which was pretty valuable, the library paintings et cetera. They were put up for auction in London. Two days after he died, George came to see me.'

He could hear her breathing heavily in the darkened room.

'When I came here I looked around for a house and fell in love with the place I have. It was much too expensive and quite impracticable. Finally, Tavisham said he'd buy it for me and I could pay him back £250 a year without any interest at all. I suppose I shouldn't have, but he was a very wealthy man so I accepted with thanks.'

'You gave him a mortgage?'

'Oh, yes, he took me up to see his solicitor.' She gave a sad little half laugh. 'The old gentleman was rather disapproving about it all. When Guy died, I'd paid off £1,200 but there was still £2,000 left, although, of course, the value of the property had increased. Guy had left me £500 in his will, but it still meant that I should have to get £1,500 in the normal way. Anyway George offered to take it over, interest free. I felt I couldn't agree and said so. In the end George in his gruff way, said, "Then I'll make it two per cent." So that was that.'

'You had papers drawn up?'

'Yes,' she said, 'George got it done locally. I suppose I owe the estate in the region of £1,300.'

Harry felt a sense of anti-climax.

'I'm not too good at this sort of thing,' she said.

'Before, I'd known George as a friend of Guy, and occasionally I got an invitation to drop by for tennis in summer. But the transfer seemed to entail George popping round quite a lot. In fact I experienced the usual female query in my mind, but I was sure that he didn't collect girls. Anyway, when I got to know him and like him, he told me a very peculiar story.'

He rose and went towards the light switch.

'No, don't put it on,' she protested. 'It's pleasant as it is. Now you're probably familiar with the fact that a child that Guy knew was brutally murdered?'

'I've read the file.'

'I heard about it from my twice-weekly woman soon after I arrived. She even brought round an old Sunday paper.'

'Was she warning you against Tavisham?'

'No, she was vastly impressed whenever Guy called. His was one of the original families in the county and the older generation still are impressed by the name. Anyway, one evening George came round, or popped round as he called it, to invite me for tennis. He suddenly came out with the statement that somebody had tried to frame Guy for this murder and that he'd narrowly escaped.'

'He was serious?'

'He seemed deathly serious,' her voice was grim. 'Of course, I asked who. It was a most peculiar business, he said in his dourest Scottish way. Tavisham had told him one night when he was particularly low and just had to talk about it. Apparently the man who disappeared—Marcus—had previously gone out of his way to ingratiate himself with Tavisham. Guy thought he was after something and, of course, he suddenly went off with a woman. But Guy thought it was all somehow connected.'

'Did Marcus go off with a woman?'

'Of course he did,' she said scornfully. 'Otherwise why would he run off like that?'

'It may be,' he said, feeling amused. 'So anyway Tavisham didn't mention names to George Stryver?'

'George said not. Let me see. He said Tavisham made a few rather vague statements that he would have to check on. Anyway, Guy had said that he had written down what he knew of the affair and put it in a safe place, but he was adamant that he wanted no scandal, as he wasn't a hundred per cent sure, by any means. George had influence enough to approach Guy's solicitor the day after he died and get the answer that the firm held no "to be opened after my death" type of thing. So he asked me to search Tavisham Hall.'

'So that's why you were in the hay loft.'

She laughed. 'That's why and if I ever saw a man's face thinking the worst I saw it on yours that day. To make it brief I've been through everything in the house with a tooth comb. George came up a couple of times, giving out that he might buy the house, but after that he thought he'd better keep away.'

There was silence for a minute. Then she said in a tight voice, 'You don't believe me, do you?'

'My dear!'

'That's about all,' she said dully. 'Of course, George made it into full-scale cops and robbers. He'd telephone at work and just name a London street corner. I'd sweat up to London by train, and, of course, I never had anything to report. What with my job, and this house and garden, there never seems enough time, and I had to squeeze more hours out of the week up at the Hall. I know every crack, every wall by now.'

'You only communicated that way?'

'Sometimes he called me by telephone, but always from a public callbox. Oh, he took it seriously. I got to be very fond of him, so I humoured him as I thought.'

'He never came to your home?'

'Not after those first days. He always impressed me that I must never allude to the matter when I met him socially. Once at tennis I whispered that I had finished the attics, he called me up next day and was really hopping mad. Oh, there was one time, a day or so before he died. The doorbell went around oneish and I staggered out of bed. I put the chain on and it was George. He came in and told me that he'd decided to let a professional detective have a go at Tavisham Hall and could I get the man—I think it was Belcher, some name like that—into the house on the pretext of wiring repairs. I was a trifle short with him, I'm afraid. I was very tired, so I said I'd see. He went off like a disgruntled schoolboy, I'm so sorry now.'

'Hm,' Harry slowly filled his pipe. 'Are you going to the police, officially I mean, with that story?'

'What do you think?'

'No, no. I think you quite definitely shouldn't, Elizabeth.'

'I rather thought that,' she said.

'Can you remember any small details that Stryver mentioned, if any?'

'I jotted two things down last night. I couldn't sleep. Yes, he mentioned a company called Steel Auxiliaries, and I'd never heard of it. On the other occasion he asked me if the name of Farqueson ever meant a thing to me. I said it didn't.'

'You know, Elizabeth, I've never been in this situation before. In our work it's usually rather shady people, a tap on the shoulder and "I've instructions to nick you, Bill, better come along." Let me think.' He fiddled with his tobacco pouch and finally said, 'As a friend I should tell you that it's known that you stayed at the same hotel as George, a grubby sort of one, at least once on those London trips.'

She caught her breath. 'My God! Have you ever considered that the most innocent action can look black when you people get hold of it.'

'That's the point, Elizabeth,' said Harry firmly, 'we are people, just like juries, barristers, or your old char. with her Sunday paper.'

'I told you,' her voice came fiercely, 'that I went to London once a month to meet George. I usually met him at some unlikely place around ten, had some coffee with him, and then he'd push off. We'd join up about fourish—the entrance to the National Gallery, places like that, and we'd go on a tiny pub crawl and then have dinner.' She gave a cross between a sob and a hiccough. 'George was very much the detective at bay, glances over shoulder, etcetera, but he knew a lot about London. He used to take me to places south of the river where the food was good and the people very amusing. He had a talent for getting into conversation with people. We had some good evenings....'

Her voice changed. She spoke like an automaton. 'I suppose it's no good trying to explain. On four occasions we missed my last train. Once George had been walking with me through White-chapel—he knew its history right down to Jack the Ripper. Another time he'd found a pub where the last of the real coster-mongers go. He was passionately interested in people. He said that was partly how he made his money, knowing how people tick.

'He could have driven me back, but he always said it was too risky and we'd have to find a very quiet, unobstrusive hotel. As you say, they were crummy, all four of them, near railway stations mostly.'

'Did George always book a double room for himself?'

'Always,' she said, her voice businesslike. 'You'll find that if you ask his friends. He always said that hotel beds were too small for him.'

'First thing tomorrow morning just write a simple note—no explanations—and give the dates and places. Drop it in to me at the station.'

'You advise that?' Her tone was doubtful. 'Some one I knew said it was always better not to volunteer information.'

He sighed to himself. 'In this case the police will know within two or three days, Elizabeth. It might be better to have it on record that you freely volunteered these facts.'

'All right.' She sounded like a little girl, he thought.

'Elizabeth! I think you knew a Farqueson, though.'

'I knew one?'

'When you were training in London a man named Freddy Farqueson had a flat next door.'

'Lord! you're right.' She sounded flabbergasted. 'An oily little man, separated from his wife. He had plenty of money. The flats were expensive ones and I had a room with a distant cousin.' Her voice was distant as she looked back over the years. 'Farqueson had ingratiated himself with my cousin's husband to the extent that he got an invitation to sherry occasionally. I usually made an excuse to be out. He could undress you at a glance, could Master Freddy. I think I told you that before I came here I only met Tavisham once or twice? One of those occasions was when he called on me at the flat. He stayed only half an hour, he was catching a plane. I was showing him out just as Farqueson rang the doorbell. He was returning a book he'd borrowed. I had to make a formal introduction and I remember at the time that for a moment Farqueson looked as though he'd seen a ghost. Just for a second his jaw dropped. I'd always rather laughed at the phrase, until I saw it happen.'

'Did Tavisham recognise him?'

'No. I don't think he took much notice of him. He was worrying about his plane. Guy was one of those people who are always convinced that they'll miss their transport.'

'That's very interesting,' said Harry, sucking his pipe. 'You're right about Farqueson's character, too, by the way.'

'Harry,' her voice was almost inaudible. 'You knew where I lived. I suppose that means...'

'I read the file.' His voice was weary.

'Oh.' It was a gasp. He heard a flurry of movement, saw her for a moment silhouetted in the doorway against the hall light and then the door closed.

He sat there without moving for ten minutes.

Miss Walsh was at her kitchen door as he walked towards the stairs.

'Is your friend still here?' She called.

'She went a few minutes ago.'

'Such a nice girl, but looks as though she hasn't slept since last Shrove Tuesday. Come and join me in a drink. Everybody's out and I loathe drinking on me own, a pernicious habit Guy Tavisham used to say.'

He chose a tankard of stout rather than gin.

'But a very nice girl,' said Miss Walsh cunningly. 'She said her name was Holland.'

'I bet you asked her,' said Harry.

'Go on with you. Us old ladies have only got our curiosity left. Would she be Guy's executor?'

'One of them.'

'I thought it might be. Guy always said she was dead straight. He told me her real name, too, and that the trouble she was in nearly broke her up.'

'She took it hard?' He kept his voice non-commital.

'Very hard, Guy said. That's why she lives among all the old fogies around the Strand. A girl like her who should be having fun.'

He swallowed his stout. 'Thanks. It's an early night for me, got a heavy day tomorrow.'

He seemed to have been asleep only a few minutes, when there was a knock on the door. It was Miss Walsh, her breath distinctly alcoholic. 'The phone for you.'

He apologised and followed her to the kitchen. He glanced at the clock; it was well after eleven.

'This is Rhonda Gentry.' Her voice was steady and deliberate.

'Oh, hallo,' he said embarrassed.

'I'd be most grateful if you could come round.'

Ignoring Miss Walsh's quizzing eye, he threw on some clothes and got his bicycle from the backyard.

Elizabeth Holland had changed into slacks and her face looked paler than ever. He declined her offer of a drink.

Her manner was a trifle formal. 'Please sit down.' She carefully avoided using any name. 'Now I'd much appreciate it if you'll just sit and listen.'

According to her story, she was twenty-three when she had become engaged to Ivan Goldsmith, five years older than she, a very handsome, blond man of athletic disposition. He lived with a widowed mother in straitened circumstances, but his prospects were bright.

'The engagement lasted three months,' she said, 'we liked each other, found each other fun, but, well I guess I wasn't ready for marriage.'

However, friendship had persisted, in spite of the wagging tongues of the small town. She worked at the county hospital and when she was on an evening shift Ivan would get off the London train and spend an hour in the dispensary before catching his bus.

'There was very little to do in the evenings except clerical work,' she said, 'and though I suppose it was strictly against the rules, nobody objected. I'd give him a cup of hospital cocoa and we'd talk.'

One night in July he called, appearing very agitated. He asked if she could get off for an hour and she managed to arrange it on the score of some very urgent private business.

'We went into a horrible old pub near the station, deserted except for us and cobwebs. It made it far worse, somehow.'

Ivan would always make a clean breast of any worry to Rhonda. He told her, almost out of his mind with distress, that he had embezzled £2,700 from a trust account and with his own small savings invested it in a company concerning which he had secret information of a future take-over bid.

'He bought at 16/3d.' she said, 'and they touched thirty shillings as the rumour spread. Then came the crash. The company passed over its six-month dividend, announced heavy losses, and of course the take-over offer was so much poppycock. The shares dropped to 2/10d. apiece and it was difficult to find a buyer even so.'

Ivan was safe until the next trust audit, two months' ahead. Then he was faced with ruin.

'The uncle was a sanctimonious, stiff-necked man who appeared to think the world revolved round his business. Ivan didn't think he'd prosecute because of the family name, but he would certainly see that Ivan left his profession.'

She had urged him to try to raise the money. 'All I had was £120 which I said he could have.'

The next few weeks were a nightmare to Ivan. He approached all his friends, using a pretext, and including Elizabeth's money, obtained promises amounting to a little less than a thousand.

'I persuaded him to tell his mother, finally. She had her bit of jewellery valued, but with the insurance policies and everything she possessed, Ivan was still nine hundred short. As he said it had to be all or nothing.

'We were then in June. I was feeling as limp as I feel now. The audit was three weeks off. I forgot to tell you that Ivan got himself another girl, not one I'd have chosen for him, but that doesn't matter. She was the daughter of quite a prominent barrister who had a country house in the district. I used to go to the tennis club on Sunday afternoons and to my surprise Ivan and Suzy turned up, which wasn't their usual practice.'

She took a cigarette from a cedarwood box and Harry lit it for her.

'Thanks. Ivan was in mad form as he could be when he wanted. He fairly bubbled over with a kind of mad gaiety. Suzy always thought of her dignity. My heart leaped because I was sure that he had somehow raised the cash. I found one opportunity to get him alone. Of course several people saw us and that was one ground for suspicion against me. I asked him if things were going to be all right.' She held her hands for a moment against her head. 'I shall never forget what he said. He flashed his tremendous smile and said, "It's going to be all right, girl." I hate to recall it. Then we were interrupted by Suzy.'

'I see,' said Harry, 'and on the way home he took poison. I suppose he took it from the dispensary.'

She nodded. 'There'd been an accident and a fire there so that they couldn't tell if hyoscine was missing.'

'But good God, my foolish girl, you had only to tell the police what you've told me....'

'My aunt's little maid was friendly with the local policeman's son, so we got the news almost immediately. I hurried round to Mrs. Goldsmith. She begged me to keep silent and help her to prevent his name being smeared. So I did.' Her chin jutted. 'I'm not a fool. There was no evidence against me.'

'And you got old Specs to represent you?'

'Ivan had told me fascinating stories about this man. So I rang him up and almost fell down when he told me his price. Nevertheless I knew I had to have the best and not the nice bumbling old gentleman who did my uncle's work. There'd been a Scotland Yard man down, a red-faced horror who could insinuate things in a few words. I saw he was bent on getting me to argue with him—Ivan had told me about such things—so I clammed up and at the right time got old Specs down to flatten everybody.

I could see that even he really thought I was guilty,' she said bitterly.

Harry rubbed one set of knuckles against his forehead.

'Is his mother still alive?'

She nodded. 'We exchange cards two or three times a year. A little after Ivan's death she moved to a small cottage in Upand, a village in Bucks. I haven't seen her since I left to come here.'

He nodded.

'Elizabeth,' he said, taking a decision, 'I believe you innocent of anything to do with Stryver's death. But I do suggest that you consult old Specs or somebody in the same class. I can give you half a dozen names, although perhaps I shouldn't.'

She could be stubborn, he realised, as she shook her head. 'Not this time. To hell with them. I didn't do it, I can't be convicted.

He rose and stood looking down at her, wondering why the hell he, Harry James, ambitious young policeman, should find himself in this situation. She held something out to him, an envelope. 'The dates and hotels are in there, Harry.' There were dark patches of purple under her eyes.

'Don't see me out, Elizabeth.'

She started to get up. 'I could drive you home. One of the women at work is holidaying abroad and she lent me her car.'

He gently pushed her into her chair. 'I'm in a walking mood.'

Back at Fanny Walsh's he set the alarm for six-thirty and an hour later he was standing outside a drive-yourself agency as a sleepy man hefted the roll-up door.

He hired a car, ruefully reflecting with a fragment of his mind that this week would mean another dip into the savings' account. He drove with controlled savagery, his knuckles taut on the wheel. He stopped twice to dash water on his face from the canister he had put on the back seat. He arrived at the tiny village of Upand, Bucks, as the church clock was striking ten-thirty.

The sub post-office gave him Mrs. Goldsmith's address. It was a small bungalow with minimal land round it covered with parched grass and some struggling nasturtiums, not a gardener's house.

He rang the bell and waited as the minutes dragged by. The door opened with the faint dragging sound of warped wood. The woman who opened it leaned heavily on a crutch, her left leg twisted under her. Age or suffering or both had sweated her face and body to a frame of bone, but the eyes were still alive.

He showed her his warrant card and noted the flash of apprehension in her face.

'I'm here more or less unofficially, Mrs. Goldsmith,' he said, 'on behalf of a mutual friend.'

The living-room was dead and rather airless. Harry subconsciously noticed what he classified as souvenirs attached to the wall.

'It's Miss Rhonda Gentry, Mrs. Goldsmith,' he said slowly.

Her face was blank.

'I know she now goes by the name of Holland and lives in Bradshaw.'

The wary look grew less. 'I am very fond of her,' she said, 'by any name.'

'So am I,' he said, 'which is why I don't like to see her mixed up in another death from hyoscine.'

Mrs. Goldsmith's head slightly jerked against the padded back of her high-backed chair and there was a bluish tinge around her mouth. Harry came out of his chair fast.

'No, no,' she said, 'I'm all right.'

He watched her rest while her breathing became normal.

'Another!' she said.

He nodded. 'The first was your son. Now it's another, the Stryver case. You probably know about it.'

'I read something, the papers are full of it, but I didn't know that Rhonda had anything to do with it.'

'The reporters haven't got to that angle. They will.' He leaned forward slightly in an effort to impress her. 'Police work being what it is, somebody being a suspect in one case is likely to be doubly suspect in a subsequent, similar one.'

As she twisted her hands he noticed how swollen the knuckles were.

'Sergeant,' she said, 'Rhonda and I share a dreadful memory and please believe me it has weighed heavily that I placed her burden on her. My son committed suicide because he stole from his uncle's office.'

'He told you?'

She nodded. 'Whatever way we thought, we could not raise the money. It was . . .' one swollen hand gestured, 'what does it matter now? I suppose only Rhonda and I ever think of him. Time was rushing by, as it does. I suppose I was a coward, I should have seen his uncle, a hard unforgiving man, God rest him, but he kept saying, "wait another week, mother".'

'Had you considered he might choose that way out?'

'I was afraid. That particular Sunday he kissed me goodbye as he always did. I knew he was meeting his fiancée at the tennis club, I had checked. I sat at home ... telling myself it was all right ... until ...'

He waited.

'Rhonda came round. It came out that she knew and I made her promise to keep silence, a foolish, stupid prideful thing, but I suppose I wasn't quite normal....'

'So it never came out?'

'I suppose I under-estimated the police,' she said, faintly. 'I never knew Rhonda was a suspect, even when she moved away I thought it was just because she had never cared for the villagers and their gossip.'

'What about his uncle?'

'There again,' she sighed. 'He never referred to it. Two years later he died. His business name was everything to him—my husband's elder brother. I've always feared that the discovery broke him. He was kind to me in his will—I have enough.'

Harry nodded. 'Thank you Mrs. Goldsmith. I'm sorry to have caused you pain, but I think that the important thing is the living....'

'I'm old and ill,' she said matter-of-factly. 'Oh, no it's not a matter of commiseration, I'm in no pain and I'm not in misery. My husband died young, but for some years we saw a lot of the world. It's the living.... Could you get me a sheet of paper and a pen from there?' She indicated a small table in the corner of the room 'so that I can write something briefly.'

She placed the paper on a book and wrote laboriously.

He thanked her and prevailed on her not to come to the door.

CHAPTER SIX

HE REACHED BRADSHAW at two, checked in the car, and
found Richman in his office. 'Do you mind glancing at this, sir?'
He extended the paper and the Chief Inspector read it aloud.

'I, Emma Goldsmith, 69, of 3 Bath Place, Upand, Buckingham-
shire hereby swear that my son, the late Ivan Goldsmith, told
me that he embezzled £3,750 from the office where he worked.
I believe he committed suicide for that reason.'

'How did you get this, Sergeant, it's dated as of today?' He
looked at his watch.
'I hired a car.'
'I hope you don't expect to get that on expenses.' Richman's
smile was thin.
'I shan't put it on.'
'I see. In the old days I believe that they called a ship's captain
who spent his own money on paint and gear a ship's husband.'
Suddenly he rapped. 'I do so hope you are not experiencing any
emotional involvement, Sergeant.'
Harry disliked lying, but he bravely said, 'No, sir.'
'Ah, most of us do experience it,' said Richman seriously, 'one
time or another. I think the only thing for a copper is to marry a
copper's daughter. They understand us. My father-in-law was a
sergeant down in Kent.' He gave his charming smile. 'But for the
fact my eldest girl turned eleven last month I'd invite you to
dinner.'
He stared down at the document. 'The old dame must like
Miss Gentry.'
'She thought her incapable of murder.'
'Of her son's murder,' Richman gently corrected. 'This will
probably get Miss Gentry off Hawker's list. But, of course, the
premise remains. She had had first-hand knowledge of the lethal
effect of the poison. Her innocence of one murder does not logic-
ally effect this one.'
Harry felt a sickness in the pit of his stomach.
'In a way it's better for us,' said Richman. 'We could have the
inquest on the young man re-opened and a suicide verdict

recorded. Therefore we could perhaps introduce that as evidence of association regarding hyoscine. The previous open verdict meant that we couldn't introduce it.'

With nothing better to say, Harry dumbly produced the envelope. 'She listed the places she stayed at with Stryver. Her story is that the old gentleman was playing cops and robbers, with "Who killed Tavisham?" the mainspring.'

Richman registered distaste. 'I thought I told you before to keep Tavisham et al. well away from me. She can tell all that to her solicitor.'

Richman pushed over a green folder. 'I had an urgent call from Stryver's brother. He was down to make arrangements for taking the body back north for interment. The servants have been making the house ready for closure—eventually it'll be put up for auction including furniture, perhaps next year when the fuss is over.

'They'd packed up George's possessions separately, clothes for the Salvation Army, his books and pictures for the family. Among the books was an old-fashioned blotting book, about fifty sheets of blotting paper with a hole through the centres so that one can see if there's another letter underneath what has been signed already. George had had it in his business office for years and took it with him. He used to keep it on the bookshelf—it's an unwieldly size. The brother leafed it through and found two or three carbon copies that hadn't been filed, business letters, but then there was this.' The inspector turned the folder open revealing a photostat. 'Read it,' he invited.

Harry read it. It was typewritten except for the signature, and an addition.

Sunday

'My dearest little girl,

I was very worried by what you told me in London. As you said I could easily let you have the money of which you are in need, but it would poison the sweet relationship between us. I have told you that I have made some provision for you in my will: all I may hope is that I can enjoy a year or so more of you.

You need not trouble about the mortgage repayment on your cottage. Of course, how could you have thought otherwise?

Yes, I do realise that the £500 Guy Tavisham left you as his Executor is inadequate for what you are required to do. But you are entitled, as I told you, to relinquish the duties and if there is any question of the £500 I would reimburse you.

On the question of marriage, it has always been understood between us, for reasons affecting us both, that this has never been envisaged.

All love,
George Stryver.

P.S. I must ask you never to call round except on the usual Sundays.'

The signature and postscript were in handwriting. At the bottom of the sheet was one line of writing. 'Returned to me without comment.'

Harry's eyes met Richman's. 'Could be motive,' said the Chief Inspector.'

'Circumstantial,' said Harry.

'We'll need a bit more.'

Harry remembered the learned judge's dictum that circumstantial evidence was the fact that if you saw a man coming out of a public house it was a fair inference that he had taken a drink: and counsel's addition, that if you could smell beer on him, surmise became certainty.

'There's a handwriting expert in the district,' said Richman. 'As good as any: he usually takes the police cases up here. I sent a car with the original, he should be here soon. Meantime take a look at the rest of that file.'

Richman had been thorough. He made allowance for the lack of date, impartially examined the evidence that it had been sent to Miss Holland, and included a sketch map of Stryver's workroom in relation to the rest of the house.

'Could have been planted,' Harry dared to say, 'particularly in view of the lack of a definite date.'

'Anybody *could* have slipped in the back entrance and planted it,' agreed Richman, 'but it would have to have been on the morning of the murder, otherwise too much risk. Any of them at the tennis party could have nicked in the back door, that's true and that's what'll be said, no doubt. But it depends on whether this letter truly reflects the circumstances. Anyway, we'll see about the handwriting. These are no liftable prints, only smudges.'

The handwriting expert was a wispy, elderly man with bright unblinking eyes.

'The signature looks all right,' he said.

'You'd swear to it?' pressed Richman.

The expert sighed and nodded. 'You're not Forgery?'

Richman shook his head. 'That branch never came my way. As you know it's specialised.'

'Well, Chief Inspector, I'll give you a very short lesson. The only manuals that exist are the Bank of England standard one and your own. If you trace a signature, it would take me about two hours of photographic work to establish the fact beyond doubt. If you sit down carefully and copy it, the same thing. What a good forger does is to practise free-hand for maybe a week. Then he has a good night's sleep, comes down in the morning and dashes off the signature he wants to fake. Like this.'

He unscrewed his fountain pen and wrote rapidly, 'George Stryver.'

'Damned good,' said Richman, holding the sheet of paper. 'I can't tell the difference.'

'Oh, yes,' said the wispy man. 'It could easily be established that this was not written by the pen—a common one, by the way—that deceased used. Neither is the ink the same. Ball points, of course, are pretty much hell for us. I'm too old for a forger, you need to be under sixty, preferably much younger.

'Anyway, when we get one of these cuties, it's close work with various measuring devices, curves, angle, stroke thickness, all that. The signature I examined comes within the recognised tolerances.'

'So it's genuine.'

'Please, Inspector,' the wispy man spread out his palms. 'In the box I shall say that in my opinion it is a genuine signature. Opposing counsel will establish that what I am saying is that there is simply no evidence that it is forged.'

'Fair enough,' said Richman. 'I suppose I'm being naive, but do you get any evidence as to mood or character from writing?'

'That's the dubious periphery of our profession,' the expert smiled charmingly, 'but—and not for evidence—I'd say Mr. Stryver was under the influence of some emotion when he signed. He was writing faster and heavier than usual.'

'It could be a forgery?' asked Harry.

The old gentleman fumbled in his pocket and produced a ten shilling note. 'Oh, yes, so could this be. But it would be a bloody good professional job.'

After he had gone Richman turned to Harry.

'Eventually we'll have to ask Miss Holland about this letter. Y' know, I think we'll find her a young lady difficult to pin down—enough brains to spot an untenable position before she's pinned down. Meantime, the typewriter. A few of the copies in Stryver's files have a facsimile of this type-face. His desk has got a large Royal and a small, half size Olympia. According to the book this is an old Remington. The housekeeper says that George used to keep an old machine at his Club, the Constitutional. You'd better get round and look.'

As Harry got up, the Chief Inspector added, grimly, 'I think that tomorrow we'd better think about a search warrant. I'll take the necessary advice.'

The Constitutional Club exuded rather gloomy comfort and the decor leaned to teak panelling and enormous chairs.

'Mr. Stryver's typewriter?' The head steward was a small, dapper man with a whimsical Irish face. 'This way, Sergeant.'

The writing room was large, with curious desks, green leather covered. The typewriter reposed on one of them. Harry took the cover off. It was an old Remington portable, in fact very old. He tapped a couple of heavy keys.

'An old friend, Mr. Stryver used to say, nearly forty. It had been round the world with him seven times, he reckoned.'

'Was he a good typist?'

'Quite fast, sir, but a lot of exing out, not expert.'

'He kept it here?'

'Yes, you see the old fellow used to come in here once a week to do his personal letters.'

'He left it lying around here?'

'What you'd be wanting is to know if other people used it. Yes, sir, it was available to anyone—Mr. Stryver was a generous man.'

'Was it used much?'

'Well, sir, it was a bit of a joke among the regulars—the official typewriter, that sort of thing, and old Mr. Stryver was always saying the committee should buy the ribbons. But it worked that if any member felt he wanted to type something out, he'd use this machine.'

'So it wouldn't be an uncommon sight to see somebody using it?'

'No, sir, commonplace you might say.'

'And you are a busy club?'

'Yes, sir, the club acquired valuable investments many years ago and offers very good amenities.'

Harry left a receipt for the typewriter. Back at the station it took him only a few minutes to see for himself that the battered type-face matched that of the letter.

On his way home Harry stopped for a steak and, contrary to his usual habit, two double whiskys at a gloomy pub with brass fixtures and cracking leather chairs and surprisingly good food. He felt more cheerful than he had all day until he saw that a small Morris was parked outside the house.

He smiled at Elizabeth Holland as she stuck her burnished head out of the window.

'I thought it was you a second before I saw you,' he said.

'I telephoned, but they said you had gone.' Her words came with a rush. 'Could you come with me to Tavisham Hall?'

He started to reply, saw the strain in her face and then walked round and got into the passenger's seat at the front.

'No good chewing this over until we get there,' she said shortly, 'and anyway I don't want to talk.'

From force of habit he noted that she drove the little car skilfully and carefully and relaxed as he lay back in the seat She drove into the drive of the deserted house, swung to the left at the old stabling and pulled up before a small, rather neglected looking cottage.

'This is Tallent's place,' she explained shortly.

A short red-faced man with a halo of white curls round his bald pate opened the door. He wore slacks and a sports shirt, but there was a deftness about his movements that made her introduction unnecessary.

'Sergeant James, this is Mr. Barry, Mr. Tavisham's former butler.'

Barry gave a short bow and ushered them into the little living-room. It had been tidied up and the window was open, but there was an unpleasant staleness in the air.

'Let's sit down,' said Elizabeth Holland.

Harry found an uncomfortable black painted chair and found himself looking at an alarm clock and a green china owl on the mantelpiece, plus a photograph of a much younger Tallent in khaki and puttees.

'I came here this morning at noon,' she said, 'mainly because I wanted to be alone. Tallent wasn't about and I got no answer when I knocked at his door, so I pottered around weeding and then went for a walk. When I got back I ran into Mr. Barry.'

'It was like this Sergeant.' Barry had a faintly husky, rather ingratiating voice. 'We live at the seaside and the wife's relations decided to spend a fortnight. They're all right, but, well, I like a bit of peace these days—kids and all that—so I said "Righto, old girl, I'll sheer off and drop in on some of our old friends at the old place". I sent Jim Tallent a card, saying I hoped I could have a bed for maybe a week, but when I arrived there was no Jim and no answer when I knocked. I was prowling around wondering what to do when Miss Holland came up.'

'I thought something was wrong,' the girl said. 'We got a crow bar from the stables—the windows were locked—and Mr. Barry got in. We found Tallent in his bedroom in a bad way.'

'It's drink with Jim, I'm afraid,' said Barry. 'After his wife died he was that way, but when the house was open and the master was alive it wasn't too bad.'

'We got the doctor,' Elizabeth said. 'He's been drinking too much, eating too little and has a bad respiratory infection. Tomorrow he will go into hospital if he's not very much improved.'

'He came again when you were gone, Miss, and gave him a shot to quiet him. He's sleeping now.'

Trying to keep annoyance out of his voice, Harry said, 'I don't see how this concerns me. If there's anything I can do, I would, but...'

He felt sorry when he saw how tired she was.

'Perhaps you'll explain, Miss,' said Barry, his manner uneasy.

'He wants to see a policeman—not, he insisted, the local one. It's,' she hesitated and went on with a rush, 'about that child who was killed.'

The little house seemed to grow more oppressive and momentarily Harry had the impression that the walls of the dingy little living-room had shrunken.

Barry's face was blotched with white. 'I tried not to hear none of what he said. I'm seventy-two, Sergeant, and I've earned a bit of peace, sir.'

He checked an angry retort. 'Look here,' he said, 'the man had a temperature.'

'He was light-headed,' the girl said, 'but not wandering. He found the child's body.'

'I'll go and see how he is,' said Barry, hurriedly.

'We have to be pretty careful,' said Harry, 'about what we do. You are certain he asked to see a policeman?'

'He asked for you.'

They were silent until Barry came back and his face brightened at the lack of conversation. ''E's sleeping nice. The doctor said it would put him off for three hours or so and we're to get him again if his temperature hasn't dropped.'

Harry consulted his watch. 'I'll come back in an hour or so. Will you be all right?'

They nodded and with a sense of relief he went out of the door and strode for a mile along the country lane until he reached the village. He borrowed an evening paper from the publican and settled into a chair with a pint of stout. He noted that the Stryver murder had been relegated to page four with the emphasis on Glasgow. He dawdled on the way home, savouring the dying heat of the summer evening and the smell of clover from the fields.

'He's come to,' excitement fought with trepidation in Barry's red face.

'You'd better stay here.'

The bedroom was elaborate and untidy. He guessed that somebody must have put away Tallent's clothes: their usual place would be on the floor. Quart bottles without tops were under the dressing-table and the room smelled of perspiration. Elizabeth Holland turned, a thermometer in her hand. 'Very slightly above normal,' she said. 'Shall I stay?'

'Better leave me.'

He sat gingerly on the end of Tallent's bed. The old man looked shrunken, his hair looking wet as it fell about his forehead. Harry saw a set of dentures in a glass beside the bed.

'How goes it, Mr. Tallent?'

The man's voice had a wheezy quality about it. 'It's this heat. I was working out in it until I felt queer, just as though I'd eaten something poisonous like the Master.' His glance was sly.

'You wanted to see me?'

'Yes, I've had it on me mind. Now just you listen. Write it down if you like.'

As he produced notebook and pen Harry gave the usual warning.

'To hell with you.' The old eyes were savage. 'I went through France with Sir Richard, the master's father. Right through the first war. I ain't afraid of police or nothing. Now just write it down.'

On the day in question, Tallent had been repainting the kitchen in his capacity of general handyman. At seven o'clock he had something to eat and went to the village for a drink. There was nobody in the bar that he liked, so after a morose pint by himself he bought a quart bottle and started for home taking the small track which led through the Tavisham property. A few hundred yards from the house he passed an old stone shed, part of a ruined cottage.

'I had me torch as it was a dark night and no moon and I flashed it up against the shed. Now the latch had gone and I'd put a stone up agin the door and I saw that it had been moved and the door was swingin' in the breeze. I looked in.' He gave a retching sound. 'I got a strong stomach, but I brought me supper up. The kid was lying on the floor.'

Harry handed him a water glass and he sipped it gratefully.

'I kept me head and went to the back of the house. No lights. Barry and his missus used to get to bed early in the winter, but I had me own key. The Master's in his room among his books. He sees my face and asks what's up.'

'Was his manner normal?'

'Now you just shut up and don't go puttin' words into my mouth.' The hard eyes glared.

'I told him what was up and we went down through the front entrance. He 'ad two cars, a big Alvis in the garage for long trips and a little car he left parked in the drive. He opens the door and I go to get in, shining the torch, when I see smears of fresh blood all over the seats. I showed it to him, and then we walk along to the shed. I bent and turned the body over and it's little Monica who the governor knew as well as if she was a daughter.'

Tallent's hand shook slightly as he reached up to wipe sweat off his forehead.

''E never swore, but now he says, "Jesus, Tallent! Take the Alvis and get to the constable! See that he telephones Bentleigh first thing."

'"Just a minute, Master Guy," I says, "where were you this afternoon?"'

A funny look comes into his eye and then he says, as though he's far away, that he motored around the lanes behind Eaglesham, stopped and walked in the wood there, lay down and read a bit and then came home a bit before seven.

'"Then," I said, "you'll be putting your head into a noose so they can pull the end." I never see a man before or since stand so still without movin' a muscle.

'"Get the police, Tallent," he said, and so I knew I 'ad to talk faster than ever in my life. "Look," I said, "now you listen to me,

Master Guy. They'll put you inside and not look for anyone else. I'll get rid of the body where they'll find it later and give them a chance to find who done it."

'We argued for a bit, but then he got my point. Finally he says, "You know I'm innocent of this?" I said I knew he 'adn't done it—as I did in fact.'

Harry looked at him sharply. Tallent's face wore a triumphant smirk.

'Finally I persuade him to go back to the house as though nothing 'ad 'appened. Then I move fast. I gather up the poor little mite and, sweatin' like a pig in spite of the cold, get back to the small car, blood and all, and drive a mile past the village. I put 'er little body in a culvert and covered it with dead leaves.

'When I'm back I put the car in the garage beside the Alvis, turn the lights on and get to work. I'm good with my 'ands. I strip down the upholstery and scrub every piece of it until finally there's not a bit that hasn't been scrubbed three times over. There was a thick cloth mat in the back and I take that right out and soak the floor with neat ammonia.

'That's that and it's close on three in the morning and I'm shaking every time I hear a car on the road. I go back to the shed, thank God there was a tap there, and start scrubbing there until I've gone over every mortal thing with scraper and water. It was past five when I'd finished that. Back at my cottage I changed into overalls and took paraffin out to the incinerator. I put my clothes and shoes in it along with the car mat and get it going nicely, I remember it took longer than I thought and about three gallons of oil.' Tallent showed his gums in a kind of laugh.

'I take a bit of breakfast and about nine the stuff in the 'cinerator is all ashes, so I bail them out very carefully and take them into the greenhouse and flush them down the sink, collecting the buttons and bits which hadn't burned. I got a pick and dug a hole and put 'em in that. There's one more thing and that's to get a pail of whitewash and give the inside of the shed two coats. By that time I'm half dead so I tell the Barrys I've got a chill and go off to bed.'

Harry stared morosely at his pothooks. 'You did a thorough job.'

The bright eyes narrowed.

'One thing,' Harry said slowly. 'You said you knew that Tavisham hadn't done it.'

A spasm of coughing shook Tallent's chest. 'The car,' he wheezed. 'Mr. Guy had the habit of leaving things in it. He once left a salmon in the boot of the Alvis for a fortnight in summer. Every time I cleaned that car I fancied I got the stink of it. So when I saw the little car outside on my way to the pub, I flashed my torch inside. I'll take my oath there wasn't blood anywhere then. So I knew. Somebody smeared it over with a bloody rag.'

'Did you tell Tavisham?'

The old man's mouth clamped together and he shook his head.

Harry was astonished into saying, 'You could have cleared him, man.'

'If I'd told him Master Guy'd have made us go to the police for sure.' He finished the glass of water and glared at Harry. 'It was Johnny Lushington's bull that stuck in my mind.'

'Delirium!' Harry thought for a moment.

'Yes,' said Tallent. 'Johnny bought this bull for forty quid and I was there when the lorry come with it. Before the lorry got out of the yard Johnny says to me, 'There's something wrong.' The beast could hardly stand, as I said in evidence at the Court. Took my solemn oath. There's a little old man with a loud voice to 'im for the other side. "Was I quite sure?"' His voice filled with harsh mimicry. 'A nasty little fellow. You'd give him a straight answer and he'd sneak up behind and sink 'is teeth in yer arse. The verdict went against Johnny.' He cleared his throat. 'That's what the bastards'd 've done again. Aren't yew Mr. Tavisham's paid servant?' he mimicked.

The English countryman, thought Harry, meeting the blood-shot eyes. Part dogged loyalty, part bravery, a dash of sneaky malice, cunning as a fox, silly as a two-bob watch, surviving wars and depressions and prosperity unchanged.

'You'd better rest,' he said, 'I'll send somebody in with a drink. Meantime I'd appreciate it as a favour if you didn't talk about it.'

He rather congratulated himself on his diplomacy. Order a man like Tallent and, unless perhaps years of habit or ingrained social precedence were involved, you got back a bite, but to request as a favour, well that produced the ingrained peasant reaction of delight in making a gesture that did not involve hard cash.

In the living-room he said to Barry, without preliminary, 'Was Tallent in the habit of looking to see if Mr. Tavisham had left anything in the car?'

The butler looked relieved at the innocuousness of the request, 'That he was,' he said eagerly. 'The Master was careless, you'd find his keys or maybe his wallet on the seat. Once he left a fish in the boot. Old Jim never got over that and used to check regular.'

'He'd better have a drink of milk, or whatever the doctor said.'

'I'll do it.' Without giving them time to demur, Barry rose hurriedly.

Harry looked at Elizabeth, laying back in the one armchair. 'If he's quite rational in the morning, it might be an idea if you or Barry told him that a statement made in these circumstances is quite inadmissible unless he makes it again when he's quite normal. Put it in words he understands and impress upon him not under any account to start confiding in anybody else.'

She nodded, her eyes half closed with tiredness.

'Harry,' she said. 'Shall I be arrested tomorrow?'

He shook his head. 'Highly unlikely. But I've advised you to get a solicitor before things get any worse. Now, what about letting me drive you home.'

'I'll stay the night,' she said, 'I brought a change of clothes. In the morning we'll see what can be done with Tallent. But you take the car, there's no transport at this hour and it would be difficult to raise a taxi. I shan't feel like driving in the morning.'

He took her at her word.

With some difficulty he found Wickstraw's house in a sub-urban road tangled by cul-de-sacs and crescents several miles beyond Bentleigh. The house was in darkness. He looked at his watch, which showed 1 a.m. and after a momentary hesitation pressed the bell.

After a few minutes Wickstraw blinked at him out of sleepy eyes. 'All right, come in, and it had better be good at this hour,' he grunted but did not sound unfriendly.

He led Harry into a surprisingly elaborately furnished lounge, modern pictures on the wall and chairs which looked frail even if they probably were not. Wickstraw scowled around.

'Come into my room.' He led the way into a smaller, sparsely furnished room which smelt of tobacco smoke and whisky.

'Now let's have it.'

Harry told him slowly, picking his words carefully. By the time he had finished Wickstraw was sweating slightly.

'Just a minute while I get a pipe.' He fumbled in a desk drawer, and sat down, breathing heavily.

'The last thing I bloody well wanted was that old case resurrected. It's more than eighteen months now since the press had a crack at us for not solving it. You've read the file. The lab. found traces of blood in the car and in the outhouse—under the fresh whitewash—but this fellow, uh, Tallent, had done his work well enough so that they couldn't definitely prove a blood grouping, the girl was in a rare classification and we could have nailed Tavisham on it.' He brooded, eyebrows touching. 'Can we charge Tallent?'

Harry had been turning this over in his mind. 'There's no property in a corpse, of course. An accessory to murder I very much doubt. There's obstructing and the various ordinances about moving corpses and reporting death, but...'

'Yeah,' grunted Wickstraw, 'but is the operative word.'

'The man had had a temperature of 101 and I don't think anybody would take a statement made in those conditions into court, unless there was a hell of a lot of corroboratory evidence, which there isn't.'

He saw the Superintendent's face brighten and went on, 'I'd say Barry will keep his mouth shut. He likes a quiet life. I told Holland that when Tallent was normal she might have a word with him pointing out that if he insisted on making a confession I supposed we'd have to charge him with something, but that on the other hand if he kept his trap shut I didn't suppose anything would happen.'

Wickstraw nodded, his black eyes fixed on Harry. 'I'm rather glad they sent you down, Sergeant. Only one thing, now that Tallent's talked once, suppose he starts meandering on the subject in pubs. Next thing is the press'll have it and up she goes, only worse for us.'

'Might be a matter of dragging Tavisham's name through the muck.'

The Superintendent nodded slowly. 'I'll do it personally at the first opportunity. And Elizabeth Holland's got too many worries of her own. But I'll put a man on to take out the file for study, so that if the balloon does go up we can say we've been working on it. After all these years....'

Harry felt momentary happiness at being treated as an equal.

Wickstraw went on, half talking to himself, 'I've read the reports ten times or more. The girl's mother was in hospital getting her appendix out, so the child stayed nights with an aunt in the next village. She caught the bus after school. The aunt wasn't bright and when Monica didn't turn up she thought the girl had gone home to her father, so the disappearance was reported at noon next day. His black eyes flickered at Harry. 'That's what saved Tavisham.'

'If it had been reported the previous night the search party would have nailed Tallent at his work. Do you think he's telling the truth?'

Harry shrugged in sheer weariness. 'I'd say he has his wits about him, and I can't see the point of him lying. Although he must be seventy and is a heavy drinker for his age. He might have known Tavisham was guilty and fabricated this out of addled brains: it might all be true except for the bit about knowing that the car was clean when it came in.'

'They went over Tavisham's clothes and they were clean,' grunted Wickstraw. 'Mrs. Barry accounted for all his suits. Oh, well. As for you, Sergeant, don't trouble to come in early tomorrow. I'll tell Richman.'

Harry parked the car outside Elizabeth Holland's cottage, put the keys through the letter box and walked home, almost groaning aloud when he saw that the light was shining through the kitchen door.

'Come in for a minute,' his landlady called.

She was clad in a voluminous red silk gown and smelled of gin.

'I'm very tired, I'm afraid,' he said.

'Then a stout and a gin chaser will help.'

There seemed no escape and he seated himself at the table. He drank as quickly as seemed polite, while Fanny Walsh stared at him fixedly.

'Take this quick before I change my mind.'

It was a manila envelope, crumpled and stained.

'Tavisham left it with me,' she said. 'At his most mysterious. Skating all around in fancy figures, saying that if there was any great trouble about his estate I should give it to the authorities. The Holland girl's his executor, isn't she? That means the estate.'

He took out his pen.

'Kept it sewn in my corsets,' said Miss Walsh ginnily. 'Only safe place I always say, and then not impreg,' she stumbled, 'not completely safe.'

'Sign your name over the flap, that's procedure.'

Her signature was bold and sprawling.

'I'll see it goes to his solicitor,' said Harry.

He left her staring owl-like at the row of empty stout bottles.

CHAPTER SEVEN

WICKSTRAW CAME OUT of the police station as Harry neared it. He thought it might have been by design.

'I've been through to the local doctor, Sergeant,' said the Superintendent. 'He says Tallent should recover, but he's hospitalised him, says he needs six weeks rest away from the booze. I'll have an eye kept on him.'

'Oh, God!' said Wickstraw, 'you've made my morning. Suppose it's a confession! We'd have to get the inquest re-opened and experience God knows what difficulties proving the document. The coroner here's dry as dust and his family have some vague kinship with the Tavishams. Ah, well.' He got into his car.

Inside he thought Richman greeted him a trifle sourly.

'I had a talk with Colonel Rodgers last night, Sergeant, wangled a social meeting through Wickstraw. He's a shrewd old gentleman with a pretty good idea of the kind of firm Tony's with. Six months ago he persuaded him to sell out. But here's the point. He told him that if he sold at a loss he'd make up the difference because he had a pretty good idea that Tony had borrowed money to buy in.'

'I still think we should take a good look at that situation, sir.'

'We will, if the case against Holland falls down. The position is that the DPP's office telephoned to say that they wouldn't act unless the hyoscine angle was considerably stronger, but they authorise me to apply for a warrant to search her premises. I've got a technician on poisons due in at noon, so we'll make it immediately after lunch if she's in.'

'Hardly think she'd hang on to the stuff,' Harry grunted.

'Ninety per cent of them do. There I go, talking like Hawker. I've had other reports. She's been well and truly on her beam ends for money. Apparently the uncle who brought her up fell on bad times just before he died and she's helping the widow. She owes the trades people a fair bit. Notice her clothes?' He rapped the question unexpectedly.

'Not particularly,' said Harry, feeling surly.

Richman gave his short, barking laugh. 'You ought to study

clothes. I do. She wears all last year's stuff at the latest. Now you can give me a hand getting the reports correlated.'

At one Harry went to a solitary lunch.

The poisons expert was a cheerful man named Rice. He was raw-boned with wrists projecting a little too far out of serge coat sleeves.

The police car drew up outside Elizabeth Holland's cottage. Harry could smell the scent of stocks hanging on the heavy air.

For a moment the girl closed her eyes as she opened the door.

'We're just checking,' chirped Richman, 'and wondered if you'd co-operate.'

'Co-operate,' a corner of her mouth twisted upwards, 'and what co-operation is it now?'

'We have to make a check on poison, hyoscine in particular, in the district.'

'I suppose you've got a search warrant anyway. Very well, look all you wish.'

She turned away, leaving the door open.

Richman gave Harry one of his inscrutable looks. 'You better take the garden, Sergeant.'

With relief Harry went to the back of the house. He checked the small lawn meticulously and then the flower beds. There was no sign of earth having been turned. A concrete path intersected the lawn between the beds and he checked for signs of reconcreting.

A paling fence ran around the garden and he meticulously examined it to make sure that the tired old ruse of a taped tin or envelope had not been used. The garden incinerator yielded nothing but ashes. Only a tiny shed in one corner remained. It was padlocked and Harry peered in the window through the chicken wire. There was a spade, a couple of rakes, an oldish looking lawn-mower, trowels, a few pots and on a shelf a mess of tins and packets. He did not feel inclined to go into the house and contented himself with prowling moodily around the lawn.

Richman and his two assistants were quicker than he had thought possible. The Chief Inspector answered his unspoken question: 'Only two of the rooms are really furnished. There's a spare single bed in another, but that's about all. It was mainly the kitchen and bathroom that occupied us. Nothing there.'

Harry jerked his thumb towards the shed.

'Ah, yes,' said Richman, 'she gave me the key. A very co-operative young woman.'

Harry hated him at that moment until he made himself realise that to the Chief it was just another case, and Elizabeth merely another face in a procession of faces.

Richman opened the door and peered in. 'Too small for comfort, Mr. Rice. I'll hand the stuff out to you.'

Rice spread sheets of paper on the lawn and methodically emptied out the various cans and cartons.

'A sucker for patent gardening stuff, evidently,' he grunted. 'Yes,' he caught Harry's eye, 'I always empty everything out since that Glasgow case—maybe you remember, attempted poisoning. He covered his white arsenic with two inches of french chalk. I sampled from the top and it fooled me. If he hadn't confessed we'd have been in trouble.' He worked rapidly, talking as he went.

'Nothing here. Just one more check on this stuff. No, no, laddie, nowt here but a stomach ache if you ate the lot.'

He neatly repacked the containers.

'Do you fellows mind coming here, please?'

Richman was standing where the shed met the side of the fence. There was a gap of a few inches and the Chief Inspector was stooped, shining a powerful pencil torch into the aperture.

'There's something down there. I'll have the tongs, if you please.'

He manoeuvred with the expanding device and drew them back with a small vial clutched between the tips.

He gingerly withdrew it. It had originally contained twelve aspirin tablets.

'We'd better dust it for prints,' he said.

The graphite powder yielded only a smudge when it was brushed on.

Richman handed the vial to Rice who took his bag and went into the shed.

'I've got a feeling,' the Chief Inspector said flatly.

They waited in silence for about fifteen minutes until Rice appeared. He was whistling tonelessly.

'About seven grains of a white crystalline substance,' he said and sighed. 'You can take it as five to one on that it's hyoscine.'

'And that would seem to wrap it up,' said Richman. His voice rather sad.

For a moment they stood in silence.

'We'd better ask her about it,' Richman said.

He led the way in by the kitchen door. Elizabeth was washing down a wall.

At Richman's suggestion she led the way into the living-room.

'Now Miss Holland,' said the Chief Inspector. 'You know your rights. You need not make any comment. I found this in between your potting shed and the fence.'

The vial looked insignificant on his broad white palm.

Elizabeth glanced at it, white faced, but calm.

'I am one of the rare cases with an allergy to aspirin. I have never seen that before.'

'I won't take up any more of your time,' said Richman. He paused at the front door. 'Miss Holland,' he spoke gravely, 'it is no business of mine, but I would urge you to consult a solicitor.'

She said nothing.

'How long will it take to make a positive identification?' Richman asked Rice in the car.

'An hour after I get back to the lab. I'll phone you at once.'

Back in the office, Richman took up the neat folder, product of their morning's work and the neat distillation of hundreds of man hours, and said, rather hesitantly, 'That would seem to clear it up, Sergeant. I'll cope with the rest of it, a couple of days and the paper work. So you'd better return to London, you might take the copies down with you. And thank you very much.'

It was a polite, discomforting dismissal. Harry wondered what kind of personal report the Chief Inspector would put in, not a good one he thought.

He shook hands and went back to the lodging house. What he considered to be his one recent piece of luck was the fact that his landlady was apparently out. He left a scribbled note of thanks on the kitchen table with his week's money and telephoned for a cab.

Extravagantly he decided to pay the cost between third and first and tried to sleep, eventually leafing through the file. Richman was excellent on paper work. It looked pretty bad. Well, he thought, so she's guilty, that's the end of it and I hope I don't make that mistake again. The journey was long and slow. At his destination he picked up a cold roast chicken and a pound of tomatoes and went straight home.

After the luxury of a bottle of wine he sorted through the files and placed them in a brief case for next morning. He looked at Tavisham's mysterious testament. 'A person in authority', Fanny Walsh had said. Hell, wasn't he in authority. He tore it open and extracted the single foolscap sheet, slightly yellow around its edges. The signature was precise and neat, 'Guy Tavisham'.

He read it twice. No names, stilted diplomatic prose. Tavisham had been old and frightened. He had seen similar statements by elderly embezzlers, foggy, complaining, shuffling away from reality with an old man's step. He put the envelope in the brief case and dozed in the armchair in front of the opened window through which came a slight breeze. He guessed the heat wave was nearly over and fell asleep.

His wrist watch showed eleven when he awoke abruptly with a dry winey mouth, his mind filled with an idea. After washing his mouth out he reached for a scribbling pad. It was midnight when he took the brief case and waited in the street until a cab passed.

'New Scotland Yard,' he croaked, conscious of the driver's curious glance in the mirror.

Hawker was still in his room. The desk lamp lit a fierce spot on the green blotter. Harry watched spatulate fingers crowned by little tufts of grey hair gather up working sheets and replace them neatly in the top drawer.

'Shoot,' said Hawker.

He talked until there was a dryness in his throat.

Hawker got up, throwing a tall shadow across the desk. Harry heard him pace to the window, footsteps surprisingly light.

'I'll be sorry to leave this office,' Hawker grunted, 'soft slippered ease. For a few years young blokes like you will tell the young 'uns, "You should have known an old bastard named Hawker"....'

'The case,' Harry said through the cotton wool in his mouth.

'Ah, yes, the case,' said Hawker. 'There are two cases, aren't there? The cases you were sent on and the murder of Stryver. I can act on the first, the second is Richman's pigeon.'

He padded back and the swivel chair creaked under his weight.

'Tom Richman had the dubious pleasure of serving three years as my factotum before they stepped him up, eight years ago now. You get these protocol things. I think Tom will play: it might not do him any credit if you're right, but he's a good policeman.'

The hands moved into the area of light, holding a notebook and a ball point pen. Hawker wrote quickly and meticulously.

When he had finished the old man gave a chuckle.

'If you're wrong, Sergeant, well, ever heard of the parrot dept.?'

'No, sir.'

'In the Commons they give you a peerage. Here it's alleged

there is a parrot dept. filled with once-bright young men who now deal with old ladies who've lost a parrot. There are 9,000 old ladies in Greater London who possess parrots and the incidence of losses is high.'

'And you, sir?'

He could feel Hawker's malevolent gaze. 'Batting average! One duck to four good innings, over the years. It's time I got a duck. But you, I'll throw you to the parrots.'

'I don't believe it.'

'Should have stuck to the accountancy,' grunted Hawker, tilting his chair. 'I'll tell you something you haven't got a grasp of fully. Tonight you'll see the machine from the top, and a staggering one it is. I'm going to get some top brass out of bed and by the morning, if necessary, we'll rout out the Archbishop of Canterbury.' Hawker's spatulate index finger was already dialling the house phone.

'Hallo, sir, Hawker. Yes, it's late for me, but...' Harry felt his head droop and supported it with his hand, elbow on his knees. His eyeballs stung as the room filled with light. Hawker stood looking down at him so that Harry blinked up at the tobacco burns which honeycombed the old fashioned white broadcloth shirt.

'Out to it lad?'

Harry shook his head.

'Get upstairs and take a cold shower if you want. Then join me in room 78 with a book and a pencil. You'll be taking notes for me. Or would you rather knock off and let me tell you about it in the morning?'

Harry got to his jellied legs. 'Shorthand note, sir?'

Hawker nodded. 'Richman's on his way, not too pleased.'

Room 78 had a wall-to-wall carpet and a refectory table, beyond which were three small tables with typewriters, play-back machines, hard chairs and two civilian stenographers. At the big table seven men sat with telephones, one of them Hawker.

Each telephone was linked to a tape recorder and periodically Hawker threw off his tape into a wire basket. Harry retrieved it, fed it into his play-back and typed.

In Gloesham, Bucks, a farm-labourer named Alf was awakened from beery sleep.

In his house at Wimbledon a Permanent Secretary jolted awake as the red telephone by his bedside gave its discreet bleep-bleep.

The Minister in the Zurich Embassy said, 'Christ, the things they give us.'

At a little after three Richman came in, eyes scoops of grey jelly below sleepless lids. He went to the bald-headed man in command at the head of the table, whispered for several minutes, and then gathered up the pages of reports.

Zurich. The Minister was speaking German-Swiss on the telephone.

'Every co-operation, Herr Direktor, every co-operation, as you know. Yes, the utmost discretion. Bitte, bitte, remember at all times our utmost consideration....' He replaced the green handset and looked at his assistant.

'Don't know whether this is much, like squeezing an empty tube, but get this away in code....'

Fenchley, North Devon. 'Yew dew remember, dad, now,' said the youngish fisherman. 'Yew had Elsie and me down while you mended the net and we heard him scream, now, and you dropped the net and ran.'

'Ar,' the grizzled old head nodded. 'I'd told him not to meddle earlier I do recall.'

Gloesham, Bucks.

'I saw him get into the car, sir,' the man Alf said. 'But only the back view, not taking much notice. Stocky and athletic in a plastic raincoat and brown hat.'

Harry's head nodded at times over the typewriter.

Presently the telephones grew still. His wrist-watch showed a little after five. Only the bald-headed man at the end of the table, Richman and Hawker remained.

Because nobody told him to go he remained. Presently three men came through the door.

There was a man who looked like a frog, broad nosed from which hairy tufts spread unmolested from the nostrils, who sat in the corner with an air of not being there, in spite of his ugly brown suit.

Two men, one of them in sponge-bag trousers and black coat, represented the Director of Public Prosecutions, all of them with the bleary-eyed look of men aroused from deep sleep.

At last the man with the sponge-bag trousers rumpled his grey hair. 'You have a *prima facie* for murder of George Stryver, not too strong.... I don't know.'

'They're going to skip,' said Hawker, slumped in his chair, his little eyes bagged in folds of flesh.

An assistant coughed, 'Perhaps if the arrest were made after he had, er, skipped ... presumption of guilt.'

The frog-faced man rolled an ominous eyeball.

'Air tickets to the Lebanon on Thursday, just in case,' said Hawker.

The man in the sponge-bag pants paused to commune in silence with his political maker.

'There's no evidence....'

'But a bloody scandal if it happened,' said Hawker, with greasy relish.

'A few days,' said sponge-bag trousers, 'we don't want the charge of being precipitate.'

'Very good, sir,' said Hawker, glancing at Richman. 'Mr. Richman will record a minute.'

Sponge-bag pants flickered his gaze at the frog-faced man. 'Well, Superintendent, go ahead. We'll have to have Treasury counsel at the preliminary hearing—they'll try to rush it, of course. Do you think we'd get any admissions?'

Hawker shrugged. 'More likely a bullet in the abdomen.'

Sponge-bag looked disapproving at the mention of violence.

The frog-faced man spoke, his voice, surprisingly, a light and expressionless tenor. 'A little general conversation before arrest. This could fit in with me. If it doesn't, the nest will empty as soon as the press get the arrest.'

'Judge's rules, you know,' said sponge-bag.

'Ah, yes, of course,' said frog-face. 'Judge's rules, of course.'

'Well, then, we'll leave it to you gentlemen,' said sponge-bag pants in some relief.

The Commander seated at the end of the long table spoke in an Army voice. 'We don't want a hullabaloo, and the local force is efficient so they can be drawn on. Can you handle it, Mr. Richman, remembering that it's essential that we get vigorous reaction.'

'I think so.' Richman was staring at his shoes.

'All it's necessary to take is Sergeant, um, James who knows the people. And of course, you'll wish to go?' He addressed the man in the loud brown suit.

'I'd better be in on it from the start. I made arrangements to ease in ten of my men by the first train this morning. It's all right—market research cover.'

Briefly the Commander chuckled, 'Used to be newspaper circulation in the old days, eh? Very well, gentlemen.'

Eventually Harry found himself with the anonymous man in the back of a Humber. Richman sat with the driver. Fifty miles from Bradshaw the car stopped and he was roused by Richman shaking his shoulder.

'Five hours' sleep, Sergeant.'

It was an old discreet inn, or so it impressed Harry, who registered little other than the large red spots, against a green background, worn by an oversize woman who showed him to his small bedroom.

He kicked off his shoes and it seemed the next minute that a knock came on his door and a hoarse male voice informed him that it was 10.45. He found his brief case where he had put it under the bed, took out his electric razor, and went to find the bathroom.

He was the last to reach the small foyer, feeling shabby in his crumpled suit, Richman somehow preserved the illusion of immaculacy and Harry suspected that he had somehow contrived a clean white shirt. The frog-faced man, in the same gruesome suit, merely looked indestructible.

'We'll push on,' said Richman. 'We can eat when we get there.' Harry got into the same seat as earlier and listened to his stomach rumbling.

They halted at the main police headquarters in Bradshaw. Wickstraw's office was large and imposing and by forethought or organisation had provided coffee and ham sandwiches. As they ate, the Superintendent said, 'Bad thing this, Mr. Richman. I'm glad it's Yard.'

Richman finished his first ham sandwich before replying, with equal blandness. 'You were informed of the procedure, Super?'

'Oh, yes,' said Wickstraw. 'You go in at 1.15 and ten minutes before that I'll have the road blocks operative. I'd better accompany you.'

The coffee having cleared his head, Harry felt an inward admiration of the way in which Wickstraw hedged his bets.

The frog-faced man seemed to have no name. Harry had been staring blankly at the unpleasant brown suit, surmising that it must be made of some synthetic material because it had remained uncrushed during the journey.

'It's dangerous, you know,' said the frog-faced man. 'Not that they'd resist arrest, no percentage in that and they're quite professional I imagine. But a ten minute telephone call might make all the difference, perhaps, and if that is so they'd shoot to get at it.'

'There are three extensions at the house,' said Wickstraw.

'Oh, that! I've arranged for the line to be non-operative ten minutes before we get there. But public telephones. I'd like a man outside every one within a radius of half a mile.'

The Superintendent picked up the intercom. and spoke briskly into it while the others finished the meal.

'All right, gentlemen,' said Wickstraw at last. 'We now move off in one car, with an Inspector and four other men following us.'

'My own men will converge at 1.25,' said the frog-faced man.

At 1.15 precisely Harry was last in line as Richman led the way to the door of the house. He watched the Chief Inspector deftly brush aside the housekeeper who opened the door and followed the procession along the wide hallway into the living area.

He stood and looked down through the open windows at the small terrace a few feet below upon which the fat Chow lay on his back asleep, paws curled into the air. Below in the former quarry the blue tiles of the swimming pool made the water look doubly inviting. There were a few people outside the dressing sheds and he recognised the squat muscular figure of Burke.

Without turning, he heard Richman say, 'We are here officially, sir. You know Superintendent Wickstraw and the Sergeant.' He made no attempt to introduce the man in the brown suit.

'I had no apprehension that this was a social call, Inspector,' Lester Monck's voice was very cold.

'Well sir,' said Richman, 'I must advise you that you can have a solicitor present and that you are within your rights in making no comment at all, because it may well be that I shall take out a warrant against you.' He read the prepared sentence from his notebook.

'Do you mean that you suspect my husband?' Gladys Monck was outraged contralto and raised eyebrows.

Richman did not reply.

'I think you should phone the Chief Constable, Lester.'

Monck glanced affectionately at his wife as he sat down on the arm of a chair. 'I think we'll have to hear the Inspector out, old thing. The machinery had got fouled up somewhere and we'll soon put it right.'

'Mr. Monck,' said Richman abruptly, 'people connect your name with the Moncks who were lords of the manor here. In fact your family had no connection with them. You were a Devon family.'

'A very old Devon family,' interposed Mrs. Monck. 'I think I should like you to pour me a sherry, dear.'

Monck's face was blank as he walked to the sideboard. 'No good tempting you fellows, I guess. Right-ho, two only.'

His hand was quite steady as he handed Mrs. Monck her drink.

'Let's see. No, Inspector, I have no means of knowing whether the Moncks hereabout were collaterals. Not much interest anyway.'

'We should really be with our guests,' said Mrs. Monck. 'It's so offhand.'

'An old family,' Richman ignored her. 'So old that in 1914 one representative remained, Sir Simon Monck, a widowed diplomat and his ten year old son. The family estates had been sold and Sir Simon was not wealthy.'

He paused. Monck looked at him levelly over his sherry glass.

'The son was a sickly boy in July, 1914. Sir Simon took him on a leisurely tour through Austria and Hungary. There was a train crash. Sir Simon was killed and his boy, Lester, was in hospital with injuries. Then, of course, war came. The Swiss Red Cross reported that the boy had recovered and had been taken into the home of a Hungarian official who had known Sir Simon.'

'I cannot imagine what the devil you are reciting my life history for,' said Monck. His ordinarily impassive face was wrinkled into a scowl. He suddenly looked very tough, Harry thought.

His eyes took in the room. Richman had nicked himself when shaving. Wickstraw's mouth was pursed and accentuated his jowls. The anonymous man had crossed to his side at the window. The light glinted on the broad planes of Monck's cheekbones.

'Bear with me,' said Richman. 'After the war, the diplomat moved to Berlin. Sir Simon's family solicitor went across and found a boy,' he paused and stared levelly at Monck for a long moment, 'a boy in good health and very much a member of the family. Money needed to be husbanded and the solicitor thought it best for the boy to be left where he was. Difficulties arose over his return—he was studying this and that, his educational reports were wonderful, so when he finally came to England and to his father's old Oxford College, Lester Monck was a man of slightly over 20. He did quite brilliantly and joined the diplomatic with six languages to his credit.'

'What you're saying,' said Monck, concisely, 'is that I'm not Lester Monck.'

'Exactly,' said Richman, quite amiably.

'My late father,' said Monck, 'used to say that a gentleman took one sherry, and one sherry only, before lunch. But on this nightmarish occasion I'll have a second.'

Richman's eyes met Harry's, not particularly happily. He swung towards Gladys Monck.

'In 1935 Mr. Monck was en poste at Shanghai. He married a Miss Gladys Glover, daughter of medical missionaries who had worked and died obscurely in China. We can't find anybody who knew Miss Glover more than one year before her marriage.'

'My God, Lester do you hear this man?'

'Leave my wife out of it, do you hear?'

'Very well. In 1912 there was a boy named Marcus holidaying with his parents in Devon. With them was staying a young schoolmaster who subsequently became his guardian. Marcus struck up a friendship with young Monck. One day they were fooling on the beach and Monck gashed his thigh on a broken bottle.'

Richman's cold eyes were deadly now.

'If it hadn't been for the father of a companion, a fisherman, Monck would have bled to death. As it was he was three weeks in a cottage hospital with thirty stitches in his thigh. Years later Marcus became the M.P. here and of course he was not the man to mention a youthful friendship. But when he came to swim here he noticed the absence of any scar. In fact he wrote to his guardian about it, who had no memory of the event.'

Monck put his sherry down with a crack on the glass topped table.

'Inspector, I must warn you of one thing. I have very distant cousins named Monck, and Lester is a traditional family name. One of the pitfalls of history is precisely this kind of thing.' His voice was dry and patient.

('Any K.C. could drive a horse and cart through that evidence,' the man from the Home Office had commented.)

Richman went on as though he had not heard, staring down at his shoes. 'Marcus discovered he was dying....' He paused and suddenly looked hard at Monck whose mouth had opened in an O of surprise.

'Our experts say he had about a year left. He was a tidy, brave little man. He planned to get his affairs in order, to resign from the House, but one piece of unfinished business troubled him—you. Those days were different from these, mercifully—discretion, caution, etcetera. He had previously approached Guy Tavisham, who I think may have acquired certain doubts about you, Mr. Monck.'

'Two dead men,' said Monck, his teeth showing between his lips.

Very slowly Mrs. Monck reached out to a cigarette box and lit a cigarette. Her large white face looked merely thoughtful.

'Lester,' she said, 'get these men out of here.'

But Monck was squinting up at Richman.

'Oh, in a way we have a voice from the dead. Tavisham left a statement—you suspected that, of course—but it wasn't in his house, it was in the corsets of a Miss Fanny Walsh.'

'Oh, get these lunatics out, Lester.' Outrage was in Gladys Monck's every feature.

'I see,' said Monck.

'A very guarded statement, indeed,' said Richman. 'He was a careful man. Now, I think Marcus laid a few little traps for you and so he had to go. However, he had been an M.P. and if he was discovered murdered, well, there would have been a very big manhunt.

'So there was a man named Whelks, who was a petty crook with political affiliations. The point about him was that he was a brilliant mimic, and Marcus had a very distinctive voice. I think those calls to establish the fact that he was in London the day he vanished were made by Whelks, and that Marcus never left Bradshaw.'

Monck made no comment.

'Whelks had no stomach for murder, but there was plenty of time to get rid of him before he suspected.'

Monck cleared his throat. 'This seems a lot of ingenious, and I may say quite false, speculation. In any case I thought you wanted to discuss poor old George Stryver.'

'I just want to be perfectly fair to you,' said Richman suavely, 'and give you our complete background.'

('And try to get that background to a jury,' the Home Office official had grunted.)

'You see,' said Richman, 'a planned murder is like a stone in a pool. The ripples go out. It can't be contained, as the murderer requires. In this case we have Guy Tavisham fully occupied during the war, but with a little worrying cyst in his mind. Your record stresses that you are an amazing judge of character and you knew that sooner or later Tavisham would overcome his class loyalty, his desire not to stir up mud and go with his doubts to M.I.5.'

Harry glanced out the window and saw Burke's brown body float in a graceful arc from the diving board.

'And so...' There was a white line round Monck's mouth, and his eyes were slits.

'Ah, Tavisham's rather far-fetched code was such that he wouldn't associate with anyone he suspected. You made overtures, he kept away. No chance of a friendly meeting with Tavisham without other people present, so he had to be discredited.

'One of his hobbies was morbid criminology—he had a large section of it in his library. It was well-known and I think it suggested a train of thought. Who would believe a man convicted of a brutal sadistic murder of a nine-year-old girl?'

Very slowly, Monck flushed, upwards from his throat. 'Inspector...'

Richman, speaking fast, steam-rollered him. 'Three men were needed. They were named Smith, a brute from south London, Farqueson and Case. All three wanted money desperately, and a damned good psychologist spotted that they wouldn't puke at murder.' ·

'I remember that we were in Rome when that regrettable murder occurred,' said Monck, slowly.

Richman nodded. 'Why not? Smith to knock the child on the head, Farqueson master-minding and Case to run interference if necessary and I think he'd have enjoyed the mutilation that followed. The body was put into a shed on Tavisham's estate, some blood was smeared in his car. Who'd believe a man who murdered and mutilated a nine-year-old child?' His finger stabbed down at Monck.

Wickstraw had been looking at a painting on the wall. He said, benevolently, 'I think perhaps Mr. Monck would like a solicitor present.'

Monck sat silent. His wife reached for another cigarette.

'Smith had withheld £400 from a bookmaker who employed him. The bookie said it was a question of settlement or acid in Smith's eyes. Farqueson had embezzled from his aunt's estate,

186

Case was being blackmailed. Good psychology. It might interest you to know that previously or subsequently all three were killers.'

A smile crinkled Monck's eyes. He seemed about to speak but thought better of it.

'The scheme failed in its full intention. One of Tavisham's servants, extraordinarily loyal to his master, as they seem to be hereabouts, found the body. Tavisham was no fool and he could see no way out of the trap except to remove the body elsewhere, clean his car, and bluff it out in the face of suspicion. But it broke him personally, he was never the same man again.

'I don't know about his poisoning. Tavisham was extraordinarily unobservant concerning food: if he found a piece of veal and ham pie in the refrigerator in his hide-away cottage, he'd have eaten it.'

Richman stopped talking and walked deliberately to the sideboard, chose a tumbler and poured himself a glass of water.

A laugh floated up from the pool. Otherwise the silence was unbroken. Harry recognised an old scene, nothing but the voice of the police officer, a time when the accused sat in silence, listening and thinking.

The Chief-Inspector set down his glass and walked leisurely back. The Moncks might have been wax-work figures.

'A man stayed the night in an hotel a few miles from the cottage, two days before Tavisham acquired the fatal dose. They arrived late and left early. The night porter gave us an interesting description, 5 ft. 6 inches, broad white face,' Richman's glance strayed towards Mrs. Monck. 'The night porter didn't like the man, thought he was effeminate.

'What could have been the same—er—person, was seen in Bristol at the time Farqueson fell down a lift shaft. And another strange fact, Farqueson was seen with the man Case the day before his body was found in a Wiltshire ditch.

'Case had a history of blackmail and the man Smith was his acquaintance around the London dog tracks. By what we think was another act of murder Farqueson had become a wealthy man and I think Case and Smith started bleeding him. But Case's nose told him that there was bigger game behind Mr. Farqueson and he went sniffing around. So were eliminated and, to close up another pipeline, Mr. Farqueson went the same way.'

'I think, Mr. Richman, that Mr. Monck might want to ask some questions at this stage.' Wickstraw bowed slightly from the waist like a slightly sinister Mr. Pickwick.

'I see no reason to question a farrago of nonsense.' Monck's voice was a trifle hoarse and he seemed lost in his own thoughts.

'Well,' said Richman, 'if there's no question, we come to the outstanding matter, Mr. Stryver. I admit that, perhaps because I never met him, I under-estimated him badly. On the surface he was an eccentric old gentleman, given to the perusal of spy stories, but, of course, he had had a very successful career and he was a tough, intelligent man of great tenacity. And he had been pretty high in financial counsels during the war. In his accountancy business he had struck a foreign registered company, Metal Auxiliaries, which didn't seem to do much except receive a great deal of Swiss currency. Nothing illegal about that, Mr. Monck, except that I think he received some indication that you were the J. T. Robinson who signed the cheques on the Metal Auxiliaries' accounts.'

Mrs. Monck stirred. 'As this nonsense seems endless, I think we should tell our guests we shan't be serving drinks.'

'I would really prefer you to remain here,' said Richman.

'I suppose I'll have to telephone them afterwards and apologise,' she said in tones of resignation. Monck gave a faint nod of agreement.

The Chief Inspector was watching the woman closely. 'In police work we often don't know exactly what we are looking for. We just keep paying out the net and examining a hundred useless articles in the hope that something will turn up. But when we know what we are looking for, that's another story. For instance it took us five hours to discover various things about Metal Auxiliaries that had taken Stryver, a private citizen of influence, nearly a year. Nowadays the Swiss authorities aren't so reticent about certain types of business as they used to be—the class of business in fact they would sooner not have, as for instance Metal Auxiliaries which they believe is merely an agency for a foreign government.'

Monck turned to his wife. 'I don't think...' His voice held interrogation.

Harry came in on cue. Monck jumped at the sound of the voice behind him. As his eyes sought Monck's, Harry's momentarily brushed against Gladys Monck's flat, grey gaze.

'The clincher, Mr. Monck, is the order that people left the tennis party. Miss Holland walked out with you, Colonel Rodgers was talking to Mrs. Burke, Mr. Burke was with Tony Rodgers. The missing capsule was found in an old drain.

'We presume it was burning a hole in the murderer's pocket. Even so the risk, however slight, of being seen in the act of disposing of the capsule would be unthinkable unless in the company of a confederate. Now work it out. Elizabeth Holland came back, but Burke was within sight of her and they walked out together. But you and Mrs. Monck were alone together when you walked to the gate at 12.30.'

Harry jumped. Mrs. Monck slumped in her chair and the sherry glass was in shards upon the coffee table.

'Look out!' Richman bellowed.

Monck's heavy shoulder bashed Harry's breast bone so that he reeled, swerving to avoid the open window and sprawling to his knees, his face over the lintel. He watched Monck's heavy jump towards the terrace. Roused from slumber the old Chow rolled sideways. Monck instinctively threw his feet to one side and with equal blind response the dog snapped his teeth into one trouser leg. He saw Monck reel, the dog twisting between his ankles. Cloth ripped and Monck staggered, caught his thighs on the narrow wall and was over. Harry had thrown himself over the lintel, feeling his ankles jar upon the polished stone. As he looked he could see Monck hitting the concrete edge of the pool. Above the snarls of the Chow a woman screamed.

He raced for the long stairway down and was conscious of being passed by the man in the brown suit. But they reached the bottom almost together.

'An accident,' said the man quickly.

'Mr. Burke,' said Harry, over him. Burke's flat eyes met him impassively. 'Keep everybody together, will you please.'

As he turned to the stairs he heard Burke's deep reassuring voice. Richman had almost gained the bottom, and, way up and foreshortened like an Emmett station-master he saw Wickstraw's paunch and chest.

'Get back quick,' shouted the brown-suited man and Harry sprinted, surprised that he could do so. Adrenaline raced his heart as he swung up and into the living-room.

Gladys Monck's head sprawled over her tightly encased chest, cheeks blue. There was a slow, drawling gurgle from her lungs. He rushed to the front door and summoned the police driver.

'Get the surgeon and an ambulance.' The man gaped, collected himself and swung in behind the wheel.

He got back to find the others there.

'I've sent for the surgeon and an ambulance,' he told Richman, who, bent, was cupping a glass over the slack mouth, white under the lipstick.

'Nothing there,' said Richman.

'It's a version of prussic acid,' said the brown-suited man, 'with various other things. No pain guaranteed and death in ninety seconds. It would have been in the cigarette box, of course.'

He stepped back a pace. 'She was the boss. We heard her give him his orders to break for a telephone!' He sighed. 'They wouldn't have talked. Now what I want is the phone on and fifteen hours. I'd like more, but I doubt I can get it. Is the coroner O.K.?'

Wickstraw nodded.

'I imagine the top brass will want to discuss presentation,' said the brown-suited man.

Wickstraw nodded. 'That will be right.'

Harry went back to the police station to report to London. Then he waited for the others. Wickstraw was rubbing his hands. He smiled at Harry.

'As good an ending as could be expected. Double suicide while being questioned as to the death of George Stryver—a one day sensation.'

'You had some vague suspicions, I think, sir,' said Harry.

'Oh, my word,' said Wickstraw rubbing his nose. 'An old copper gets instincts, but, now, what was there to it? A vague unease—Fanny Walsh—she's seen a lot of life—felt it, too. Silly old cow, sitting on that letter. But there we are. Maybe I should have stirred the pot around, but a millionaire like Stryver, a distinguished F.O. careerist like Monck.' He wagged his head.

'You presented the case magnificently, sir,' Harry said to Richman, who was filling his pipe.

'I thought I did well,' admitted the Chief Inspector, 'as good a production as I've ever turned on. But it was thin, too thin. We had nothing—you youngsters don't spend enough time studying law of evidence,' the cold grey eyes flicked against Harry. 'No, we broke him on the wheel and he knew it. Something I found out, he had been called to the Bar after he left Oxford. His main job at the F.O. was on the drafting of agreements with other countries. Blimey,' Richman lapsed into humanity, 'get that driver of yours to rustle up tea, could you Super?'

After his first cup, Richman said, 'The wheel we broke him on was his paramount duty to get a telephone call through to some-body. Otherwise he'd have sat tight. Oh, we might have got him, probably would, on some protracted and messy security angle.'

'Cold-blooded swine,' said Wickstraw.

'I wouldn't go quite that far,' said Richman. 'An army officer, probably devoted to country. The police surgeon says the skin on the abdomen is that of a man of sixty-eight—his official age was seven years younger, so when he came here he was twenty-eight, not twenty-one. At a guess, she was the killer, and I'd hate to know what kind of hell hole she served her apprenticeship in.'

'He'd have been primarily a paymaster?' said Harry.

'Yes,' said Richman. 'I understand that's the snag, getting in and distributing what amounts to a considerable sum in cash each year.

'In fact there's a special section to watch money movements: they'll have some sore backsides over this. And of course his knowledge of people: who might be a possible approach etcetera. But still, there's Marcus and the man Whelks, so your men will have a spot of digging to do, Super.'

'Around that quarry, I'd guess.'

Richman shrugged. 'The Moncks used to charter a forty-foot cabin cruiser from Deal several times a year. I'd guess well-weighted canvas sacks and a good knowledge of charts and currents. Ah, well. Now you, Sergeant, better take the five p.m. back. I'll authorise a taxi. I suppose you may be paying a call on the way to the station.' The hard grey eyes were impossible to read.

Harry shook hands and went down to wait for the cab. The Desk Sergeant popped his head through the door of the little cubicle. 'Call for you, Sergeant.'

It was Hawker. 'Deputy Inspector?'

'What?'

'You heard. I got the impression that the powers-that-be were powerfully moved by the fact that your suspects died so tidily.' Hawker laughed, 'But don't make a habit of that.'

'Well, thank you, sir,' said Harry.

'Oh,' said Hawker casually. 'There's no divisional vacancy for a D.I., and you're about two years too young anyway.' The old man savoured his moment of suspense. 'In fact I'm the only man with a vacancy for that rank.'

'My God,' said Harry.

Hawker allowed himself a small cackle before putting down his handset.

He ordered the taxi to stop opposite Rhonda Gentry's cottage, and nodded to the policeman who stood, apparently idly, on the opposite side of the street. She gave a little gasp as she saw him, and taking off the chain, swung the door open, her wide, apprehensive amber eyes staring past him.

Gently he pushed her inside, conscious of the softness of her shoulders. 'It's all over, Rhonda, you have nothing, nothing to fear.'

He waited while she cried, and then took her briefly in his arms. In spite of the tear-drenched cheeks she was still beautiful.

'I'm catching the train back, Rhonda,' he said. 'I'm now a Deputy Inspector,' he added, feeling rather shy.

'Is that important?' she asked, ambiguously.

'It'll provide a margin for a luxury or two.' He found himself breathing rather fast. 'I have a little flat in Bayswater; it's in the book. Next Saturday, I could meet the first train.'

She gave her deep laugh. 'Bachelor flat. No, it's not the attempt at seduction.' She shook her auburn head. 'No, it's being expected to do a week's washing up, clear out a stinking dustbin, hoover the carpet.'

'I could fix it with the cleaning woman,' he said seriously.

'You do that and go catch your train.' She opened the door.

In the car he opened his engagement book and under 'Saturday', wrote 'Cleaning woman?????'